FLORA BUTLER SCREAMED. SHE SCREAMED AGAIN AND AGAIN. . . .

They weren't screams of pain. They were screams of ecstasy. Flora enjoyed having babies.

Flora thought, as the baby was placed in her arms, *She is the most beautiful baby of the lot.* The Lord had favored her. She would call her Emily. Yes, she would always think of her as that. And then, in one horrible moment, she wished with all her might she could keep the baby.

She looked up. The nurse was holding out her arms and waiting for the baby, who would be taken to the couple who were waiting for her. Lucky couple. *Good-bye, baby. I wish you a good life. May the Lord protect you. Never forget who your mother really is.* . . .

Books by Judi Miller

Hush, Little Baby
Save the Last Dance for Me

Published by POCKET BOOKS

Most Pocket Books are available at special quantity discounts for bulk purchases for sales promotions, premiums or fund raising. Special books or book excerpts can also be created to fit specific needs.

For details write the office of the Vice President of Special Markets, Pocket Books, 1230 Avenue of the Americas, New York, New York 10020.

HUSH, LITTLE BABY

JUDI MILLER

PUBLISHED BY POCKET BOOKS NEW YORK

This novel is a work of fiction. Names, characters, places and incidents are either the product of the author's imagination or are used fictitiously. Any resemblance to actual events or locales or persons, living or dead, is entirely coincidental.

Another *Original* publication of POCKET BOOKS

 POCKET BOOKS, a Simon & Schuster division of
GULF & WESTERN CORPORATION
1230 Avenue of the Americas, New York, N.Y. 10020

ISBN: 0-671-43182-X

First Pocket Books printing January, 1983

10 9 8 7 6 5 4 3 2 1

POCKET and colophon are registered trademarks
of Simon & Schuster.

Printed in the U.S.A.

With loving memory
for two people
who would be most proud:
my parents, Ruth and Joe

Acknowledgments

I wish to thank two busy authors who helped me with my research on surrogate motherhood: John Kelly and Dennis L. Breo. Also many thanks to Bruce Leonard, audio engineer, ABC radio. And to my cousins, Beth, Joey and Bobby Goldman, for showing me Atlanta.

I am most grateful to Susan Ginsburg, my editor, for her efforts. As I am to David Alexander and Bruce Becker for their support. And Eric Drew for his much-appreciated assistance.

But most especially I want to thank my agent, David Cogan, for making everything come together for me.

"And Sâ raī said unto Abram, Behold now, the LORD has restrained me from bearing: I pray thee, go in unto my maid; it may be that I may obtain children by her . . ."

Genesis 16:2
Holy Bible
King James Version

HUSH, LITTLE BABY

Chapter One

The sky was milky and the uneven grounds were brightened here and there by patches of moonlight. Ralph Butler paced up and down in front of the parked Dodge van. He looked at his watch. They would be breaking soon.

He stood staring at the dark outlines of the pines on the hillside. With the air so clean and crisp, the earth so fragrant and the moon so round and full, he felt he was the only man on earth. He spoke softly. "You created all this, Lord. And you created man and woman. So they could have children. Lord? I think we're tampering with your plan. Ya see, we're still having children, but not necessarily the way you planned it."

"Daddy, can I have something to drink? I'm thirsty."

He turned. Towheaded Amy had opened a van window and was hanging half out of it. Ralph looked up toward the sky. "I'll have to continue this later, Lord." He mouthed the words. "I just thought you should know what was going on." He hung his head. "We're straying, Lord. And there's no one around to tell us if it's evil or not. It feels right to her. But the damned apple felt right to Eve. Excuse me, Lord." He gulped. "Well, it's done. But I don't mind telling you right now I got second thoughts."

"Daaaaaaady!"

Ralph turned back to the van. Benjamin, Carl and Dennis were asleep in a jumble of arms, legs, blankets and leaking pillows. Starting with Amy, the oldest, age eight, they had come two years apart. They would have had another baby this year, but they couldn't afford it. Ralph opened the door to the driver's seat, stepped up and took a thermos of milk out of a large paper bag. He poured some into the thermos cup and handed it to her.

She drank some and made a face in the dark. "Daddy, it's warm."

"Okay. Look, here's an orange in the bag. That's cold. Feels it to me."

She grabbed the orange and disappeared under the blanket. When he looked over at her a few minutes later, he saw she had fallen asleep.

He studied the view again, sitting in the van, with the door open. The next kid would have been an "E." Elizabeth, Edward, something like that. Oh, well. Looking at his watch, he saw that it was after ten. He got up at five every morning to be at the plant. Wouldn't change much after they got that money. Not with inflation the way it was. Still, it would help.

He yawned. They were probably talking now, having coffee. He could knock on the door and get a cup. But the smartest thing at this hour would be to sneak a little nap. His wife wasn't going anywhere without him. He rolled back sideways on the front seat and brought his knees up slightly. He wouldn't think. He would sleep better when it was all over. But it got to him sometimes. It did something to a man. He never thought he'd feel this way, but he did. Like a fifth wheel. Like a baby sitter. Like . . . like—his face contorted and he forced out the idea— like a man who did things to the bodies of other men.

* * *

There were coffee mugs and teacups and saucers neatly stacked on a table. On another table, with a centerpiece of fresh-picked flowers, were homemade bread and slices of cheese. One of the women was serving. Flora Butler stood in the middle of the room biting her lip.

The minister was gingerly drinking tea from a cup. In his saucer was a folded napkin to catch the excess water. Flora watched carefully, and when she saw him stand alone for half a second she saw her opportunity and went over.

The minister couldn't help but smile at the woman. The Lord had blessed her with perfect beauty. Clear, cornflower-blue eyes, hair the color of spring wheat, cheeks with the tender blush of a baby rose. No wonder they had called her Flora. Flower. The loveliest woman in the Church of the True Believers. And the most disciplined and devoted.

Flora lowered her eyes when she saw the head of the church. "I've done something without consulting the church or getting permission," she said shakily, almost whispering.

The minister nodded. He put his half-finished tea down on a table. "We shall go into a private room," he said. "But first let us pray together." They neither bowed their heads nor closed their eyes but stared straight ahead. Others saw their stillness. A few stood silently with them. Flora was trembling.

"Mama," a husky, babyish voice said.

Flora Butler turned around. It seemed to her that the word *mama* was coming from every direction, tapping the windows like the fresh, light spring shower. The pine trees had whispered, "Mama," to her as she hurried from the church to the van with a newspaper over her head.

In one motion she turned around, scooped up her two-year-old son and put the baby on her lap, taking his thumb out of his mouth. She smoothed out the silky blond hair that fringed his face. Then she kissed him on the forehead and whispered, "Mama's here. Go back to sleep, Denny." The child curled up in her lap like a cat.

"How'd the Bible reading go?" her husband asked, one eye on his lovely wife and the other on the dark night.

"Very fine, yes, very fine." Flora's eyes shone.

He nodded.

"And did you tell Minister Haver?"

She nodded and mumbled. "He said it was the Lord's way of doing His work." Flora bit her lip. He hadn't really said much of anything. That's what bothered her.

They drove quietly for a while.

"I got a letter from my mother today," she said.

"What did she have to say?" Ralph stole a quick side glance at his wife. Her nose was tilted upward, her lips were forming a frown. He couldn't see her body shaking with fury, but he could sense it.

"What did she have to say?" he asked again.

"*She* said daddy thought it was a fine idea, but she could never give me her blessings. Said there was something unnatural about it. Something *ungodly*. But if that's what I wanted to do, I was a grown woman and she couldn't put any sense into me." Flora's voice was a low rumble, almost a growl. "Mama's just jealous. She only had me. She couldn't have any more children."

"Now, honey, don't get yourself all riled up. At least your mother was honest. You can't blame her for having her own thoughts."

Flora's lovely features stretched lopsidedly into a grotesque scowl as she turned on her husband. "You

always take my mother's side," she cried. "I sometimes wonder why you didn't marry *her!*"

Ralph winced. He said nothing, just kept his eyes
straight ahead on the road.

In the space of seconds, Flora's face became
serene and composed again. She looked down at the
sleeping boy in her lap and cuddled him close to her
breast as if he were a little baby again.

Mrs. Haver sat in front of her dressing-room
table, plaiting her hair into braids. Her husband was
in bed.

"I think it's disgusting."

"Now, now," said the Reverend Haver, who was
a high-school teacher as well.

"I read something about this. But usually no
money changes hands."

Her husband clasped his hands over his chest.
"Yes, that's the part I don't like. But I didn't want to
say anything."

"Do you think it could be called adultery?" she
asked, snidely, putting a rubber band on the tip of
her long braid.

"Interesting question. However, it's in the Bible.
We all know that. Genesis. Hagar did it for Sarah
and Abraham. It's the Lord's way, Catherine. And
it's done."

She pinned both braids on top of her head and
thought of an interesting phrase, "rent-a-womb."
But she wouldn't dare say it.

"Well, if you ask me, she's fooling around with
Mother Nature. At least Hagar went to bed with
Abraham."

The two children lay in the same bed. Amy was in
the top bunk, and Benjamin, in the bottom. Benjamin was sucking his thumb because it was dark and

no one could see him. Both children were awake way past their bedtime. They had been wakened out of a deep sleep getting out of the van and weren't tired anymore.

"Benjamin," Amy said in her smug, older-sister voice, "did you know mama's gonna have a new baby?" She enjoyed knowing things that Benjamin didn't, like the fact that one day they would have to add on another bedroom because she and Benjamin would be too old to share one.

"But her tummy's not big," Benjamin said, confused.

"It will be."

"Where'll the new baby sleep?" Benjamin asked.

"It's not coming here."

Benjamin sat up. He was frightened. "Not coming here? You mean the stork's taking the baby back?"

Amy snickered and hiked her nightgown up under the covers, playing with her fingers in the crack between her legs. "No, silly. Don't you know how babies get born?"

Benjamin wished sometimes that Amy would let him be. She always mixed him up. But he had to know. "Uh-uh," he said finally.

Amy had learned a lot from hanging around the older kids down the street. Mama had said they weren't good Christians and she was not to play with them. She didn't. But she listened to what they talked about. That's how she knew. "Look," she told Benjamin. "The man's part fits into the woman's part and his seed and her seed kiss and then they have a baby from that but it grows in the mother's tummy. You could also have a baby if you french-kiss too much."

"Then how does the baby get here if the stork doesn't bring him?" Benjamin asked, almost on the verge of tears.

"It pops out."

"Pops out of where?"

"Go to bed, Benjy. You're yuchy. Just a yuchy little boy."

"How come mama won't bring our new baby home?" the little boy demanded, fighting sleep.

"She's selling it."

Benjamin didn't understand any of this. He thought Amy was making up stories. Then she started to laugh. He loved it when Amy laughed like that. It made him silly and giggly, and then they were both laughing. Though he didn't know why.

The loud laughter spiraled down the hallway until Ralph came out of the big bedroom at the end of the hallway and opened up their door. There was silence until neither child could contain his giggling any longer.

"Amy and Benjamin? Now you kids go to sleep. You'll wake up your brothers."

Ralph finished unbuttoning his plaid shirt as he walked back down the hall. When he opened the door he saw Flora slipping into a thin, light blue nightie. She turned sideways. No swelling yet. Just the full, ripe breasts. He grinned. He wanted his wife. He had been afraid he wouldn't be able to.

In his urgency he seized her and pressed his lips down hard on hers. When he felt her resistance, he pressed tighter. For a second she yielded, and then she squirmed out of his embrace and pushed him away.

"No, Ralph. It's . . . it's not right."

Ralph looked at her, stunned and stricken. "But, why? You pushed me away! You're still my wife, Flora. We always did with the other children."

Flora shuddered and moved toward the window. "I meant it isn't right for *me* tonight."

Ralph stared at her longingly. It had always been difficult for Flora to loosen up. He wouldn't have minded working doubly hard to get her in the mood, but just then he lost his urge. That hardly ever happened. He didn't feel like trying. "I'll take a cold shower, Flora."

Flora turned, and her long, wheat-colored hair swung with her. Her blue eyes glittered as she smiled approvingly at him. "That's a good idea, dear," she said sweetly.

Then she turned her back to him and continued to stare out the window. She was grateful he had put up no struggle as he sometimes did. Truthfully, there could be no sex with her husband until after the baby was born. For her it wasn't just two sweaty bodies colliding in the act itself. It was something spiritual. And she had another man's seed growing inside her.

In the bathroom Ralph mixed the ice-cold water with hot water and lathered up. She didn't want him anymore. His own wife had told him to take a cold shower. As rigid as Flora could be, she wasn't the kind of wife to reject a husband. She considered it her wifely duty. He turned his eyes toward the ceiling. "Lord, I wanted to continue that conversation we had before. You see, the thing is, it was all Flora's idea. She answered an ad in the newspaper. This doctor's in New York City. Now, don't blame Flora, Lord. She ain't no Eve. She likes to be pregnant. She was born to breed, and she wanted one more child. It's really my fault, too, Lord. I persuaded her. You see we can't afford to have any more, and you know we could use the money."

Just then he stopped quickly.

Flora called in. "You talking to me, Ralph?"

He came out, a towel wrapped around his middle, his hair dripping wet. "No, honey. Just thinking out loud."

They fell asleep, backs to each other. Ralph was asleep in seconds, as usual. Flora stayed awake thinking. It had helped to talk to Minister Haver, but she still had this burning in the pit of her stomach. Nerves. Yes, she was scared, but she'd never admit it to anyone. Sometimes it felt like the fires of hell in there. And she had all these fears she hadn't had before. She would never tell anyone, not even Ralph. But she was afraid to drive and take a shower alone, and she was terrified that one of the kids would get hurt. She didn't even like to look in the mirror when she was alone. Flora Butler was deathly afraid God would punish her for taking life into her own hands.

Chapter Two

Amanda stood with her feet spread apart and her hands on her hips. Her gold hoop earrings bobbed a little as she spoke to the short, bald-headed man sitting behind the massive walnut desk.

"I mean it, Murray. I'm giving notice, and nothing you can say will dissuade me."

Murray twisted a silver and sapphire ring around and around on his pinkie, brushed an imaginary speck from his cream-colored suit, then picked up a well-chewed pencil, which he rolled between thumb and forefinger. "I'm not trying to dissuade you," he laughed. "How much is MacNulty & Small paying you, Amanda, dear? I'll top it."

Amanda plopped down on a love seat. She waited until she had sunk fully into it. Then she stretched out her legs until they bumped a chrome and glass coffee table.

"Now, Amanda, you needn't slouch. Just give me

a figure." Amanda looked out through the windows of Tower Place, where the ad agency had moved not too long ago. This was the fashionable business place to be in Atlanta. She would rather have been at home this gorgeous June day. Rather have been helping Mavis with the party.

"What?" she said suddenly. "No, I'm not going anywhere else. I'm just resigning. My God, I'm giving you six months' notice. Is that all you can think of? That I'm deserting you? I'm giving you a chance to recruit from New York."

"You're *not* going to another agency?"

"No, Mur, I'm not. Think. Think. What have I wanted for so long? What have I missed days of work for?"

Murray got up from behind his desk and came up to her. He kissed her cheek. "Amanda. You're going to have a baby."

Amanda opened her mouth. Somewhere off in the distance an art director and a copywriter were doing a lousy imitation of Ginger Rogers and Fred Astaire. Amanda could feel Murray's eyes slip down to scan her slim white skirt.

"Close, Murray, dear. We're adopting a child."

"How lovely. But you could still work. Perhaps three days a week? Two days a week? Free-lance?"

Amanda shook her head to all of it. "No, Murray. You can't get half-involved around here. I'd be coming in more days before you know it. Just because I won that Clio award. You're always saying you do advertising that sells, not wins awards."

"That's because I hardly ever win awards. Awards bring in the clients, Amanda. I'll be sorry to lose you."

"I believe in being a full-time mother. I'm ready for it."

He went back to his desk, shrugging. "Congratulations, then. Just remember, Amanda, if you decide you want to come back to work, at any time, I'll always take you back. Even if I've replaced you with a new associate creative director."

"How?"

"I'll fire the person I hired to replace you."

Amanda laughed. "Thanks, Murray. I've got a lunch date. Gotta run." She ran out of his office because she suddenly felt like crying.

She walked quickly to her own office, the one she had decorated herself. Then she shut her door on the clacking of the typewriters and the laughter coming from her art director's office, next to hers. On all of it. It would be so good to leave it. To really be a full-time mother. To kiss the sweet-smelling hair and cuddle to her the soft, fragrant little body, the precious baby that she had waited so long for. Amanda sat at her desk, put her head down and cried bitterly.

Not far away, in a renovated ante-bellum mansion that housed WABG, Branch Whitney pulled off his earphones, cued his engineer and ran his fingers through his hair. He got up and stretched, then walked out into the hall, humming.

When he got to the door of the men's room, he decided he was going to do it. Why not? He had built a career out of being himself. His wife would probably kill him—crucify him would be more like it. But he could bring her around. He remembered that song that had the lyrics "wrap yourself in Saran." Sure enough, a woman waltzed through the studio dressed in nothing but Saran Wrap. Of course, they had a security guard now. He had built his career on women, God love them. He smiled. He was going to do it.

Then he grimaced. This would be nothing compared with what it would be like when he told her about the other thing. He couldn't think about it now. She wasn't going to like that. No, not one bit.

Amanda took two Kleenexes from the box on her desk and blotted her cheeks. She sometimes wondered if she shouldn't see a shrink. These sudden bouts of depression would overcome her. She seemed bursting with sadness. Lately all she did was cry, when she had everything to be happy for. She remembered the elation of thinking she was pregnant and the plunge when she had to scrounge around for a Tampax. She used to watch the paper flushing away round and round in the whirlpool at the bottom of the toilet. Then she'd cry. And how many times had that happened? She'd lost count. But now she'd have a baby for sure.

She flicked on the radio, just in time to hear the bing-bong-bing theme that was his musical signature. "Branch Whitney . . . bing . . . bong . . . bing . . . WABG AM . . . let's get together . . . from ten to two . . . spend time with Branch Whitney . . . I care about you."

God, how Amanda hated that ditsy little jingle. She was sorry she had written the words. He couldn't sing either. Not paying much attention to the radio, she picked up a piece of copy one of her writers had done on a co-op ad with Rich's. She had tuned out the soothing music, the bouncy commercials and the charming Branch Whitney patter.

Then she sat straight up and stared at the radio. She couldn't believe it. "And so we're having a name-the-baby contest!" The resonant voice of Branch Whitney. It caressed the microphone, and every housewife mopping the kitchen floor, making beds, having coffee, spinning fantasies, loved him. She sometimes wondered why he didn't get his vocal chords insured. Amanda chewed on her pen. Surely he meant a gorilla or elephant born in the zoo. Branch wouldn't do something like that.

"Just send a three-by-five index card to Branch Whitney, WABG, Peachtree Street, to the attention of Name Amanda's Baby and of course to good old Atlanta, Georgia, which is the best place to be on this sunny June day. Just as balmy and breezy . . ."

Amanda clicked the radio off. How dare he! He had never told her about the contest. And before she had a chance to tell their friends about the baby. She was saving that. Now he had made the formal announcement with a contest. Everyone would know they were adopting a baby. Adopting a baby. That was funny. Even she was beginning to believe it.

Mavis Appleton had just finished polishing the silver coffee service. She took a pack of cigarettes from her housedress and lit one, exhaling. She never inhaled. Looking out over the windows to the side, she saw the sunlight dancing with fiery feet on the creek that filled the ravine that ran up toward the woods. It was a steep incline crowned by the magnificent white-columned Georgian house at the top of the hill. From the front road it was almost hidden by the crisscrossing of sweet-gum trees and pines. The house had been in the family since 1900. Mavis was third-generation help working for third-generation Whitneys. Except everyone knew these Whitneys had no real money, not the money their grandparents and the Whitneys before them had had. These Whitneys had to work.

Mavis stubbed out her cigarette just as the phone rang.

"Mavis?"

"How are you, honey?"

"Tell me what they're going to name the baby, so I can win me a free dinner."

"What baby? What are you talking about?"

"Your boss just announced it on the radio. They're going to have a baby, and there's a contest to name the baby. Now, c'mon, let me in on it."

"She ain't having no baby," Mavis replied sharply, but she began to feel the sickening downhill slide of insecurity. They hadn't told her.

"No, you know what I mean. They're adopting a baby. Now, what's the name? C'mon, it's dinner for two. I'll take you."

"I don't fix no contests, Lilah!" she said crossly. "Now if you want dinner, you go make it yourself!"

She hung up. The sun had disappeared behind a cloud. She felt a chill. She looked out the window. The ravine stood dark and threatening. She watched the mailman's car driving slowly down the street. Then she took another cigarette from her pocket. The folks were adopting a baby. A baby. The sun came out again, but everything seemed dark and dreary. *Why hadn't they told her?* She should have been the first to know.

Amanda's lunch date had canceled out. "Oh, well, who wanted to have lunch with the client, anyway?" she mumbled to herself. Especially a client who felt the flu coming on. She flipped through her book to see if there was anyone who might be free. She didn't want to be alone. Not today. Branch had made her a celebrity. She made a few calls. Everyone was in meetings. She could drive home and help Mavis, but there really wasn't all that much to do. The party was being catered. She didn't feel like going shopping.

Idly she stuck a piece of canary yellow copy paper in her electric typewriter. Actually, they had until December. She who named fast-food snack shops and hosiery colors and wines had been reluctant to think up a name for the baby. She should call Branch . . . and . . . her fingers had typed something. She looked at the paper. Danielle. Danielle? She hadn't really been thinking at all. She had just typed it. Well, it was obviously in the back of her mind. She typed again, but more consciously. A little boy. Daniel. Dan. Danny.

She reached in her drawer and pulled out a three-by-five index card. Printing DANIELLE carefully on one, she addressed it. Then she giggled and took out another one. She lettered DANIEL on it. The first one she signed Amanda Whitney, and the second, Mrs. Branch Whitney. She would say nothing to Branch about the announcement on the radio. That would drive him mad. She'd pretend she hadn't heard the show. She found some stamps and slipped into her white suit jacket. There was time to kill. Everyone took a two-hour lunch at Rogers & Harrisburg, Inc. She'd go for a walk and then grab a hamburger some place.

After mailing her letters in the building, she walked around the corner of Piedmont Center and Peachtree. Looking up at the shimmering blue skyscraper she had just left, she was struck suddenly by the stark futuristic statement of the mirrorlike building. But then all of Atlanta was being given that sleek, streamlined look. It was an architect's haven. A city of tomorrows. She wondered what her tomorrows would be. Her todays were getting rather complicated.

Two women passed her by, and she studied them behind her sunglasses. Junior League ladies. She could spot them a mile away. Impeccable lineage, the too-high voices, the vapid, gay patter, the life of lunches and charity work. Iron butterflies she liked to call them. But they all had babies. Between their functions and their decorators, they had babies.

Everyone had babies. In fact, she had never really met a woman who couldn't. But she wouldn't be like the Junior Leaguers when she became a mother. A mother. Her tomorrows were in that one word. She took a deep breath. A baby. The sun came out in full force, bright and hard, and her spirits lifted. Suddenly she was starving.

Stopping at the curb and waiting for the light to change, she found herself staring into the face of one of the most beautiful women she had ever seen. She looked like an old photograph, a lady out of the nineteenth century. Her strawberry blond hair and eyebrows looked touched by gold in the sun. Her brown eyes sparkled with amber flecks. She had an aura about her. Then Amanda saw why she looked so fresh and beautiful. She was pregnant.

Under the crisp white maternity smock was a big belly with a baby in it. Amanda wanted to ask her if it was her first. To say she was going to be a mother soon, too. But that was ridiculous. She in her slim skirt. Then the lovely woman crossed the street and Amanda stayed rooted, feeling confused, ashamed, envious. She was thirty-seven years old, and there were no more miracles to pray for. She had truly almost made herself sick trying until six months ago, when her doctor said to give up. Why couldn't she just accept it?

The caterer had supplied two maids and a butler in uniform. They were starting to circulate among the small crowd that had begun arriving. Cars were lining up in the long, winding driveway. Only a select number of cars would park on the street, those that had to leave early. Everyone else would want to stay. A Whitney party was a choice invitation. Plus a chance to see the fabulous family mansion.

Mavis was in charge of the kitchen, caterers or no

caterers. She nagged the hired help and supervised every detail, driving the caterer to the brink of quitting. Her confidence had been restored. Just before the party, Mrs. Whitney had taken her aside.

"It was an accident what happened today, Mavis. You know how Mr. Whitney is. I would want you to be the first to know. I need you to help me with the baby."

Mavis's cheeks had dimpled and were so round it looked like she had two peaches tucked in either side. "Oh, yes, Mrs. Whitney. Don't worry about one little thing. With three kids of my own, I sure know what to do."

Amanda was at the door greeting the guests as they arrived. Branch had disappeared. She hadn't seen him since he ran upstairs to change. It was odd. He hadn't even complimented her on her new backless red crepe gown. She had taken the ruby and gold earrings and necklace from the safe. Her lustrous brown hair was pulled back at the nape of her neck into a low chignon.

"Amaaanda! You look as lovely as ever." Amanda turned. Mrs. Magnolia Mouth. The bothersome wife of Branch's equally bothersome program director and boss, who insisted on playing some rock music and sneaked the music right into the program log made up beforehand. There was a continuing battle. Rock wasn't Branch Whitney, and he didn't feel it was his fans, either.

"Amanda, darling, we can't stay too late," she was saying. "It's the maid's night off and our baby sitter has to leave early. You know what it's like having four children. And, oh, congratulations, I hear you're going . . . to get a baby."

The words were cloying, the voice, whiny, almost a syrupy drawl. Amanda stood stunned for a moment. She pictured a woman coming up to her and stabbing a dagger into her stomach, then the pain, then the blood spreading all over her dress. She smiled. "Yes, we're adopting a child."

"How lovely for you, Amanda. A boy or a girl?"

"If you'll excuse me, I have to find Branch," Amanda said quickly, and walked into the growing crowd. *He has to go throw a contest,* she thought to herself. *It would have been just an ordinary party, and now, questions, questions. And he isn't even around to answer them, the coward.* Oh, she would find him. He was in the house somewhere. She smiled in spite of herself. Branch. Unpredictable, childlike, lovable Branch Ashworth Whitney. Life with him could never be boring. She hadn't been bored one day in the ten years they had been married.

Turning into the morning room, she thought that soon that old chinoiserie wallpaper would have to be replaced. The upkeep of the house would baffle the Atlanta Historical Society, who would love to get their hands on it one day. *Not for sale,* she thought firmly. She loved living in a colorful museum. One of the many tall clocks chimed the hour and she jumped. She could only allow herself five minutes to search for her husband.

She sank her burgundy sling-back heels into the pearl gray and pink Persian carpet outside the library door and stopped. Voices. She tried the door knob. Strange, it was locked. She leaned closer. Branch's voice, yes. But who was the other person? It sounded softer, cajoling, yet she couldn't make out the words. She knocked. She waited another minute. No one answered. It was probably nothing. Then she remembered they couldn't hear the knock if they were talking. The door was too thick. She debated, then turned, stumbling and catching herself. Who was locked in the library with Branch? Who was missing from the party? She entered the main ballroom and realized it would be impossible to tell. The place was mobbed.

Inside the library, Branch was poking the fire. His stomach was in knots.

"You have to tell her, the sooner the better," the voice from the couch said.

"You don't know Amanda. . . ."

"There's no other way to handle it. I checked. She has to know. She would find out about it anyway. There's no way of getting around those signatures, Branch."

Amanda was talking to Murray and some people from the agency when she spotted Branch coming into the room. He was standing underneath the big crystal chandelier. She smiled and relaxed, laughing inwardly at herself. It was only Justin Hirsch with Branch. She studied them for a second. Justin was the more handsome of the two if you liked dark, sensitive, movie-star looks. He was short, just about five seven, Amanda's height. And then there was Branch. Six foot one, salt and pepper hair, impossible, irrepressible and terribly sexy. She couldn't imagine not being in love with Branch Whitney.

Branch came over to his wife's little group and shook hands with Murray. "I hate to lose Amanda," Murray said, "but I guess the competition is too stiff."

Branch smiled graciously and winked at Amanda. She gave him a long, searching look. If she asked him why the library door had been locked, it would seem as if she was spying on him. Besides, it wasn't important. Knowing Branch and Justin, they were swapping dirty jokes. She studied his eyes, trying to figure out if that was all it was, when Joyce Hirsch came by.

"Can you slip away for a minute, Amanda?" Joyce said. "I've got to see that nursery."

Amanda brightened, and looked around. The

room was filled with chattering, munching, drinking people. It was a good time to break away. Joyce was the only one who knew about the existence of the special little room.

"I'll just be a minute, darling," she told Branch, then left with Joyce. They made their way through the huge room of people, who stopped to congratulate Amanda. Then they took the back stairway. On the second landing they turned down the hall. Right next to the master bedroom, with its enormous marble bathroom, was the baby's room. Joyce released a soft gasp when the door was opened. It was done in pale yellows, ice-cream pink and soft mint green. The walls gleamed with fresh white paint.

"This is like stepping into a storybook room," Joyce squealed. "You didn't really design this all by yourself?"

"I did," Amanda said, proudly.

There were little lamps with clowns for the base, a mobile of little bunnies and baby chicks, stuffed animals of every size and shape pyramiding one wall, and a little crib with a ruffled canopy.

"God, what could anyone give you for a baby gift? You've got it all."

Amanda laughed. "I guess it is kind of cute," she said, appraising the bright, cheery little room with a designer's eye.

"Lucky baby," Joyce said, smiling. "Oh, Amanda, I'm just so happy for you. You wanted a baby so badly." She sat down in the white rocking chair with the heart-shaped pink pillow and rocked, sticking her legs out. "Now, you'll have your baby. It's terrific!"

Amanda turned her back on the petite blonde. She burst into tears. Joyce sprang out of the rocker and rushed over to Amanda, putting her arms around her.

"What is it, Amanda? You're scared, aren't you?

Well, you'll do just fine, believe me. You'll make a good mother."

Amanda crumpled under a fresh outburst of tears. "What is it? Can I help?" Joyce said softly.

"Joyce, everything I tell you is in the strictest confidence. I have to tell someone. Promise you won't tell anyone, not even Justin?"

Joyce nodded, and suddenly she felt uncomfortable. She didn't want to hear this.

"We're . . . we're not adopting this baby," Amanda said.

Joyce had the urge to run from the room. Anything but to stay and listen. Calmly she forced herself to say, "But you said you were. Branch even announced it on the radio."

"It can pass for an adopted baby. But it's really Branch's child."

Joyce was silent.

"I know what you're thinking," Amanda went on painfully. "That Branch had an affair and I offered to take the baby. No, it's nothing like that. It's worse. There's this doctor . . . I mean . . . we're paying a woman to have this baby for us. A surrogate mother." She glanced at Joyce, who wore a blank look. "Artificial insemination. It's Branch's baby. Some woman we don't know is carrying Branch's baby so I can be a mother."

Joyce smiled slowly. "Oh, well, there's nothing wrong in that, Amanda. I read about it somewhere. Many women are having children that way." She bit her lip. She would rather not have had any children than have it be only her husband's child. She hated Branch Whitney at that moment. She had known about everything from Justin. But did Amanda know the rest of it?

"I wanted a baby so badly, Joyce. You know that, and Branch, well, you know how insistent he can be. He was for it. He made it seem so right. You have

two children. You don't know what it's like to want a
baby so much you wonder if you might kidnap the
next one you see peeking out of a baby carriage.
There were days I didn't trust myself, I swear." She
was sobbing again. "And all those tests and the
doctors and seeing the pregnant women waiting in
the offices. Smiling!"

"I understand," Joyce said, soothingly. She was
thinking, *So he hasn't told her all of it.* Poor Amanda. "Don't feel guilty. You don't have to be the
natural mother of a child to be a good mother. You
want the baby!"

Amanda looked at Joyce. "It was Branch's idea to
tell everyone we're adopting. He doesn't want the
publicity."

"It would be easier for the child," Joyce said
tactfully. "Look, everything will work out. Go
splash some cold water on your face, and let's get
back to the party."

Amanda didn't answer. She was staring, as if
transfixed, at a small panda bear that had fallen and
sat alone in a corner. "Sometimes I think I made a
big mistake," she said, her voice hollow, without
energy. "But it's too late to change it."

Chapter Three

The tall, slimly built man parted the drapes in his
Madison Avenue office and looked down at the
traffic below. From where he stood on the nineteenth floor, the cars and trucks looked like creeping

beetles. The sun was trying to penetrate through the gloom, but he knew the only end to the muggy August day would be the way it began—damp, humid and depressing, with intermittent periods of rain. It was a perfect day for a funeral.

They had buried his mother this morning. His nurse had had to reschedule his appointments. He detested being inconvenienced in any way.

The drapes slipped through his fingers as he heard several phones ring, followed by his intercom buzzer. With his long stride he reached his desk almost immediately, and pressed a button.

"Dr. Borg," said his secretary's voice, "your attorney on three, Mrs. Fields on four and Miss Benson on five."

The man's forehead creased imperceptibly. "Tell Mr. Nathan I'll get back to him before five, tell Mrs. Fields I'm with a patient and find out what her problem is. Let me talk to Miss Benson."

He pressed down another button on his beige phone.

"Is that you, darling?"

"Yes, Suzanne, who else would it be? I'm very busy. What do you want?"

"I'm sorry. I just wanted to know if you were all right. I should have gone."

He sighed loudly. "Suzanne, she was my mother, not yours." She irked him. He had told her over and over he didn't want a commitment. He'd been perfectly honest. She was getting too attached. Just like all the other women. She was going to cry. He knew it. He closed his eyes and waited for it. Why couldn't women sense when he grew tired of them?

"Barnard?" She was crying softly into the phone, trying to disguise it. "This is just so unexpected. Everything was so . . . and suddenly you're cool. I understand this is a time of mourning for you. But, have I done anything wrong?"

Have I done anything wrong? That was the funniest part. He laughed to himself.

"Are we through? Could you just tell me that? I don't understand."

"Yes, Suzanne, we are through." He sighed. Well, she asked for it.

All she said after that was a faint good-bye. He hung up the phone and smiled. Sometimes Dr. Barnard Borg thought he enjoyed the endings better than the beginnings. Of course, the two were never that far apart.

Suzanne held the phone in her hand for a moment, then slowly placed it on the receiver. There was no one around, and the door to her office was closed. "Bastard!" she screamed at the top of her voice. Just like that. The unbelievable lovemaking, the leisurely, romantic dinners, the lovely weekends at that inn in the country. Three solid months of thinking she knew him, of thinking he loved her and would change his mind about commitment. Through the pain she thought, *maybe he did me a favor by ending things.* She was attractive, thirty-three, successful. She'd go out and find herself someone else. She made a mental note never to date a gynecologist again.

There was a knock on the door.

"Come in," he said.

"Mrs. Butler is waiting in the reception room," Thelma, his nurse, announced.

He glided from his office into the cheerfully decorated waiting room. His white coat flapped in the breeze, his energy stirred.

"Mrs. Butler," he said graciously.

The woman sitting in the far corner of the couch looked up. Her hair had fallen in strands out of her bun and hung in damp tendrils around her face. Her umbrella lay on the carpeting over a small puddle. She smiled shyly at the doctor, who bowed from the waist, picked up one of her hands and gently kissed it.

She followed the nurse into a bright examining room while Dr. Borg disappeared into another small room. Mechanically she undressed and snapped on the tangerine cotton dressing gown. It always seemed as if she had it backward somehow. When Dr. Borg came in, she was sitting on the table with her bare feet dangling over the edge. The doctor was holding a file and looked apologetic, as if he should have knocked before intruding. The nurse assisted her. Flora relaxed back on the table.

Dr. Borg suggested politely that she place her feet in the metal stirrups on either side of the examining table. One of the nurses artfully draped a sheet over her belly. But Flora knew that bit of modesty was more for her own benefit than his.

Looking up at the mobile swinging gaily over her head, the white doves flying nowhere, she wondered if it really could distract a patient. When she had become pregnant on the same table, she had hardly noticed it.

She had watched only the doctor. When she saw the syringe, she thought, *There's a baby in there.* Then, after he did it, she knew there was a strange man's sperm inside her and she was conceiving. Tears ran down her face, and the nurse had bent over to ask if she was okay.

"I'm fine," she had whispered. And she was. She was joyful. Conception. A divine miracle. She always knew when she and Ralph had made a baby.

Flora studied the doctor. He was a handsome man. Tall, blond, very distinguished looking. Dr. Borg was a good doctor. She had absolute confi-

dence that he knew what he was doing. Except for
the rare times she looked into his eyes and felt
instinctively afraid.

She felt him pressing her belly, winced a little
when he probed the vaginal passage and smiled
when he said expansively, "Fine, fine, excellent
for the fourth month." But he had warned her.
There was more. She had tried not to think about
it.

"Have you ever had an amniocentesis with your
other children?"

Flora Butler shook her head.

"Well, it's becoming almost routine for women
older than yourself nowadays. It's mainly to check
against Downs syndrome. And of course you can tell
the sex of the child."

Flora Butler had tuned him out. She was having a
quiet moment of terror. What if the baby wasn't
healthy? She hadn't even thought of that. She was
twenty-eight years old. That wasn't old, but what if
she did have a retarded or defective baby? They
couldn't keep it. They couldn't even support a
healthy child or they would have had their own. If
the baby was "damaged," they wouldn't get the
money, probably. And worse, she could never allow
an abortion. It was against everything they believed
in.

She breathed deeply. Mustn't be nervous. The
Lord was watching over her. One of the nurses
handed the doctor a stethoscopelike object. "This is
an electronic fetal stethoscope," announced Dr.
Borg. He put the receiver end across her belly, and
the stethoscope, in his ears. She saw he was grinning
as if he was pleased with himself. But it was an odd
smile. Flora looked at him and thought it was a
smirk.

Thelma, his nurse, was standing to the side,
holding Mrs. Butler's hand. She looked down at the

woman on the table and thought that she was one of Dr. Borg's loveliest patients. She looked just like a Madonna. *Oh, the lucky woman who was going to get her baby,* she decided.

Dr. Borg spread grease on Flora's stomach. She shivered, though it wasn't cold. Everyone's eyes were on the ultrasound screen. "Looks like a television of sorts, doesn't it, Mrs. Butler?" Dr. Borg commented. All it produced, she noticed, were shadows and silhouettes of the fetus. They weren't clear to her at first. Then she gasped out loud. She could see the images clearly. She had seen legs, arms and a torso, bobbing, floating. Dr. Borg smiled at her. "That's the baby, Mrs. Butler."

She said nothing. It wasn't Flora's way to react to something immediately. She shut her eyes tightly while Dr. Borg turned off the machine and until he completed the tap, withdrawing the champagne-colored fluid from her amniotic sac. When Flora opened her eyes, she saw what she had seen on the screen, though it was now blank. She had seen her baby before it was born.

After she had dressed, the nurse escorted her down the hall to the doctor's office.

"*'Be fruitful, and multiply, and replenish the earth.'*"

"I beg your pardon?" the nurse said, just outside the doctor's door.

"It's a quote. From the Bible."

"Oh."

"Genesis. 9:1. When God blessed Noah and his sons and . . ."

The nurse wasn't listening. She was tapping the door, which was slightly ajar. "Enjoy your talk with Dr. Borg," she said, smiling. "And have a good day."

Dr. Borg opened the door and escorted her to the plush, beige-fabric chair in front of his desk. Then he sat down. Flora waited while he inspected her file folder with as much scrutiny as he had just examined her body. The beige drapes billowed out in front of the air conditioner.

"I want you to take it easy for this pregnancy. It's important not to overdo," he said.

"I don't do much except cook and clean and sew for my family and go to church."

"Well, sometimes there are clever ways of cutting back, saving steps. . . ." He looked at his watch. "I'll call you, Mrs. Butler."

She looked at him blankly.

"About your amniocentesis. We should have the results shortly."

"Yes, of course." A tiny crease of sweat began to line her forehead. A defective, deformed baby. What then? But, no, God wouldn't let it happen. God was good. She pictured the husband and wife who had suffered all these years, trying, trying, probably getting into debt for the baby they wanted. The husband would be a God-fearing man like her Ralph. And the wife someone just like herself. Dr. Borg had said every effort was made to match. The poor woman was probably knitting or sewing for her baby right now. God wouldn't let Flora disappoint them.

"There is something else I wanted to ask," she said softly.

"Yes, Mrs. Butler," he replied, trying to keep any hint of impatience out of his voice.

"It's about the birth. . . . You see, all of my four children were born in a hospital, but my husband was with me during labor and delivery."

"That's fine."

She was standing now. He saw her fists were clenched. "I don't take drugs, doctor. I don't believe in them."

"I don't foresee the need for anything, Mrs.

Butler. I'll keep all your requests in mind." He wondered if she would ever leave. He would be running late today.

"And one other thing," she said, standing straighter. "I don't like my babies to be born with forceps pressing into their heads."

"Oh, I agree," he said. *This wasn't her baby,* he thought. "Everything possible will be done to make it a natural birth process."

"Good, then you understand."

"You can count on me, Mrs. Butler. Now if you'll go to the desk, my receptionist will schedule your next appointment."

He watched her walk gracefully across the room to the door. She resembled a huge cat. *A perfect breeder,* he thought. Would that he could find more like her. He glanced at his watch. It was way before five, but he had to return Harvey Nathan's call. It turned out to be just a question on a rewording of the surrogate-mother contracts. A minor detail. Before they hung up, he said, "One more thing, Harv."

"Anything, Barn."

"That redhead who came up to you at that party last week. The one with the fantastic tits, small waist and full hips . . ."

"Huh? Last week! Wait a second, the redhead in the flowered sarong thing?"

"Yeah."

"She's a singer. Don't know her number, but maybe I can try to . . ."

"Do you know where she sings?"

"In a little club in the Village. You know, she's pretty good. The Blue Willow. That's where she sings. A little jazz club."

When they hung up, Harvey Nathan drummed his fingers on his desk. What would it be like to be Dr. Barnard Borg? The man could have any woman he wanted. He had never had that kind of luck when he was single. But Barn? He attracted them just by lifting his eyelids slowly. Which just went to prove that most women were masochists.

Chapter Four

The rush-hour traffic was about an hour away. As Flora Butler walked down Madison Avenue, she wasn't sure if it was raining or if the air conditioning from the huge office buildings was spraying moisture. Her sandals squished in the dampness. Her raincoat was clammy next to her skin. But still she walked. She had to think.

Down Madison Avenue to Thirty-fourth Street. All the way across town until she came to Gimbels, where she caught the PATH train to Hoboken. She followed the Conrail signs. There she waited with a paper cup of tea in her hands for an old Erie-Lackawanna train to take her to Wananwa, New Jersey. Then she'd have to take a cab.

The ancient, dusty train rocked and bumped until it seemed to collapse on the track. Flora climbed the steep step, her tea jiggling in her cup, her mind elsewhere. When the train finally pulled out, rocking and chugging, she held her belly with both hands and shut her eyes.

Suddenly her eyes blinked open. She shuddered, though the train was a good fifteen degrees hotter than it was outside the dusty, steamy windows. Another woman would get the baby. She nodded and held her stomach. It was the Lord's way. And it was a blessing. From her womb to another woman's arms. She didn't care what anybody said. There was nothing unnatural about it. A tear sneaked out and slid down her cheek. Flora always hid in the closet to cry. But now, for one joyous moment, she felt unashamed. It was a happy tear. Another tear escaped from the other eye, and she wiped it onto her hand.

A tiny, plump, gray-haired lady leaned across the aisle and touched her arm. Flora jumped. "My dear," the woman said, her voice vibrating with the train, "I thought I might get you some water. You seem to be feeling ill." She looked down at Flora's belly meaningfully.

Flora looked up into the face of the lady with the kind smile. "Oh, no, I'm all right," she said. The lady didn't retreat. "The Lord has blessed me," Flora said. The eyes. Flora could always tell from the eyes. "'Blessed are ye that sow beside all waters, that send forth thither the feet of the ox and the ass'—Isaiah," she said.

"'The morning stars sang together, and all the sons of God shouted for Joy'—the Book of Job," the woman said, after scarcely a beat. "The Lord works in wondrous ways, doesn't He?" She turned toward her seat, but leaned back to Flora one more time. "May God bless you and your husband with a healthy baby."

Flora smiled weakly and her lips formed an "amen." The woman sat down and became a stranger again. Flora kept her face to the window, watching the familiar scenery fly by. The blurred stretches of grass, the junkyards, the beginnings of a shopping center. She thought of something. She couldn't tell Ralph about that test she had taken. What if the baby was damaged?

* * *

Amy was playing outside near the driveway. She was banging the little boy who lived across the street with a rolled-up magazine until he cried out in pain.

"You take that back, you little bastard!" she screamed, giving him a few seconds' reprieve.

"I'm going to tell your mama you use bad words," the little boy shouted.

Amy went quickly behind him and pinned back his arms while Benjamin walloped him all over. "Stop!" he cried. "Okay, I'll take it back."

"Say it," Benjamin insisted.

"I won't say your mama has babies and sells 'em."

"I won't say it no more," Amy prompted him.

"No more."

They watched him run across the street, and Amy yelled, "Better not. It could have been a piece of wood with a nail. And Aaron? . . ."

The little boy stopped and turned fearfully. "What?"

"You're not a Christian, Aaron. That's what."

The little boy started to run. Amy and Benjamin burst into laughter.

"Turd," Amy shouted.

"Naaa!" Benjamin said, jiggling his fingers, one hand in his ear, the other on his nose.

"Look, there's mama!" Amy said, spotting a cab turning the corner.

"You're gonna get it. You better have a story."

Amy looked down. Her new homemade pink dress was filthy and ripped. She wasn't even supposed to be wearing it. It was for church. Benjamin was right. She was going to get it. Unless she thought fast. She turned her head toward the treetops and rolled her eyeballs around. Too bad she didn't have an onion. It was easier to work up a cry.

Flora paid the cab driver, thinking how expensive that trip had become. They needed the second van.

But she wouldn't get the rest of the money until the baby was born. She spotted her kids running toward her. As she got out of the cab, she said in one breath, "Where's Carl and Denny? Why are you crying, Amy? What happened to your new dress?"

"Carl and Denny are playing inside," Benjamin said, his big brown eyes enormous. Amy was going to get it this time.

Amy walked alongside her mother, wringing her dirty hands and crying piteously, "Mama . . . mama . . ." They reached the kitchen.

Flora stopped to get her wind, then sighed and took a deep breath, throwing her shoulders back. "Amy, go and change. Wash up, and come into the kitchen and tell me what happened when I went away. Benjamin, go take Carl and Denny outside. It's too nice a day to be shut up inside."

Amy didn't move. Her sobs became billows and her little chest heaved in and out as if she couldn't catch her breath. She gasped quickly and violently until she could speak. "The kids around here. They say bad things about . . . you. Mama, they never leave us alone. They hit us and make us run." She resumed her tortured singsong sobbing.

Flora turned the girl's smudged face up to hers.

"What do they say, Amy?"

"They say . . . they say . . . you make babies to sell, mama."

Flora stood still. Amy held her breath. The branches of the elms rustled outside the open window. A bird cawed. Flora didn't move. Amy took a short breath. Then Flora walked to a chair and sat down heavily.

Children learned from parents. "Have you been playing with any children other than your playmates from church?"

"No, ma'am," Amy said.

Flora opened her arms, and Amy looked for a

second, then ran into them. Then Flora put the little girl's dirty blond hair to her breast. "'A day in thy courts is better than a thousand. I had rather be a door-keeper in the house of my God, than to dwell in the tents of wickedness.' Psalms," Flora said intensely.

Amy was careful not to squirm. She wasn't going to get a spanking or be punished. Her mama never hugged her. She liked it.

"You're eight years old now, Amy. A big girl. It's time you understood what life is all about. It's time to begin your Bible study."

That evening in Atlanta, Amanda and Branch Whitney had cocktails in the Regency Hyatt. They watched the bulletlike outside elevator shoot people up and down. They held hands and listened to the piano player's renditions of mellow old tunes.

"Know what this reminds me of?" Branch remarked.

"That little piano bar we used to go to when you were trying to convince me to marry you?"

"Convince *you?* I was the biggest catch in Atlanta, and you knew it." He put his hand on her thigh, admiring her tan cashmere skirt and cream-colored silk blouse. "I'm nothing without you, Amanda," he said seriously.

Amanda fingered her gold chains, lowered her head and smiled. "Thank you for that, darling. Thank you."

"This place reminds me of that old movie *Grand Hotel.* I like to look up at all the hotel rooms on each landing and wonder who's in each."

"Why, Branch, you have the most marvelous imagination. The kind of imagination that dreams up baby-naming contests."

"I knew you knew! All along. That's why I never

said anything. You really had me nervous at first, though. But it's okay now, isn't it?" His face looked so like a little boy's Amanda laughed and cupped his chin with her hand. "Naughty, naughty," she said. "Let's go to dinner."

They walked hand in hand out the door of the hotel, oblivious to head-turners. Some people knew who Branch was; others admired Amanda's striking loveliness. They had decided it was a second honeymoon night. They were celebrating the full moon. Branch was praying for a miracle.

"Here's to the mother-to-be," Branch said, raising his glass of red wine after they were seated and waited on in the restaurant.

"And here's to the father-to-be," Amanda said, raising hers. She felt that same quick depression come on her again.

"What's wrong?" Branch said.

"Nothing. No, well, it's something. I just wish I were the mother-to-be in reality." There, she admitted it.

"Amanda," Branch said, the tone of his voice unsympathetic, almost stern. "Stop punishing yourself. We tried, honey. For five long years we tried. You *are* the mother-to-be."

Amanda nodded and tried desperately to switch to an upbeat mood. "Do you want a boy or a girl? I never even asked you that."

"Just a healthy baby," Branch replied. It had to be a healthy baby.

Amanda picked up a celery stick. "I guess I want a girl. I love those little dresses they have in the stores. Lace and ruffles and checks and plaids. They're so cute."

Branch laughed. "You want a doll. You'll dress her in designer jeans!"

"I will not!" She looked down, feeling guilty.

What kind of mother would she be? "Okay, I guess I just want a healthy baby, too." She felt a sudden rush of genuine enthusiasm. She wanted so much not to ruin it for him. To be as excited as he was. "Oh, Branch, I am happy. Really I am. Just think, we'll have a child."

Branch looked into her light green eyes and smiled. "I'm happy when you're happy," he said sincerely. Then he looked down. "But there's something you have to know, Amanda."

He was acting serious. The joking was over. "What is it?" Amanda asked. "Is something wrong? With the baby?"

"Shhh. Not with the baby. But . . ."

The waiter arrived with their steaks and he stopped talking. "Medium rare for Mr. Whitney and medium for Mrs. Whitney." With a shaking hand, she picked up her wine glass and spilled some. Deftly, the waiter produced a napkin and wiped the spilled wine, saying nothing. Just as expertly he disappeared.

Amanda stared at her steak. "What is it, Branch?" She was almost shouting.

Branch looked at her hard and long. Then he picked up his knife and fork and began eating. "The thing is, Amanda, I have to disqualify you from the contest. I mean, you'd win and I'd have to reveal the winner's name on the air." He reached inside his jacket and pulled out her two postcards. Amanda looked at him, shook her head and started to laugh. She laughed so hard people turned around to stare. Then she started to cry.

Branch looked at her thoughtfully. "Try some of this," he said. "Not bad. It's Maurice's own steak sauce."

"Hey, Maurice!" he called. The owner, a little man with a twirled mustache, arrived at their table instantly. Amanda had pulled her compact out of her purse and was checking her makeup, dabbing a smudge of mascara with a Kleenex.

"You know, you should bottle this, Maurice. Amanda could write you some advertising copy, and I could plug it on the air. 'Maurice's Own Steak Sauce.' There's a good name," he said, carefully watching his wife. She made a face at the name. She wanted to say she'd be busy with bottles filled with something other than steak sauce, but Maurice got very excited. "No, Mr. Whitney, please. I invented the sauce for my favorite customers, like you and Mrs. Whitney. Now please, eat. And dinner is on the house tonight. To celebrate the new baby."

They smiled at him, and tears came to Amanda's eyes again. "Weepy," she explained. "Branch, let's talk about the baby."

"Okay," he said, trying to be cool.

"Do you think he or she should go to private school?"

"Oh, absolutely."

"Me, too. Music lessons?"

"Everything lessons."

"What about Sunday school?"

He stopped, his fork in midair. Then he put it down. "Oh, I don't know, Amanda. Maybe let's wait for him or her to decide. I'm not especially religious."

"Me, neither. But I wonder if that's solid enough for a child."

He winked at her. "Listen, Dr. Spock. We've got a couple of years to figure that one out."

"Sweet of Maurice to give us dinner on the house," she said.

"Order two desserts," Branch replied, his mouth half-full.

Then they started laughing like two little kids.

"It's the wine. . . ." Branch said airily.

"It's the Grand Hotel. . . ." Amanda said, doing a poor imitation of Greta Garbo.

"Want to spend the night there?" Branch said, sticking his knife in his mouth and flicking imaginary cigar ashes, doing a fairly good imitation of Groucho Marx.

Then they were quiet, looking at each other across the table, through the glow of the shimmering candlelight. "Not a bad idea, kiddo," she said, and winked saucily. But there was a lump in her throat. Because it was such a nice make-believe anniversary. And because she was such a hopeless romantic.

Branch looked lovingly at his beautiful wife. Who said marriage wasn't terrific? He was a lucky man. Then he thought of what he still had to tell Amanda, and he felt queasy. He might not be able to finish his steak after all.

After dinner they had crème de menthe parfaits and brandies. When they left, everyone turned to watch. Amanda kissed Maurice. Branch was smiling. Then Amanda turned and waved to the employees, her eyes sparkling. Everyone who had dinner at Maurice's that night had the same thought: the Branch Whitneys were the beautiful people of Atlanta.

They were quiet as they drove home. It was a chilly night for August. The ravine was as black as the sky. Pinecones had blanketed the grounds again, and Amanda made a mental note to have them raked. As they drove up the endless driveway, Amanda said softly, "The stars are really out tonight."

"Hmmm," said Branch.

"But the best star of all is sitting next to me."

"Hmmm."

"Branch! Don't you want to play disc jockey? Where are all the smart remarks?"

"Amanda, could we get a bottle of brandy and just go to the library and light a fire?"

Amanda turned to look at him. It was dark. She couldn't read his features. "Of course, darling, but I thought you would want . . ."

"Not tonight, honey. I have a headache."

She got out of the car. There was something strange in his voice. Hard to tell if he was joking or not. "The steak sauce. I didn't put any on mine," she quipped, her mood still light. He said nothing. She opened the back door and he crossed ahead of her toward the library. His back was to her. Had she seen his face at that moment, she would have been terrified. Branch Whitney had never looked uglier in his life.

Chapter Five

He stole a look at the beautiful redhead lying naked next to him. A natural redhead.

"Wow, did you take lessons somewhere?"

"You might say that," he said, smiling.

"You really know women."

"I make it my business to."

She sat up on one elbow, her hair spilling over her shoulders. "Say, what kind of doctor are you, anyway?"

"A gynecologist."

She collapsed back on the pillow and giggled. "No wonder."

"You have a lovely voice," he said. The arts

escaped him. He had never had time to cultivate a taste for them.

"Thanks. But no one digs jazz, really. You can make it in rock or disco. It's hard to be Sarah or Dinah or Ella. . . ."

He was thinking about something. It gave him a headache. His grandmother. She was a redhead.

"You'll be a doctor when you grow up." She had left him money for it. Nana, his Grandmother Tucker, had big, big, billowing breasts. He wanted to unbutton her dress and put his face in between them. But her hair. That was it. Nana's hair had never really turned gray. It was always red. Like this woman. Nana had died when he was fourteen. He had cried. And then when he grew up and went to college, it was her money that financed him through medical school. But she left him with something else—the truth. What would his life have been like if she had died before telling him? No one else would have.

". . . so I just kept struggling. But I have a good manager. He wasn't there tonight. Say, I'm glad you stopped in just like that to hear me sing. It was a beautiful one-night stand . . . or will it be more?" She giggled.

"I'll call you. We can go to dinner."

It was the look on his face as his eyes brushed over her naked body. She felt somehow he wasn't looking really at *her*. He was strange. She was used to freaked-out musicians making love on dope or playing a fantastic gig and being high on success. But this was different. He wouldn't call her. She knew it. And she liked him.

"How can I reach you?" she asked, hating the touch of fear in her voice.

"I'm in the book." He gave her a swift hug. He was wearing a suit and tie. She had on nothing but her high-heeled mules.

"Norman Tucker," he said, turning to leave. Then

he smiled over his shoulder. "Norman Tucker, M.D."

"Babe?" Branch said, stroking Amanda's hair.

They were relaxing on the couch in the library, before the fire. Her heels were off and she was curled up, her knees bent, her head on Branch's lap. She stared at the fire until her eyes started to burn a little, and then looked up at Branch. His tie was loosened, and he seemed to be concentrating on a corner of the carpet. He seemed extraordinarily self-absorbed.

"What is it, Branch?" Amanda asked. She felt something was wrong. He was off. But with Branch she couldn't be sure in which direction. It was a favorite ploy of his to invent horrible make-believe stories. Then the actual story would be easier to take.

"There are some papers you have to sign," he said, with no emotion.

"Okay, give me a pen. What kind of papers?"

"About the baby."

She sat up. "What about the baby?" She swallowed, and in an instant she knew the evening they had just spent was a setup. Did he want her to sign away all rights to her child to him? Was that legally the way it was done?

"Amanda, I know this sounds like something out of *Gone with the Wind*, but there's this old will that's been passing from generation to generation in my family."

Amanda stood up and straightened her skirt. She laughed nervously. Now she wasn't sure what he was up to. "Oh, c'mon, Branch. You can do better than that!"

Branch looked at her, sadly. "I'm not making anything up, Amanda. I wish I were. I should have told you from the beginning. Please don't make it harder for me." She sat back down on the mauve velvet couch. She found herself praying for the punch line, hoping it was a trick.

"Let me begin very simply," Branch said, gazing into the dying fire. "Before the Civil War and even after, the Whitneys made their money in cotton and railroads. I mean, it wasn't the Atlanta Coca-Cola fortune, but it was always considerable."

"Spare me the history of your family, Branch. It's all over this house, really," Amanda snapped impatiently.

Branch sighed. Amanda had never heard him make a sound like that. It was the sigh of an old man. "Well, okay, I'll spare you. At the end of the Civil War, my Uncle Noble, on my father's side, had a clause written into his will. It was buried because there was just so much money no one really knew where it all was coming from. When I was growing up, the money started to dwindle. Justin's father was my parents' lawyer, and now Justin is the family lawyer. Look, Amanda, I know this is unbelievable, but it happens to be true. If I'm married and have a child, the estate releases more money to keep the Whitney line going."

"Does it have to be a boy?" Amanda said dryly, still hoping it was one of his jokes.

"No, it doesn't."

"Oh, honestly, Branch, do you expect me to believe this cockamamie story?" She got up and started pacing in her stocking feet. "Why wasn't your mother well off? She had you. If I remember correctly, we paid for her funeral. She didn't have any money at the end. She was entirely dependent on us."

"She was divorced from my father."

Amanda turned. "I beg your pardon?"

"Look, my parents had so much money they didn't even know where it all came from. Then their fortune dwindled. Poor business management finished them off. Plus, they were like children when it came to handling money."

"But, Branch, you said they were mismatched . . . you said your father was a womanizer, a playboy. . . ."

"I know, Amanda," he said sternly. "But had they known my money could have supported them, they would have stayed married, believe me."

Amanda sank into a chair across from him and pressed her fingers to her temples. "Your family gives me a royal headache, they really do." Then she looked up slowly as the reality of the situation began to penetrate. "So this is really true, about the money?"

"Yes! The money was held in escrow for the next generation."

"And just how much did they get per year for having you?"

"One hundred thousand a year for life. It passes on to the child when he or she has a child."

Amanda let out a low whistle.

"Of course, with inflation, it's not very much, but then . . ."

Amanda cut him short. "Branch, this is unreal. . . . I just don't understand. . . ." She realized she was shaking. "Or . . . maybe I do. The child can't be adopted?"

Branch looked down. Well, one way or the other, it would be over. "No."

"But as long as it's the seed of your seed and all that crap, it fulfills the conditions of that will."

He nodded miserably.

Amanda jumped to her feet. "You tricked me! I was never ecstatic over the idea of a surrogate mother having your baby. You conned me. You pressured me. You . . . lied to me." She looked him directly in the eyes, and he slumped down into the soft cushions of the couch. For one fleeting moment, Amanda saw a Branch she didn't know. He was weak, repulsive to her.

"Is that why you wanted us to have a baby?"

"Hey, wait a second, honey. The baby was your idea. You woke up one morning and said, 'Branch, let's have a baby.' I knew about the will all the time, but I would never ask you to have a baby to get the money. I just thought, since you wanted a baby so badly and we couldn't have our own, that we could kill two birds with one stone."

"But, why, Branch? You were proud we earned our own living. We could have adopted."

"You said you didn't want to be a working mother."

"I don't. But your income is more than enough. And we own this fabulous mansion."

Branch shook his head. "Ever hear of inflation? Taxes? The added expenses a child can bring? Career insecurity?" He looked straight at Amanda, who was staring back, icily. Then he threw his hands up, no longer playing the passive role. "Because, dammit, Amanda, I'm not getting any younger, that's why! Because I'm a big fish in a little sea, and that's all I'll ever be. Branch Whitney. The famous DJ of Atlanta. Why? Because Atlanta loves me. I tried New York and L.A. before I met you, babe, and they didn't love me. Only here am I a star. But I don't make star money. Why not live well? You have a baby. We have a house and money and security. Is it so wrong?"

"You're having the baby, not me. I had nothing to do with it!" Then she said more softly, "I don't consider Atlanta a little sea. There's always television. You said you wanted your own talk show."

"I tried, Amanda. No one wants me to do it. I'm a DJ."

Amanda stared helplessly at the floor. In the space

of minutes her life had turned upside down. Everything had been so wonderful. Had it? She had been ambivalent about another woman having her baby. Branch had told her she was being silly. She was right. A surrogate mother. It was demeaning. "I believed in you," she said pathetically.

His face was a study in anguish. "Hunh?"

"I could believe in getting a baby this way because I believed in you. That made it seem right. Now it's not right. Not for me."

"It will work out, Amanda. I promise you. You'll think it's your baby."

"But it's not. And why should I ever believe you again?"

"For godsakes, Amanda, be reasonable. Can't you understand my position? And get angry. I can deal with that. Let it out. But don't just stand there like that, so quiet, so calm. It's . . . frightening."

"You lied to me. You tricked me," Amanda said, not moving. Her arms hung at her sides, her feet were together, her eyes stared past Branch's shoulders.

"I made a practical decision you'll thank me for one day."

"The whole world has to know we're adopting, though. Is that a condition of the will, Branch?"

"It's a protection against cheap publicity for you, for me, for our child."

"There you go again! Our child. *Your* child, Branch."

"Amanda, please let me get you some brandy. Your face. It's white. Please, darling, listen to reason on all this."

"Can we cancel it?"

Branch shook his head. "No, it's too late for an abortion. Besides, a baby is not a dinette set."

"Your timing was just perfect."

"What?"

"When you told me. It was past the point of no return," she said, color returning to her face, inflection to her voice.

Amanda looked around the large room. In the massive bookshelves were rare editions of books, some of them copyrighted as far back as 1848. She looked at the ecru rug. At the aging, faded, priceless couch. At the antiques scattered about as bric-a-brac. And this was only one room. Then she saw a baby crawling on a blanket, crawling off the boundaries to reach, discover. She watched it grow up. A toddler having an accident on the one-of-a-kind antique chair. She swallowed the lump in her throat. No one would know it was his and not hers. Maybe in time . . . it was a baby . . . oh, God, she still wanted a baby. Nothing could ever change that.

Branch waited, holding his breath, looking at his attractive wife and loving her more at that moment than he ever had in his life. Finally, she glanced at him. He breathed easier. It was okay. There was a hint of a smile.

"Leave the papers on the desk," she said. "I'll sign them."

Branch stood and began to walk toward her, wanting so much to hold her in his arms.

"I'll sleep in your mother's old room. You can sleep in our room."

"Amanda, listen to reason. . . ."

Amanda squinted her eyes and growled, "Amanda, listen to reason. Since when have the Whitneys ever been reasonable? Impulsive, yes. Lovable, oh, you bet. Irrepressible, absolutely. Try selfish."

Branch Whitney left the room, his shoulders slumping. On the second step of the back stairway he could hear the harsh racking sound of Amanda's loud sobbing.

She would come around. They had had fights

before. Although never as bad as this one. A thought crossed his mind, and he tried to push it out: if he and Amanda ever got a divorce, it would involve losing a lot of money.

"Ralph?" Flora Butler rolled over to him and rested her head on his bare chest. Ralph put his arm around her, inhaling the scent of her body and the bath oil she had used. They could make love, but he didn't know if he would be able to. The thought of that other man's child in her belly. He didn't especially want her that way anymore.

"Ralph, let's . . ."

He held his breath. He had never rejected Flora. Not that she had ever asked that often. No, it had always been the other way around. He couldn't believe he would have to do it now.

". . . pray. Let us pray for the couple who will get the baby. They need our prayers. They're probably so excited and nervous getting ready for this blessed event. Hold my hand, Ralph, and let us pray together."

Ralph breathed a sigh of relief. Silently he began to pray. But not for what Flora was praying for. He was praying that, after this baby was born, it could be the way it used to be between them. That he would feel he was really her husband and she was his wife.

Chapter Six

"And a good, good morning from WABG. This is your favorite DJ, Branch Whitney, wishing you a nice breakfast, a good day and anything else your little heart desires. Now that the kids are packed off to school and you've gotten rid of your husband, let's you and I listen to Barry Manilow. . . ."

"Kill the monitor," Branch announced to his engineer. "I have to make a phone call."

The sun fizzled out of Jerry Fass's morning. Branch was in a rotten mood. They wouldn't have the easy rapport they usually did. The show wasn't going to be fun and easy. He'd have to watch out for funny mistakes, too. It was a good thing engineers weren't temperamental like DJs.

Of course, his audience would never know. Branch was a pro. He had been in the business so long he didn't even need an engineer. He could do everything himself. He was an MOR DJ—middle of the road. Soft, romantic music. No hard rock. Branch was Branch. Women liked him. But no one realized that behind Branch was his engineer and they were a team. Branch was the star.

On the other side of the glass-enclosed engineer's room, Branch was giving Flower World a hard time. "I just want to know this much. Did you deliver the flowers?" he demanded. "That was three dozen red roses to Amanda Whitney. The address is . . ." The man at the other end sniffed angrily, "Mr. Whitney,

48

you are one of our best customers. She has already received the roses, I am sure. There is no need to double-check."

Branch looked up. Jerry was cuing him for the Greyhound doughnut. "Go Greyhound," the tape sang out. Then Branch would read live copy for twenty seconds in between until the jingle came back on.

"Go Greyhound," Jerry crooned into the microphone he and Branch shared. He was greeted with a frosty silence. Branch was wondering whether to call Amanda. He knew what kind of answer he would get: "I'm sorry, she's in a meeting."

Amanda was looking out the window and thinking of running away to a lush little island somewhere in the South Seas. She was supposed to be thinking up a concept for a new campaign. A light, dry wine. Thank heaven her art director was busy. She wasn't much up to thinking.

Looking down, she noticed her wastebasket and remembered the old adage "When your wastebasket's full, you can leave for the day." Her wastebasket was full. Underneath a pile of crumpled, yellow copy paper and a *Time* magazine were three dozen dewy-fresh red roses.

Her Danish sat on a napkin, untouched. Her coffee hadn't really gotten her going. It was the first night in her marriage they had slept in separate beds while they were in the same house. She seemed suspended in a state of hopelessness. She couldn't even cry.

When the phone rang she stared at it, wishing it would stop. She wasn't ready to talk to Branch. It kept ringing. Angrily, she marched outside to the secretaries' desks. "I thought I told you . . . *no phone calls!*" Amanda screamed.

"It's a long-distance call from New York," Denise, her secretary said, her finger on the hold button. "I thought it might be important. It's a Dr. Borg."

"I'll take it in my office," Amanda said quickly. Halfway there she shouted over her shoulder, "Sorry. Just in a bad mood this morning." Then she slammed her door shut and fell over her desk reaching for the phone.

"Yes," Amanda gasped into the phone. She cleared her throat.

"Mrs. Whitney, this is Dr. Borg. I have some news for you."

Amanda clutched the side of her desk as a dizzy spell washed over her.

"We have the results of the amniotic tap. Everything looks fine. And it's a girl."

Tears were running down Amanda's cheeks. A baby. A healthy baby. A girl baby.

"A little girl?" Amanda said in a small, wondrous voice.

"That's right, Mrs. Whitney. You and your husband will have a nice package around Christmastime. How do you feel about that?" Dr. Borg said, as if she had won a big prize in a quiz show.

Amanda nodded. Tears were streaming down her face. She could cry, after all. She grunted something that resembled "thank you" and "good-bye." A girl. She had always wanted a girl. She wondered if Branch hadn't been right. Last night she had hated him for his deception. Maybe she was going crazy. But all she could think about was that they were getting a baby. She wondered how she would feel tomorrow. Or when the baby came.

Dr. Borg put down his phone. It wasn't enough to bring a baby into the world. It needed showmanship. Artistry. A woman was thanking him, as if he were God, for a natural process, birth. How many women had he seen who wanted him to take out their babies and throw them away. When it came to handling women, he had just the right touch. He was a choreographer of sorts. Everyone was happy. Except him. It was a waste of his real talents.

Amanda stood at the window, her back to the door. She was still crying. Soon the doctor would deliver a baby. A little pink and white girl. They could pretend it was adopted, but someone might comment, "Isn't it odd how much like Branch she looks?" She found a crumpled Kleenex in her pocket and blotted her nose.

Branch. She should call him, tell him. But she couldn't yet. She would have to wait until it felt right.

Puerto Rico, 1969. Twenty-six, scared, she had borrowed money to do it. She remembered what she kept repeating, though the faceless doctors and nurses ignored her: "Could you tell me, please, if it was a girl or a boy?"

The irony of it. She thought now she would have given anything to go back in time and to have kept the baby. Not to have had the abortion. If only she had known then that in her middle thirties she would want a baby more than anything else in the world.

Her last doctor had been a specialist. A miracle worker, his patients had called him. He was the one who finally told her to give up. The last time she had been on his table, he had shaken his head fiercely, ripped off his plastic gloves, thrown them in the wastebasket and said to her brusquely, "This is beginning to take its toll."

She had been shocked. She turned quickly toward the window, shielding her eyes with her arm, pretending she was squinting from the sun because she didn't want the nurse to see the tears. Again.

When she was dressed in a business suit and sitting in his office, she accused him bitterly of being a fraud. He was supposed to work wonders with women who couldn't carry children. She was willing to hospitalize herself for nine months. He had said, putting his hand on her arm, "Look, I don't think that will help. For five years you've been trying. Believe me, Amanda, if there were some way I could think of to help you, some new method, I would try it. You can go to another doctor, but I assure you, no matter what he or she tells you, it won't help. You keep miscarrying. And you're not that fertile anymore. I mean, Amanda, you're thirty-seven." She winced. "Face facts. I would say if you were twenty-seven or twenty-six we could keep trying. But you'll be thirty-eight soon, won't you?"

Amanda had looked at him and nodded dully. His hair was graying. What was he? In his forties. She looked at his desk. An accordion photograph frame. Four lovely children. She felt sick.

Twenty-six. She had had a baby flushed out of her. She had screamed, "Oh, my God, don't stick that needle in there!" A kindly nurse had held her hand, but she would never forget that pain. No one had told her she would suffer that much. That she would have to feel so demeaned, as if she were being punished for some moral mistake. She wondered if her spirit would have been more broken if she had had to wear a scarlet letter on her breast for eternity.

When she got back to Atlanta, she found out the would-be father had disappeared and disconnected his phone. It took a month for her to forget. Because nightmares are intolerable unless the mind blocks them out, and because she met Branch. He was thirty-two. They were married a few months after they met. No one had ever been as in love as they were when they were newly married.

"Let's work hard and play hard and travel whenever we wish. Let the other poor slobs have children. We

have each other." Had she said it first, or had he? *It didn't matter. They had agreed.*

She stared out the window, aware that the doctor was watching her, spending more time with her than usual. She had actually said that? *Let the other poor slobs have children?* But she had meant it. Until one morning, without warning, or so it seemed, she sat on the edge of their bed and said to Branch quite simply, "I want a baby." She was only thirty-two. It didn't seem like such a mean feat.

"Give up," the doctor said again, firmly. "Listen, you can adopt a baby, Amanda."

"No, no. There's so much red tape. We wouldn't get one right away."

The doctor shook his head. "People do it. I know you want to have one of your own, but I'm telling you that soon it's going to be dangerous to your health, physical and emotional. Adopt a baby, Amanda."

"But the next time I might succeed."

"You might," he said in agreement. "But you probably won't."

She clutched the drapes because she suddenly felt shaky. Now she was going to have a baby. But it was like getting one from a Nieman Marcus catalog. In spite of all the books she had read, what did she know about babies and children? She had wanted to take a course, but she felt out of place. All the women were pregnant.

She looked at her watch. It was only 10:30. Grabbing her bag, she dashed out of her office.

"I'm going out, Denise. I'll be back some time after lunch," she said, hurriedly, to her secretary.

"But, Mrs. Whitney, what should I say?"

"Tell whoever wants me that something urgent came up," Amanda replied.

She walked to the glass front door, out into the

hall, and pressed the button for the elevator. Inside, her secretary put her hand over the side of her mouth and said to another secretary, "What's wrong with Amanda?"

A secretary who was sitting behind her and who was jealous of anybody with a last name like Whitney giggled and muttered over her uninterrupted typing. "Maybe she has morning sickness."

There were one or two snickers among those who heard the remark.

Amanda was in her car before she knew where she was going. Rich's? Lord & Taylor, Davidson's? She smiled and began driving toward Phipps Plaza. How many times had she stood drooling in front of a certain store? Now she could walk in and buy, buy, buy. "Let me see some things in pink. Ruffles. Lots of lace. Let me see everything pink you've got," she said out loud. She would stroll into Chocolate Soup, the exclusive children's store that had tiny designer clothes, and she would indulge herself in an orgy of pink. She had time to get the usual baby stuff. Again she thought that maybe Branch had made sense, though she was still angry with him. It was a transaction all right. She got a baby. He got his inheritance. The baby got everything. And . . . Danielle . . . would think Amanda was her own mother, wouldn't she?

Flora Butler's elbows were splashed with a mustard shade of yellow. The phone was ringing. The stew was bubbling over and down the sides of the pot. She dropped the curtains she was dyeing, turned off the stove, rolled off her rubber gloves and made it to the phone on what she thought was the last ring.

"Mrs. Butler, I hope you're not busy."

"No, Dr. Borg, not at all." A drop of mustard

yellow had somehow fallen onto the living room carpet and was spreading like ringworm. There was an awkward pause.

"About that test," he began. After an eternity he started again. "A healthy baby, from what we can tell so far, Mrs. Butler. A girl."

Flora Butler was down on one knee rubbing the carpet stain with the edge of her dress.

Dr. Borg had hung up. She sat down in the chair beside the phone. Closing her eyes, she began to pray, silently, intensely. A healthy girl. Praise the Lord. No complications. They would get the money, and she would give birth again for some delighted barren woman. It was the Lord's way. She had been called, and she was answering. She felt a jerk of ecstasy and fell forward. It was a delicious and mysterious sensation. Almost sensual. Yes, the Lord must be with her. Then she remembered guiltily how much cleaning and cooking she still had to do. She said one last prayer for the anonymous woman who was getting her baby and then went back to work.

Branch pressed the cough switch that shut off his microphone, so he could blow his nose. His eyes were tearing, his nose was runny. He had been crying behind the sports pages.

Dialing Amanda once more, he got a different message. She wasn't in a meeting. She just wasn't there. It was only eleven o'clock. Where did she go? Why couldn't she call him? He could go to her office and just wait, but he had a supermarket opening and a voice-over for a bubble-gum commercial.

He was grateful when the newslady took a seat next to him and got her cue. He could think for five minutes. More flowers? Or maybe he should call Justin and tell him they didn't care about the money. The deal was off. Or maybe he should just call that doctor in New York and tell him himself. He had gotten carried away. She didn't want a baby this way. He'd call as soon as the show was over. And anyway, without the baby, they wouldn't need the money.

Chapter Seven

He was outside. It was cold, snowing. He was naked. That's why he was so cold. He fought with the silk sheets that clung to his sticky body and threatened to smother him. He struggled out of his dream and woke up. Barnard Borg looked at the luminous dial of his clock-radio. Three o'clock. The same nightmare. He was alone.

But they had been together. He had held her in his arms while she disintegrated and blew away. Even though he tried desperately to keep her together, give her some substance, he couldn't. Dr. Barnard Borg started to cry. In his dream.

Walking into the bathroom, he splashed cold water on his face and body and toweled off. He padded to the living room, naked. Standing behind the bar, he mixed himself a scotch and soda. Then he stood next to his drapeless windows and viewed the glittering penthouse view he had of the city. December. It sparkled like a Christmas tree. Twinkling multicolored lights. He had a view not many men could enjoy. Or deserved to enjoy.

Snow was blanketing the city. Each flake flew headlong into the window, stopped by the smoked glass. It looked like a frenzied galactic war. He sat on his wall-length black couch and drank his scotch. The dream. All because he had seen Rochelle again, after all those years, at the funeral.

He was glad his mother had had the good grace to die in August. Otherwise, he might not have seen her so soon. She had flown in to arrange the funeral. At the graveside she had wept. He had taken her hand for a moment, until she let it drop. But he hadn't cried. He had felt absolutely nothing.

Later, when some of his mother's old cronies from Brooklyn dropped by with little boxes of cakes and cookies, he had some precious time with her. He stared into those deep violet eyes, dark-smudged under the lids, the flawless skin, the hollow at the base of her neck he had loved to crush his lips into and the perfect mouth he wanted to tease open with his tongue.

"Did you try the herring?" she said.

"No, I have to be going," he had answered. "I have patients waiting. I'm indebted to you, Rochelle, for taking care of everything. Please send all the bills to my office."

He had felt uncomfortable standing so close to her after so many years. Her long black hair, his light, blond hair. They didn't look like brother and sister. As they talked, he wondered about that mole she hated on the inside of her thigh. Had she had it removed? She was talking to him, and he heard nothing she said. He was back in time about twenty-five years ago.

She was getting undressed. He watched from the closet, wondering when he should make his move. He had dreamed of this for months. First, her pleated skirt. Then, her angora sweater. Then her cotton bra with the pink rosebud in the center. Her breasts were bigger than he'd thought. She tugged at the inside of her panties and he held his breath. But then she kept them on and went to sit down at her vanity table. She must have seen him hiding there through her mirror. Suddenly her hairbrush went flying across the room and he ducked, laughing. "Get out of here . . . you freak! . . . you pervert . . . oooh, I hate you!" she screamed. But he knew she had known from the beginning he was watching. And he knew he could get her to play doctor . . . soon.

"When do you leave for Los Angeles?" he asked abruptly, suddenly embarrassed at his departure from reality.

"Tomorrow," she answered. "Jenny agreed to take care of all the last-minute details. She's been just wonderful with mother, don't you think?"

"Oh, yes," he said absent-mindedly, trying to memorize every detail of her face. It had been over twenty years since he had last seen her. He was just entering college. He always knew he would be a doctor, and he knew how very many hard years he had ahead of him. They had agreed never to see each other again, but he drove up one night, that important night, to her college and stood under her sorority window, howling until she got dressed and sneaked out just to shut him up. He had wept in her arms. They were a tangle of arms and legs in the back seat of his used Pontiac. She had comforted him and stroked him, and they made love, sobbing softly together. And then, all too soon, they kissed good-bye. He watched her run back to her house, stumbling a little, not looking back. To him it seemed as if she had taken on a pinkish golden halo as she disappeared from sight in the dawn.

He hadn't been invited to her wedding. Hadn't even met her husband. But he had understood. He studied her. The black tailored suit that was so elegant, but which hugged her ass provocatively, the wisp of a sheer white blouse showing through, the tiny silver earrings he wanted to nibble on and the legs. Those gorgeous legs. She had always had nice legs. Even as a little girl.

She stirred her tea, clattering the cup and saucer. He cleared his throat. "And how are my twin nephews?"

"Oh, terrible at writing thank-you notes, I guess," she said, brightening up. "Thank you for all the birthday presents, Normy. And each year the same identical gift for each so they won't fight. How thoughtful. You must come and visit us one day." Well, she had to say the last. But she still called him Normy.

They were lying on the bed, holding each other tightly, tenderly. They were naked. She said solemnly, "I never want to marry anyone but you, I don't care what anyone says." Then they heard a door slam downstairs. "Normy! Mommy's home." He held on, but she sprang out from under him, terrified, and snatched up her clothes.

It would always be that way for her, he supposed. Even if they buried the past with their mother. He had always meant to tell her the truth. But they would be ordinary if she knew, and so would their love.

He kissed her lightly on the cheek, hating to leave her. He had never had that feeling about another woman. Then he said his charming good-byes to all his mother's tiresome little old lady friends, whose turn it would be next. He walked slowly to his car, as if he were shedding old clothes. No more Normy Tucker. He was Dr. Barnard Borg. He had given birth to his personality and changed his name legally the summer before he started college. Dr. Barnard Borg, top gynecologist. One day he would be known as a top geneticist. Getting into his car, he reached up to adjust the visor and then brought his hand to his lips as it passed his face. Her perfume. Somehow he could smell it lingering on his hand. He didn't know why.

Dr. Barnard Borg turned out all the lights in his apartment and looked again at the big, round snowflakes hurtling against his windows. That was August. Now, it was December. Still, he couldn't forget her.

It took another hour of hopeless frustration before he could get her out of his mind. Then he turned his thoughts to his newest surrogate mother, Flora Butler. More snow was being predicted. He couldn't take any chances. Mrs. Butler would have to leave New Jersey earlier than they had planned. He couldn't afford any slip-ups.

Flora Butler sat on the couch, her legs spread far apart, enjoying the light of the moon that shone in through the big windows in the front room. She had flung off her bathrobe and her nightgown in a moment of agitation. She sat naked, knowing she was alone. Her long, ash blond hair hung loose, falling over the back of the couch. Both hands were on her tremendous belly. She felt relaxed.

It was almost impossible to sleep, because the baby was always kicking. Every spare moment she had, she tried to communicate with her unborn baby. To tell her about the ways of the Lord. And that in the eyes of the Lord, no matter what anyone told her, she would always be her mother.

"Mommy, I had a nightmare."

Flora jumped when she heard the voice gravelly with sleep. She said sternly, "Go back to bed, Carl. Did you say your prayers tonight?" She couldn't turn to the child.

"Amy said we didn't have to."

"Well, you do. Every night. No matter what she says. She knows better. Get into your bed and say your prayers, and the good Lord will carry you off to a peaceful sleep." She wanted to turn to see if he was all right. "Good night, Carl," she said instead, crisply.

"Good night, Mama."

The little boy lingered a moment as if he expected more attention, and then turned and walked almost silently out of the room, his pajama feet almost black. Flora looked at the clock. Four o'clock. Almost morning. The snow had stopped and the night was fresh and crisp. She felt she was the only one on earth.

She shifted clumsily on the couch to open her legs a little wider. Then she prayed. It came as before. A tremor, then a jerk and a delicious spasm that almost knocked her off the couch. It ended and she smiled, satisfied, at the moon.

From a third-floor window across the street, a boy of thirteen watched the Butlers' big front room, fascinated. He had never seen a naked lady before. Never a pregnant one. When he had awakened in the middle of the night to go to the bathroom, he had gone to the window to see if it was still snowing. He had trouble getting adjusted to the night, and then he noticed the bright light coming from the Butlers' house. At first he had thought it was just a grotesque, naked fat lady. But the more he watched, the more he thought Mrs. Butler looked round, glowing, beautiful. That's when it happened. His thing got hard. He loosened his pajama strings and let them drop. Then he stepped out of them and ran to his drawer to get his binoculars, which were triple power and no one was allowed to touch but him. He wanted to see everything. Everything. Some people were saying Mrs. Butler was weird. She made babies to sell. Wait till he told the other kids about this. Maybe she was a witch.

At around 4:30, Flora Butler slipped her nightgown over her head and wrapped her snug bathrobe around her middle. No use trying to sleep. She wouldn't. She might as well bake corn muffins for her family. Slowly she walked to the kitchen. She felt like she weighed a ton. The baby would come any day. Most women, she knew, would be miserable. But she wasn't most women. She wasn't spoiled.

Amanda looked at the tables in the conference room laden with food. There was a ham and smoked turkey and shrimp and platters filled with everything imaginable. People were joking that Amanda's retirement party was going to be better than the annual agency Christmas party. She was flattered that they had given her such a lavish one.

Branch had been invited, but he had canceled out at the last minute. Amanda had said he didn't want to upstage her, but that wasn't true. He was at home, waiting for the phone to ring. And as soon as the phone rang, he promised, he would call her. Amanda looked across a salmon mold into a sparkling white phone. Then she reminded herself. A watched phone never rings.

She was chattering and laughing and mingling, but all the time she was thinking of the woman. Mrs. Anonymous, she had named her. What kind of woman would have a baby for another woman? But whoever she was, she was going to have the baby soon. Dr. Borg had called them just three days ago and said it would be . . . "any minute now."

"So, Amanda, love, no more fights over who's better. The art director or the copywriter?"

"You're the best, Brad," she said to her art director. "I'll miss you. We were a great team, weren't we?"

"I'll miss you. I just can't imagine working with anyone else."

She knew Murray had hired someone or was close to it, but she didn't want to know. Every few seconds her mind would stray to Mrs. Anonymous and the nail-biting fact that she was close to giving birth.

Actually, her party was more like a baby shower, she mused. The secretaries and writers and art directors and media and traffic people had all brought baby toys and clothes. It was sweet. Today would be her last day at the agency. She looked at the white phone on the table in the corner.

Murray stabbed a plump shrimp with a toothpick, dipped it in sauce and handed it to her. "Try one. Listen, Amanda, if motherhood isn't all it's cracked up to be or you get bored or anything, just give me a call. For godsakes, if you decide to go back to work, don't work for another agency."

Amanda laughed. "You still don't believe I'm serious, do you? A child's formative years should be spent with the mother. All the books say that. Besides, I just want to be plain old mommy, not a busy executive."

Murray laughed. "Amanda, you could never be plain old anything." Then he said, almost to himself, "I'll never understand why a woman with your beauty, brains and talent wants nothing more than to be a mother and why women who have nothing but babies would give their eyeteeth for the glamorous life you're giving up."

Amanda shrugged. "Maybe I'll try a shrimp." Then the phone rang. The shrimp dropped onto her plate. She held her breath. "Amanda, is anything wrong?" she heard Murray say. Then another voice, "Amanda, phone call for you."

She crossed the room in a blur. Eyes, noses, mouths in motion swam before her. "Branch?" she said, not even bothering with a hello.

"New York called. She went into labor five minutes ago."

"I'll be right home."

She had to find a graceful exit to a party they made for her. Her face felt warm, and she knew it was flushed. Never had she felt so excited. Not when Branch proposed, not when she won her Clio, not when she was made a vice-president of the agency.

"Murray . . . everybody . . . forgive me, please. I have to get home. Branch . . . I . . . the baby's on its way." *There, that covered it,* she thought quickly.

She was given a round of applause as she ran awkwardly out of the conference room and down the hall. She grabbed her coat from the hook on the drawer, unlocked her handbag from the bottom file cabinet and ran out. She ran back in again. Fishing a small plastic shopping bag out of her drawer, she scooped up all her how-to baby books and took those, too.

She could hear her heels clicking down the lonely corridor as she rang for the elevator. She turned around. Silently, she said good-bye to the agency that had been good to her and to a way of life. When the elevator came and she stepped in, the door would close on the "old" Amanda. There was a strange noise and she looked up, then down the hall. It was dark.

Then she realized she was tapping her foot, waiting. That was the noise. She was tuned out, imagining she had gone to her farewell party, not in a black crepe suit, but in a big, A-shaped, red and blue jersey striped maternity smock. Something obvious. She liked that. Then she looked down and saw the sleek suit. *Oh, well, what the hell, can't have everything,* she thought practically. She *was* getting a baby.

* * *

Flora Butler screamed. She screamed again and again.

Dr. Borg glanced at his assisting nurse. Ralph Butler looked away, embarrassed. They weren't screams of pain. They were screams of ecstasy. Flora enjoyed having babies. With their own kids, he had shared their joy with her. But this one wasn't his. And now he felt angry. He had never heard her make those kinds of noises when she was in bed with him. Flora never made any noise at all.

Flora licked her lips, noticing no one until the baby was placed on her stomach.

"See, no forceps, no drugs—a natural birth with your own husband by your side." Dr. Borg said. He had never been so pleasant to Flora. She felt Ralph look away and drop her hand limply.

She couldn't believe the baby. "Look at that— golden hair and she's just newborn. None of the others had hair like that so fast, did they Ralph?" Ralph didn't answer.

Flora thought, as the baby was placed in her arms, *She is the most beautiful of the lot.* The Lord had favored her. She would call her Emily. Yes, she would always think of her as that. And then, in one horrible moment, she wished with all her might she could keep the baby.

She looked up. The nurse was holding out her arms and waiting for the baby, who would be taken to the couple who were waiting for her. Lucky couple. With her eyes she pleaded with the nurse for a second or two longer with the precious bundle. *Good-bye, baby. I wish you a good life. May the Lord protect you. Never forget who your mother really is.* The baby wasn't in her arms anymore. Flora couldn't see. Her eyes were blurred with tears. When had she started to cry? When had Ralph left? She felt so sad. She had never felt so sad in her whole life.

Chapter Eight

Flora and Ralph Butler had splurged this year. The Christmas tree was bigger. There was a big doll for Amy, who had already found it in the closet. The boys had sets of trucks, in addition to the clothes they needed. The stockings were stuffed with candy canes and chocolate Santas and tiny toys from the dime store.

Flora had been home from the hospital for a week. During the day, when no one was around, she hid in the coat closet and wept.

Just as she was pitching some tinsel on the Christmas tree, she felt two arms encircle her waist from behind. She squirmed, and her beige turtleneck twisted around the side of her body. The top of her hair was wound into a bun, and the rest flowed loosely down her back.

"The O'Sweeneys are bringing the kids home from the party, mother. Carl and Denny got so excited they fell asleep watching television. I put them to bed. Better be ready to get up early tomorrow morning."

Mother. He hadn't called her mother since before she had become pregnant with Emily. Now there were little kisses on the back of her neck, help with the dishes. Ralph was a good man. A solid man. Just like the man whose baby she had given birth to. Soon she and

Ralph could . . . Flora sat down. She felt dizzy.

"Are you okay?" Ralph asked.

"No, I'm fine. Fine. Really."

"You're doing too much, mother. You have to relax more. You haven't been yourself since . . ."

"I said I was fine!" she snapped. But she made no move to get off the couch.

Ralph studied his lovely wife. She was staring into space, looking at nothing. He looked from her to the Christmas tree. They had had so little time, and yet she had made a Christmas for them. Everything had been done almost at the last minute. His eyes turned to the mantelpiece. Hand-embroidered stockings for each of the kids. She had made them last year. Then he looked again. The stockings were full. But something was wrong. Amy . . . Benjamin . . . Carl . . . Dennis. But . . . Emily?

The spectacular winding staircase opposite the front entrance of the Whitney mansion gave the illusion that it was a never-ending stairway to the sky. Actually, the ornately carved balustrade stopped at the third floor. The baby's room was on the second floor.

Joyce Hirsch and Amanda were in the baby's room, staring down at tiny Danielle in her crib.

"She's gorgeous, Amanda. I've never seen a baby like her." Amanda smiled and looked at Joyce, shyly. "Really?" she said, as if to say, "You're not just being polite?"

"Are you kidding? A little over a week old? My kids looked like little squealing monkeys. I tried to hide them. I mean, they were ugly, Amanda." Joyce stopped herself. She had started to say they were no reward for the pain. But she had to watch what she said. Amanda had become so overly sensitive about everything.

They both watched the tiny head turned toward them. One hand lay under the pink baby quilt, and the other was under her chin, balled up into a fist about the size of a cookie.

There was a noise and Amanda turned. Branch was in the doorway with Justin. Covering Branch's face was a camera.

Amanda laughed. "Oh, no, not again. You didn't even get the last roll developed."

"The doting papa," said Joyce, beaming, enjoying herself.

"Well, he promised me no movie cameras yet. I think the lights would be too harsh for her eyes," Amanda said.

Branch clicked through the whole roll, imitating perfectly the posture of a photographer, bending toward her from the waist, standing over her, legs astride, kneeling below the crib and shooting upward. Then, as if on cue, Danielle lifted her head and opened her big, blue eyes.

Joyce gasped. "She really *is* beautiful, my God."

Branch looked down at his daughter, who seemed to be bobbing up and down like a small fish. "Look," he said, almost in awe. "Look at her hair. It's like gold."

Amanda had chestnut brown hair, and Branch's jet black hair had turned salt and pepper a few years ago. Joyce said tactfully, "Oh, her hair might darken. A lot of babies start out blond."

Branch picked the infant up and held her close, nuzzling her head underneath his chin. For a moment everyone was silent, watching the tall man holding the pretty doll-like baby swathed in pink and white pajamas. Rocking Danielle gently, he said softly, "This little girl is going to have everything her daddy can give her." Danielle seemed to hear. She looked up at her father, stretching, arching her back and chortling. Then the spell was broken when Amanda took the baby from Branch. Instantly, she began to screech. Amanda looked helpless. Branch held out his arms again, but she turned from him, clutching the crying red-faced baby.

"Rub her back a little. My babies all loved that," Joyce said.

Amanda hesitantly rubbed her back, and the crying subsided. She placed her in the crib.

"You'll get used to her, Amanda," Joyce said encouragingly. "It takes time. You're just going through the new-mother blues." And she wanted to kick herself for such a foolish slip. How could she have been so dense?

Mavis came in. "Dinner's all ready. You can serve yourselves from the sideboard. Let me babysit for a while. If you need anything, just call."

The little group left the room to celebrate Christmas Eve.

"She's a treasure, isn't she?" Joyce said.

Justin and Branch were half a stairway ahead of them. "The baby? Oh, yes," Amanda sighed.

"No, I meant Mavis," Joyce laughed. "But, of course, the baby. You're happy, aren't you, Amanda? I mean, this is what you wanted."

Amanda smiled. Joyce thought it was a little too dazzling. "Of course I'm happy. I love my baby."

"I'm happy for you," Joyce said, linking arms with Amanda. Then she burst into laughter. They had come up the front staircase before. But now she saw the huge Christmas tree at the bottom of the back stairway. Forest green, it was decorated only with tiny blue lights and a white angel. The effect was stark and stunning. Underneath the tree was a mountain of presents, including a tricycle and a rocking horse. They were each tied with big crisp pink bows.

Amanda smiled weakly. "There's no stopping Branch."

When they went into the dining room, Amanda felt strangely depressed. It wasn't that she didn't like Joyce. Joyce was one of her best friends. But she wished she'd stop acting like Amanda was some kind of an idiot with a baby, just because it wasn't hers. But it must be evident to everyone she was a failure. Every time she picked up Danielle, she cried. Every time Branch picked his daughter up, she cooed. Only a tiny baby, but she knew. She knew that Amanda wasn't her real mother.

The doorbell rang and Ralph Butler jumped up. "I'll get it!" Flora made no move.

He opened the door. "Well, looka here, Flora, some of your lady friends from the church." He winked at them, and they smiled back. Four ladies dressed in coats and boots were on the doorstep. He had expected them about now.

Flora walked to the door, but she didn't ask them in.

"We wanted to give you this, Flora," one of the ladies said. She held out a cake pan.

"What for?"

A gentle voice said, "It's our usual gift, Flora. A cake for the woman who's had a baby." Their faces were expressionless. Flora wished they hadn't bothered.

Carl and Benjamin ran through the living room and into the kitchen, then out through a door into the hall. They were screaming, playing flying truck.

Flora took the cake pan and moved toward the

kitchen, saying reluctantly, "Why don't you stay and I'll put up some coffee. There's plenty of Christmas cookies and a date-nut loaf I just baked."

It sounded like a thousand voices were babbling at once to Flora. They had food in the oven and families waiting, and maybe next week they would see her in church. Then they waved and were gone. One wore an apron under her coat, which had unbuttoned. Flora saw she was going to have a baby. But when she did, the other women would talk openly about it. They would come and chat, and when they brought their cake they would want a peek at the baby.

She closed the door and took the cake into the kitchen. Lifting the lid off the cake pan, she slid her finger across the light chocolate frosting and licked it. "Mmmm, good," she said. Then she let the cake slide from the kitchen counter into the large trash can.

In Los Angeles, Rochelle Vance lay in the pool on her back, her arms holding onto the sides. Her legs looked rippled underwater. The sun made the pool water sparkle. It was a beautiful Christmas day. She had gotten rid of her homesickness for a white Christmas years ago. Inside the house her husband, Victor, and the two boys were playing some game. The maid was preparing lunch. She had the pool all to herself. And some time to think.

Maybe she called him Barnard or Dr. Borg around people, but privately he would always be Normy. The boy she fell in love with when she was fifteen. He was her first lover. Her brother. She raised her legs to the surface of the water and spread them a little to catch the rays of the sun. Her eyes were closed. She was pretending the sun was Normy and he was making love to her.

"No one's home, Shel. It's all clear."

"I'm afraid, Normy. What if we get in trouble?"

"We won't. Promise. C'mon, Shel. You want it as much as I do."

She remembered that Sunday afternoon. She was fifteen and he was thirteen. It was the first time they did it together. He had been a better lover than her husband ever was. Why did she have to talk to him, be near him in August? They had avoided each other since college. She couldn't live with the shame. Now, what was the difference? She was forty years old and her life was half-over. An early change of life, her doctor said. Mama had had the same thing. God, she was so depressed. What was her life all about, anyway? She had the house, the pool, Victor and the boys. Impulsively she scooped up a handful of water and watched it seep through her fingers. That was her life, when you came right down to it.

A warm, drab rain fell on Christmas Day in New York City. Dr. Barnard Borg perused past medical journals for most of the day. He had refused all invitations to Christmas dinners or parties. He had no tree. He had sent no cards. Alone. He liked it that way.

He liked the silence, the precision. The way his thoughts just fit perfectly together when there was no one around to clutter his life.

There was leftover Chinese food in the refrigerator, but he wasn't hungry. He got his trench coat and slammed the door, riding the thirty floors down in the elevator. The doorman in the ornate lobby gave him a dirty look. Well, the man had to work Christmas Day. Or maybe that wasn't it. He had given the sour-faced incompetent a tip, hadn't he? He stared up at the glittering chandelier in the lobby and tried to remember. Perhaps he hadn't.

He left his apartment building on York Avenue and started walking. Walking and thinking. Letting the soft rain beat upon his face. Where was he? East Sixty-eighth Street. He could walk toward Lexington Avenue. Go to one of those junk-food places and have a hamburger and a cup of coffee. He kept on walking. The truth was he needed a woman immediately.

On Fifty-sixth Street he saw a hooker. She had short, bleached-blond hair and beautiful legs with high, high heels and a slim, compact figure under a fake fur jacket.

She turned and noticed him. He saw her bright pink lipstick and watched her flick her tongue across her teeth. She crossed her ankles provocatively and leaned into one hip. He needed her more than food. A cheap, dumb woman who thought she knew everything. A slut to show she didn't know anything. He would be in power. And when he got through with her, she wouldn't be able to work anymore on that Christmas Day.

"Twenty dollars, sweetie. It's Christmas."

The deep, throaty voice. The come-on. He came closer and studied her face. Then his stomach turned sour.

"I can show you a good time, sweetie. Fifteen bucks for you."

Red, hot anger shot through Barnard and he raised his fist. The hooker ducked, stumbled and fell in the rain. "Okay, okay, man, don't get excited."

The wig that had slipped to the side was yanked off as the man ran. Barnard Borg was shaking. They should clean up the neighborhood, he thought, as he walked in the rain. There were few passers-by, only the slim figures hiding in shadowed doorways. It was hard to tell who were men and who were women lately. But he could always tell when a man needed a shave. Why did he demean himself this way? There were women he could call. He could afford to date nicely. But there was no one he knew well enough to call on Christmas Day.

He wondered as he walked in the rain, hands in his pockets, which of his dates might be away for the holidays, which had families in the city, which might be alone as he was. Funny, he never bothered to find out. His relationships were short-lived because he liked it that way.

He passed brightly lit coffee shops that looked shimmery in the rain. But he wasn't hungry anymore. What he needed now was a drink. He would duck into some little neighborhood bar when his hands stopped shaking.

Chapter Nine

Outside the kitchen windows the white clouds were quickly being brushed into angry lumps of gray. Mavis stood at the sink, piling breakfast dishes into the dishwasher. Amanda was giggling.

Danielle, in bright pink Dr. Denton-styled terry pajamas, rolled over. She waited a beat and then flipped back to her stomach. Amanda had placed her in the little bassinet that stayed downstairs.

It was a blustery day in March. Inside, three fireplaces were going, and for the women in the house, the only world was the baby. "I love it when she does that," Amanda said, totally fascinated by Danielle. "She started flipping over like that a month ago. I think she's very advanced for a three-month-old baby, don't you, Mavis?"

"Oh, yes, I sure do. Pretty and good, too. She's a good baby most of the time."

Amanda chucked her finger playfully under the baby's chin, extracting a toothless smile and returning it with a proud grin. "She's good, except when she gets cranky."

"Oh, yes. Her dark moods are something else. But, if I may say so, Mrs. Whitney, I don't pick her up as much as you all do. I just leave her crying a bit."

Amanda looked up alertly. "I spoil her too much, I know. But it cuts right through me to hear her screech like that."

"Ain't no good for the baby, though, all that attention," Mavis mumbled in a soft voice, and then told herself to be still. That child was a Whitney, and she was going to be pampered and fussed over anyway. Probably wouldn't make much difference what they did now.

Amanda had Danielle in her arms, and the baby was trying to grab Amanda's long chestnut hair. Mavis saw them out of the corner of her eye. One eye was on the threatening sky. "You'd best wear your hair back, Mrs. Whitney, if you want any left." Amanda laughed. "Oh, I don't mind."

She had made peace with Danielle about a week after New Year's. They had been talking about breaking and taming wild animals in some drunken conversation. That night, at three in the morning, after tossing around in bed, she strolled casually into the baby's room.

She pulled up the white rocker and sat at the end of the crib, just staring at the sleeping Danielle. "Truce," she whispered. There was silence in the room. The night nurse had been dismissed. There were just the two of them. Recklessly, Amanda turned on one of the clown lights near the crib, making a wide but dim circle of light. Just enough to make the baby clearly visible, but not enough to wake her.

Amanda rested her chin in her folded arms on the side of the crib, looking down on an aerial view of the back of Danielle's head, which was about the size of a small coconut. "Okay, kid, now listen and listen good," she said firmly but softly. "I'm your mother. But I didn't give birth to you. And I'm sorry, Danielle. You don't know how sorry I am and always will be. But this treatment of me has got to stop. Now, I know you're going to be able to twist your father around your little finger. But not me. No, ma'am. And I want you to show some respect."

The tiny head turned toward her just then, and Amanda gulped. She could see the exquisite features, the perfect rosebud mouth, the long, silky eyelashes. "You see, I'm bigger than you," she continued, her voice shaky. "And I've wanted somebody just like you for a long, long time. We've got to be friends, Danielle. You're the baby and I'm the mother. But if you keep squirming out of my arms and crying every time you see me, people are going to get suspicious."

She caught a tear that fell out of her eye before it splashed onto the baby. "I'm awkward and fumbling and clumsy, I guess, but I'm trying. Aren't I, kid? I mean, have I dropped you once?"

She reached down shyly to stroke the baby's back, and Danielle woke up instantly, screeching. "Damn," Amanda whispered, unable to stop the tears almost blinding her eyes. She picked the baby up and went with her to the rocker. Then she sat down, massaging her back and talking very softly. "Please let me be your mother, Danielle. I know I'm not really, and you do, too. But let's pretend.

Because if I'm not your mother, then who am I? And I want you to like me. I really do." Her tears made her voice husky and soft. Soon the baby stopped crying and fell asleep, curled into Amanda's shoulder. It was the first time she had been able to do that. Amanda sat there, still crying but unbearably happy. She was in command. It was the beginning of a new year, and she was Danielle's mother. She looked around the lavishly decorated little room and rocked her baby. In that moment she felt a strange sense of communion with Danielle. A bond so real she was convinced it would never be broken.

After that night, everyone had noticed how much more relaxed she was with the baby. Branch was happy she had what she wanted. Mavis loved the idea of a real family in the old house again, and Joyce marveled at the change in Amanda. "So relaxed. She's just like she used to be years ago, before she almost broke her heart trying," she would tell Justin.

Amanda was happy. She was with her daughter almost every minute she was awake. Danielle never wanted for anything when she was around. And one day she cried bloody murder when Branch picked her up, and cooed when she was handed over to her mother.

Mavis had finished the breakfast and lunch dishes. "Do you want to make dinner, Mrs. Whitney, or should I?"

Amanda was watching Danielle grasp her pinkie finger with her whole tiny hand. "No, I'll make that veal dish that Branch likes," Amanda answered. "My, my," she said mockingly. "Aren't we getting domestic? Mavis? What day is it today?"

"Today, Mrs. Whitney? Why, it's Thursday. All day."

"Isn't that odd. It feels like Wednesday and I

thought it was. Doesn't matter what day it is, though. It did when I had a calendar on my desk always in front of me. But now the days don't mean the same thing to me."

The front doorbell chimed. Amanda jumped.

"We're not expecting anyone, are we?"

"No, ma'am. Not that I know of. And not in this weather. Looks like snow, if you ask me. Maybe it's one of those ice storms where the power goes out and the supermarkets close for days and days and you can't even get gas for your car."

"Oh, I don't think so, Mavis," Amanda said, feeling jittery. "There's nothing like that on the weather report. Can you get the door?"

Amanda waited. It was warm and cozy in the kitchen, but she felt a chill. The baby started to cry, and Amanda picked her up and started pacing. She hugged the baby tighter, which made her cry even more.

Then she heard humming and Mavis came back in. Amanda recognized the tune of an old black folk song.

"Who was that at the door?" she asked sharply.

"No one. Just a man. He wanted directions. Though why he drove all the way up this long driveway on West Paces Ferry Road to ask where to go in Buckhead beats me."

The baby had stopped crying. "It was a man?"

"Yes," Mavis answered, studying Mrs. Whitney. "Nice-looking gentleman."

Amanda put Danielle in the bassinet and walked into the living room. She looked out the windows facing the front of the mansion. There were no cars parked. No people inside a car eyeing the big house. Maybe that's all it was. Just a man who was lost and needed directions. Oh, when would she shake this frightening feeling? She had never said anything to

Branch, but it had begun to haunt her. In her sleeping and waking nightmares the doorbell would ring. She would open the door, and there would be the surrogate mother. Danielle's natural mother. In her dreams, just before she awoke, her body cold, but damp with perspiration, the woman was holding out her hands. From a faceless head she would say to Amanda, "I've come for my baby."

Branch Whitney woke up suddenly, wondering why, if it was time to get up, he felt so exhausted. Then he looked at the luminous dial of the clock on the night table. Four in the morning. He had done it again for the third morning in a row. It was that dream again.

He reached for a pajama top. The window was open just a little and there was a draft. But he wore nothing else. It was black out. He sat by the window that faced the woods and the ravine, watching the cloud wisps that buried the moon. He watched the earth rotating slowly, a favorite pastime since childhood. And he thought of his dream.

Every night he dreamed of the same woman. She was gliding toward him, but it wasn't Amanda. Yet it was no one he had ever met or seen on television or the movies. This woman had luxurious blond hair piled high in a Grecian style on top of her head. She wore some kind of robelike costume that lifted in a breeze. Or were they just sheets? They seemed to go on and on. And always he would try to take them off, to unwind her like a living mummy. For he had to see the sculpting of what he knew must be an exquisite form. And then he woke up in the predawn darkness, wanting her.

The woman. Who was the woman who haunted his dreams? He looked over at Amanda sleeping so peacefully. Just then the moon striped the room with a patch of light, so he could see her serene smile. Amanda smiled when she slept. Amanda was a beautiful woman. But she wasn't the goddess of his dreams. The mystery woman who would come so near and then, when he tried to hold her in his arms, would recede, her long robes trailing in the breeze. Leave it to him to have a sex dream that was like a television commercial for shampoo.

The woman. She had no distinguishable face, but he knew she was very lovely. She looked a lot like the baby. He did know one thing for sure about his strange dream. She was the woman who had carried his child for nine months. The woman in his dreams was the mother of his beautiful baby.

"Maaamaaaaa!"

The pleading cry started from the bottom floor and wound its way up, becoming louder and louder.

"Maaamaaaaa!"

Then it stopped. Flora Butler was on her knees in the attic. She sighed and stood up, brushing off her housedress. Then she turned to face her daughter.

"Don't yell like that, Amy. It's not ladylike."

Flora turned back and began collecting all the snapshots she had strewn on the floor. Bending over, she scooped them up by the handful and put them back in the box.

"Mama!" Amy said, begging for attention.

Amy's face was flushed and her hair was falling in her eyes. Flora didn't look at her daughter purposely. She would wait until Amy calmed down. Amy was too much of a tomboy, too willful. When she learned obedience to her parents and the church, then Flora would pay her more mind.

When she finally did turn, she frowned. "You have a wicked glint in your eyes, Amy Butler, and I don't like it."

Amy let her mother's words fly by. She couldn't pay attention. She was just so excited. "Mama! I got a part in the school play! I tried out and the teacher gave it to me. I'm the witch!" With that, she ran around the attic hooting and hissing and making cackling sounds.

"Stop that, Amy!" Flora said harshly. "Why can't you be a good little girl. You can be in the school play only if your schoolwork is finished, your chores are completed and you remember your Bible study."

"But, mama!" The little girl was jumping up and down. "There's more. Today when I was walking home from school I decided what I wanted to be when I grow up." She smiled crookedly, almost seductively, pleased that she could finally reveal her secret.

But when she looked up, she stared at her mother's back. Her mother was stooping, picking up the pictures again. "This afternoon when I was walking home from school, I decided when I grow up . . . and, mama, I'm only telling you, not Benjamin or the other girls at school . . . I'm going to be an actress!"

Amy waited. Her mother didn't say anything. She just kept putting those weird old photographs back into the boxes.

"Mama?" she begged, finally. "Don't you think that's good? Don't you think I'll make a good movie star? Better than Cissy Spacek or Brooke Shields or any of them, hunh?"

"Amy," Flora sighed. "You're not going to be a movie star. Don't waste your time daydreaming. Besides, you have to be pretty to be an actress. You'll get married to a nice boy from the church, when the time comes, and you'll have babies and keep his house clean for him. If you work hard in school, your father and I might manage to send you to a nurse's training school or to secretarial school, so you'll have a useful occupation if you ever want to help your husband. If you can get a husband, with your willful ways."

Flora turned slowly, and Amy stared angrily at her back. Her mother was wrong. She *would* be somebody important like a movie star. She was hurt. Her mother didn't think she was pretty. She felt a pang of jealousy. Not like the new little girl baby that couldn't come home. She had heard her mama talking to her daddy. How the baby was so beautiful. How it looked just like her mama. Well, phooey on her. Never would she tell her any secrets again. And she would not marry *any* boy and have squealing, smelly babies like Carl and Denny had been. She wanted to say, "But Maaaamaaa . . ." But her mama would have hit her. She knew when to stop. Instead she said, as sweetly as she could, her eyes averted, "Yes, mama." But Amy knew the truth. She hated her mother.

Flora glanced at Amy for a second, noticing her sad expression, but her mind was on the photograph she had been searching for. Why were there so few? It was a baby picture. One of her as an infant. It was the only reminder of the baby she had seen for just an instant. Enough time to know that the child looked exactly like her. Then she spotted it and quietly picked it up and tucked it into the pocket of her dress. It was so innocent, she thought. And she needed something.

Amy got down on the floor and studied the flat pile of pictures, picking them up one by one. "Who's this?"

It was a picture Flora had missed. "That's your Grandma Nash," she said.

Amy knew who it was; she just wanted to upset her mother.

Flora looked at the old snapshot. It was a good

one. It showed her mother with one foot on the steps holding her as an infant toward the camera on an angle. Yes, she should save that picture, as well. She looked just like her beautiful baby daughter.

Then she looked down at Amy, who was looking up at her and smiling. Poor Amy. Those awful buckteeth. There would be no money to straighten them out, either. She wondered what it would be like to be homely.

"Grandma Nash is ugly and mean, and she didn't send us a lot of presents this Christmas!" Amy blurted out.

"Shush! She's the only grandma you've got, so be thankful. Your daddy didn't even know his own parents. They were killed in a big fire, and he had to raise himself. And I must say he turned out a lot better than you promise to be. You must learn to watch your tongue, Amy. You say whatever you please, and you think only of yourself. It's not the Lord's way!"

Looking at the picture, which must have been taken around 1966, Flora remembered her own mother and her growing-up years in Maine. She had been a little older than Amy. Twelve. Her mother had eyed her with disgust. "Breasts," she had announced. "And full hips and a mouth gashed with lipstick."

"But, mother, it's light pink. All the girls are wearing lipstick."

"You're only twelve. You better watch your ways, Flora Nash, or you're going to get yourself in a whole lot of trouble." Then she screamed, "I don't want any bastard babies in this house, girl!" Flora had been confused. She didn't even know what *bastard* meant. She had looked it up in the dictionary. She knew what her mother meant when she yelled with disgust, "God never intended for a girl to be that beautiful!" But she couldn't help how she looked.

She had done what her mother wanted. She had been a good girl; she had married a God-fearing man and had babies. But it was never enough. She could never please her mama. What she had done now, she knew, would ruin her chances forever. Maybe that's why she had had the baby. She didn't know. Flora felt a ball of acid forming in the pit of her stomach. She was twenty-eight years old and her mother could still do that to her.

Well, she would never be that way with Amy. No, they had a good relationship. Nimbly she stuffed the second picture in her pocket. She'd cut her mother out of the picture and keep the little baby picture of "Emily."

"C'mon, Amy," she said, scooping up the last of the pictures and packing them away. "Let's go downstairs for Bible study. Then I'm going to teach you to bake a real cake. And before dinner mama will help you with your math problems."

"But, mama, it's the New Math. You don't know how to figure that out."

"We'll find a way together, Amy. You can do whatever you set your mind to do."

"Yes, mama," Amy said, smiling sweetly at her mother and resisting an urge to roll her eyeballs to the ceiling. She was thinking how good it felt to admit the truth. She hated her. Hated, hated, hated her—her with her beauty and her perfection. Everything *she* did was right, and everything Amy did was wrong. And the way she looked at Amy, making her feel like . . . she wasn't much to look at. Well, Amy would show her mother. When she was eighteen, she would run away from home. She'd go to New York City, and then she'd never have to see the old witch again.

* * *

Their circular bed was covered with light blue satin sheets. There were steps leading up to the bed.

"C'mon, Shel, don't pull that 'not tonight' routine. My God, I'm only human."

Rochelle Vance lay shivering, the sheets pulled pristinely up to her chin. "I . . . can't. Not tonight."

Victor jumped out of bed angrily. She turned away like a shy virgin at the sight of his naked male body.

"Damn it," he said, going down the steps toward the boudoir chair where he had left his clothes. "I've been patient and more than patient, and you know I love you, Rochelle. You're my wife. But I can't stand this constant rejection. It all started when you got back from New York. Now you have no interest in sex at all. If I didn't know you better, I would say you were having an affair."

There was a few seconds' silence. Rochelle lay looking up at the ceiling, her fingers curled over the sheets at her chin. Victor went back to her and sat on the edge of the bed, looking at the woman whom he had never stopped wanting, who belonged to him. "You do love me, hon, don't you? Don't you love your daddy?"

Rochelle turned her head slowly, like a bizarre figure in a wax museum operated on batteries. Victor had gained a few pounds, but his body was still hard and firm, athletic looking. She saw women give him the eye when they went out.

She met his gaze and smiled back. It completely disarmed him. "But, Victor, what a question. Of course I love you. You're my husband. The father of my boys."

"Shel, maybe there's something wrong. Why not see a doctor?"

"I already had an appointment with my gynecologist. I told you. I'm going through an early change of life. I feel fine." Gynecologist. The fantasies. Better than the grass she and Victor sometimes smoked. She had been afraid she was going to have an orgasm when his hands touched her. But she had to go and open her eyes. Dr. Fischer was short and skinny and balding. She had done an amazing thing, though, now that she remembered it. It had only lasted a little while. She had imagined Normy where Dr. Fischer had stood. It was Normy who was doing all those things to her. Goodness knows, they had played at it when they were kids.

"No, Shel." Victor's sharp voice brought her back into the room. "No, dear, I mean a psychiatrist. A shrink."

Rochelle looked at him. Couldn't he tell how he had just insulted her? But, no, he was going on.

"I think it was your mother's death that brought all this on. You've never been a close family. I think you're suffering from some kind of guilt. Sometimes strange things happen when someone dies. My partner—you should have seen him when his father died. He wasn't himself at all." Rochelle kept staring at Victor, hardly blinking.

"Are you bored, Rochelle? Depressed? Do you want a career? Because I don't mind. You said you wanted to open a tennis boutique. I'll finance the whole thing."

"It isn't necessary," she said dully. "I have a job. I'm a wife and a mother."

Usually the steady one in his business partnership and marriage, Victor lost his patience. "Will you go to see a shrink? Will you at least try it?"

"No."

Victor went to the closet and pulled out jeans and a shirt. For effect, he flipped on a cowboy hat. Rochelle watched him.

He walked across the thick carpeting. "You're a good mother, Shel. So that's a job you want to keep.

But I have to admit you're a real failure lately as a wife. Think about it."

Rochelle shivered again, though she wasn't at all chilly. Then she threw down the covers, yanked up her pink chiffon nightgown to her waist and spread her legs. She smiled at him defiantly. "Okay, Victor. I'm ready now. I'm ready to do my wifely duty."

Victor looked at her face. She could see he was hurt. She knew she should care or cry or something, but she couldn't do anything. His shoulders sagged a bit and, as he turned and walked out, she read the pain in his face.

It was nine o'clock in the evening when Ralph Butler eased himself out from under the old van. There wasn't much he could do. Not too dangerous, but it annoyed him. He couldn't repair it himself. Next paycheck he'd have the service station give it a going over. He sighed. Smarter to sell it, but they wouldn't get enough.

He looked over at the new van on the other side of the garage. They had bought it with the money Flora had . . . earned. That was Flora's car, for now. He wouldn't bother her with the shaky old van. Not when she was coming out of it as she was. He had the feel of the old one, anyway.

Slamming the back door to the house, he realized just about a year had passed. Last March she had told him she was pregnant. Well, they had survived it. Life went on. " 'To every *thing there is* a season, and a time to every purpose under the heaven,' Ecclesiastes 3:1." Now he had his wife back.

He could hear the low humming of the sewing machine in their bedroom. The kids were quiet as well. Maybe by some miracle they had managed to go to sleep. He wouldn't turn the thermostat off tonight. It was a little nippy for March. They couldn't afford any colds or flu, and he didn't want

Flora to be bothered with sick children. Not now when she was his again. Later, when the kids were older, they would grow up as he had. No heat at night. Even in the dead of winter.

Ralph could smell the fragrantly warm invitation of something Flora had just baked. He went to the stove, and there cooling on top was a fresh banana cake. His favorite. She was a marvel, that wife of his. A good woman. And he needed her that way as quickly as possible.

When he went into their bedroom, he could have sworn he saw Flora take something—a small piece of paper or a snapshot—out of her pocket; but he wasn't sure. He didn't want to risk making her touchy, so he wouldn't confess to spying. Besides, it was probably a picture she was copying. Many times she designed her or the children's own clothes from clippings. She even made his shirts. His heart seemed to expand with love when he saw his beautiful wife sitting so straight at the sewing machine, concentrating so intently. A few little blond hairs had curled at the bottom of her neck. The rest of her hair was sleek and smart on top of her head.

She turned instinctively, suddenly, knowing he was there. He hadn't made a sound. "Well, if you don't look like a grease monkey. Probably couldn't fix it." She turned back. He didn't answer. He was feeling happy. The fresh-baked cake, his wife sewing, his children asleep and his masculinity back and demanding. What more could a man want?

He made a move to grab her shoulders, but she ducked and pretended to scream. "Don't you touch me, Ralph Butler. It's another dress to wash and iron. Look at your hands. They're positively black."

"Take off your dress," he whispered huskily.

She kept right on sewing, turning a corner, stitching up a tablecloth she had made from sale material.

"You know very well when I'll take off my dress. When I'm finished here. As far as what you have in mind, well, we'll see when the lights are out and we're in bed, Mr. Butler."

Ralph laughed. "You like to pretend that's the way you prefer it, but I know better because I'm your husband. You enjoy it, Flora. And if I turned the lights on, you wouldn't much mind."

"Clean towels in the cupboard," Flora replied, crisply. "Get yourself a shower before bed."

In the shower Ralph scrubbed until there wasn't a trace of dirt. He didn't want to offend Flora. Yes, things had changed since a year ago. He was the luckiest man in the world. Soon he would turn off the lights, gingerly lift up and take off his wife's flannel nightie, if she'd let him, and make love to her. He said a silent thank-you to the Lord. One day Flora had been babbling about Emily, and almost overnight she was her old efficient, happy self again. That baby she had had—it was a mistake. He would never let her do anything like that again. He'd take a second and third job if they needed money. But, thank heaven, she had forgotten all about it, finally.

Chapter Ten

Rochelle Vance paced the sunken living room of her home. She knew it was late at night, or very early in the morning. She had forgotten how many scotches she had had. She was all alone, drinking alone. She poured some more scotch into a glass at the bar and started to drink, realizing the bottle was empty. Giggling, she began to dance around the living room. She wore nothing under her yellow cotton caftan.

Dancing over to the phone, she picked it up. Then she stared, surprised at her hand. This was the first time she had actually thought of calling him. Her hand lowered the receiver to the telephone. She lost her courage.

Then she picked it up again and dialed fast to make it less painful. She had memorized his phone number. Each rat-a-tat-tat of a digit sounded like machine-gun fire at an execution. But she just wanted to hear his voice. Be friendly. Victor was right. They were a cold family. She heard herself giggling again.

On the fourth ring she heard his voice. But something was wrong. He kept right on talking. He had turned into a machine. She caressed the phone that contained his voice. But then it was over and she heard a tiny alarm go off. She was speechless. She knew she was supposed to leave a message, but she was frozen. What could she say? Quietly, she replaced the receiver.

It was time to switch to brandy, she decided. After all, why not play out the whole scenario? Bored, upper-middle-class wife with nothing to do but spend her husband's abundant money ties one on. She wondered if she was becoming an alcoholic. Then she realized this was the first night she had ever had more than two drinks when she was alone. Victor had decided to go to San Francisco.

She giggled, but stopped suddenly when she heard it. An unmistakable noise behind her. She twirled around and heard someone stumbling. Everything was in darkness, except the few dim lights in the living room. But the sound had come from the back of the house. She *had* locked the door, hadn't she?

"You're sure you're not pregnant, honey?" Ralph asked cautiously, leaning over his wife, who was still in bed.

"Positive. It's just some sort of bug. And you know the way the Lord intended for us to get well. Plenty of fresh air and rest, and nothing but fresh water."

"Well, I don't know about that, Flora. It seems to me . . ."

"You go ahead to the company picnic. I don't mind. Now it's the Fourth of July. I went last year, and I'll go next year. But the kids are going to be miserable if they miss it."

Ralph stroked her smooth cheek with his finger. It always amazed him that his wife could look so fresh and dewy without all that gook women put on their faces. She was naturally beautiful. "Is there anything I can get for you? Another pitcher of water, perhaps?"

Flora shook her head and indicated a full pitcher and a glass. Then she spotted Amy hanging on to the bedroom door. "Stop scratching your scab, Amy. Come in here."

The little girl's hair was in a wayward ponytail. She was wearing a blue and white checkered sun suit, navy socks and dirty white sneakers. On her right knee was an X made by two Band-Aids.

"Yes, mama."

"Daddy's going to take you all to the picnic. I can't go because I don't feel well. Now, Amy, I expect you to help your father with the kids, you hear?"

"Yes, mama."

"Turn their eyes away if you think you see something sinful. And don't let them chew any bubble gum. The dentist's bill is high enough."

Amy turned to leave the room, then stopped with her back to her mother.

"Amy, today you're the mama of the house. It will be good practice for you. Pretty soon you'll be wanting to baby-sit and give your mama and daddy the money to buy your shoes and things."

Amy nodded, without looking back, and walked out the door. When she was sure no one could see her, she took her two hands and stretched her mouth into a horizontal line. Then she stuck out her tongue and popped her eyes wide. She didn't know Dennis was there. The two-year-old ran out of the kitchen crying, because he couldn't understand why his pretty sister suddenly looked so ugly and frightening.

Ralph opened the bedroom window just a little higher. It was going to be a splendid day. "I'll take the old van, just in case you feel better this afternoon or need something."

Flora shook her head vehemently. "Don't be silly, Ralph. The old van's liable to completely die on you."

"Nope," Ralph insisted. "I can handle that car, mother."

"Well, I don't care. The brakes are bad and you've got the kids, and I don't want to have to lie here and worry about you every minute!"

Ralph couldn't help but smile at his wife's shrewish command. Yes, Flora was back to her old spunky self.

It was seven o'clock in the morning in Los Angeles. Rochelle Vance lay curled up in a ball, unable to move. She didn't know how long she'd been there like that. She knew it was early morning because she had watched the pinkish orchid dawn turn into a bright yellowish cast. She hadn't moved since he had left, because she still wasn't sure he had really left. Maybe she would be able to get up soon. She had to call the police.

Amanda came out of the back door of the house and down the wooden steps. She was humming. On a tray were a stack of plates, glasses and bowls with snug, Saran Wrap covers. She would have to make another trip. She didn't want to bring the platter of fried chicken out until they were sitting at the picnic table. She had made everything by herself.

She would call Branch in just a few minutes. She sat down to rest on the seat of the picnic table. In the back they had put up swings and a sandbox and a baby pool. A little premature, maybe, but Branch couldn't resist it. He said he liked to look at it. Maybe if she could get him to stop taking pictures of the baby, he'd take a shot of the glorious day. It was a beautiful Fourth of July. The kind of day a camera should capture. It would make a perfect picture postcard for Atlanta. The brilliant blue sky, the fluffy white clouds, the fresh green trees and, of course, the incomparable magnolias.

Even the ravine to the side looked less spooky as the sun splashed over it, speckling it with bright spots. And the gnarled roots of the ancient trees that lined the cliff somehow managed to look gray and soft, even friendly.

Amanda wished she had a little triangle with a gong to call her family to eat. Branch was sunbathing out in the front of the house with Danielle. "Come and get it," she yelled, cupping her hands over her mouth. She got no answer. She yelled even louder. "Branch! Danielle! Lunch is being served!" Still no answer.

Sighing, she went around the side of the house.

Rounding the corner of the big house, she still couldn't see them. Then, as she came to the wide expanse of perfectly manicured lawn, she saw no one was in the white wrought-iron chairs. She spun around. No Branch. Just a baby carriage.

Panicking, she ran, almost tripping, toward it. She lifted her hands to pick up Danielle, cursing Branch for leaving her alone. Then she screamed. But she had known. The baby carriage was empty.

It was nine o'clock in the morning, and still Rochelle couldn't move. Her throat was dry. She needed coffee and she desperately had to go to the bathroom. Then she heard footsteps, and she crouched lower, trying to stuff herself underneath the couch.

"Shel?"

Rochelle began to cry. Big sobs that made her sniffle and choke all at the same time.

"Hello?" Victor said cautiously.

He saw two hands on the top of the couch when he came into the living room. Then he saw his wife rise slowly, as if she was paralyzed, and he saw the look on her face. He ran to her and held her in his arms. "Shel, what . . ."

"A burglar. Last night. I've been hiding ever since. But he didn't find me. Don't know what he took. Thank heaven the boys are away at camp."

Rochelle went into the bathroom and Victor searched the house. Great idea of his partners. Cheat on your wife. Sure, go to San Francisco and pretend it's business. He couldn't do it. See what happened when he was away? When they met again in the kitchen, Rochelle was making them coffee, and he could see some of the color had come back into her face.

"Well, the burglar took jewelry, cash, some silver,

that antique Chinese jade vase—ah, what the hell. I have insurance. The important thing is you weren't harmed. I'll call the cops."

Rochelle reached out to touch him. "No, stay a moment. Let's just sit. I'm shaken. I don't want to go through all that just yet."

He nodded and sat there.

Rochelle tried to find the words. All those hours when she was lying there, trapped, alone, she had been thinking. She knew where Victor was and what he must be up to. She hadn't really cared. But she cared that he could leave her. She didn't want to be alone. She couldn't stand to be alone. After Normy there had been Victor. She needed a man to look after her. She wasn't one of those modern, liberated women. She had to have a man to take care of her, and she was smart enough to know that about herself.

"Victor," she said, her voice quivering, "maybe we should talk." She gulped down some of the hot, black coffee she had made. This required choosing her words very carefully. "Is it a divorce you want? Because of my . . . sex problem? I don't want one. Plenty of couples manage without it, or I would understand if you . . ."

"We're not plenty of couples, Shel, and it doesn't really work for me with any woman but you. Listen, if not private therapy for you, why not couples counseling for us. See, I keep blaming you. But maybe I might be doing something wrong." That was Dr. Needleman's observation, not his. "Though I don't see what," he added quickly.

Rochelle looked at the man who had been her husband for over twenty years. She saw Normy's face. The same trick she had managed with her gynecologist, only this time it lingered. She smiled, or thought she did.

"Shel, are you okay?" Victor asked. She had a funny look on her face. Little did he know, it was the most fortunate question he could have asked her.

"Shel, are you okay?"

"I'm okay, Normy, but there's blood on the sheets."

"Don't worry about it. There's nothing wrong with you. We'll put the sheets in the machine. She'll never know."

She turned and buried her head in his boyish, but muscular, chest.

"You ought to know, Normy. You read all those books, and you're going to be a big doctor one day."

She moved her chair over to Victor's and rested her head on his chest. He stroked her hair. "Shel," he gurgled, almost under his breath. She looked up into his eyes and saw Normy's eyes. Then she was in Normy's arms. An inner voice told her it could work. She could make it work.

"Let's go to bed," she said pleadingly, wetting her lips with her tongue.

"Oh, Shel," Victor moaned, and he picked her up in his arms and carried her all the way to the bedroom.

Chapter Eleven

Flora woke up. She had dreamed of a baby. Clear as day, almost as if she were seeing it pop out of a television screen. A rosy-cheeked baby with a shaft of golden blond hair and deep blue eyes. The kind of baby everybody wanted to cuddle.

She dug with her fingernails in the night-table drawer until she found the little pouch she had made. The private place where she kept her baby pictures. She took them out and studied them. She was the baby in her dream, and yet, she wasn't.

She bit her lip. "Lord," she said. "I'm going to look at these pictures one more time. And then I'm going to forget your child, a child that now belongs to some poor, barren woman. I believe in my heart they are raising her with good Christian faith, common sense and humility. The baby belongs to them now, and they paid for it out of their hard-earned money. I belong to my husband and children, who need me. All of me."

With that she shut her eyes tightly and ripped the pictures into such tiny parts she would never be able to put them back together again. She watched them flutter into the plastic-bag-lined wastebasket she was keeping by her bed in case she had to do anything messy.

After that, she felt better. She fanned her hair out on the pillow. It was all in making peace with one's inner soul, so that one found balance and harmony.

That's what happened when one obeyed the Lord.
Maybe she would even go for a ride in the old van.
She had felt the Lord's presence. He had held her in
his hand and she wasn't sick anymore. She would be
safe.

"Branch! Branch!" Amanda screamed, almost
twisting her ankle as she ran around the side of the
house and toward the back. They weren't inside the
house. She had checked every inch.

Branch saw her about a half mile away. But he
couldn't scream to her, because he couldn't risk
straining his voice. When he got nearer he yelled,
"Amanda," but she had disappeared somewhere in
the shadows near the ravine. When he finally
reached her, she was staring into the coppery water
that slithered over the rocks in the creek. She was
crying.

"Amanda!" he said, out of breath.

She looked up quickly, like a hunted animal
caught in the split second before it knows it's going
to die. Then her eyes found him, and she grabbed
the baby from him. "My God, where were you?
Don't ever do that to me again!" All the while
she was kissing the baby's head so lavishly that
Danielle kept blinking from the constant impact of
Amanda's lips.

"Honey," Branch said gently, "I just went for a
walk with the baby. I wanted to show her off to the
neighbors."

"I thought she was in the carriage, and then she
wasn't there; and I thought she had been kidnapped
and I didn't know what happened to you. I'm
sorry." Tears were running down her cheeks. "I'm
being silly, aren't I? I couldn't help it."

"We're rich, sweetheart, but not rich enough that
anyone would kidnap the baby. She's yours. Bought
and paid for—oh, that was stupid, I mean . . ." He

let the words trail off, and right then and there would have thrown himself down the steep cliff into the ravine below if that would have erased what he had just said.

Thank heaven, he thought, *she was letting it pass.* She was trembling a little, but he could tell she was coming back to herself again. "Hey, got any food?" he said engagingly. "You've been talking about this fantastic lunch of yours, and I'm starving."

They walked around the side of the house; and, after depositing Danielle in her bright pink high chair, she ran inside to get the coleslaw, macaroni salad, chicken and lemonade. Staggering under the huge tray she was carrying, she told herself it would be all right. She knew it would. It was just that old habit she had of spoiling good moments for herself. She smiled and saw that the rolls under the plastic film had remained warm. From now on she was going to make an effort to relax. No one wanted to steal Danielle away. It was her own craziness.

Victor was in the pool. Rochelle was putting on her new black bikini. He had asked her to. The phone in the bathroom caught her eye. She knew the number by heart. Why not? She was dizzy from lack of sleep, a hangover that should have come in the morning had she gone to bed and the exhilaration of what she had just accomplished: She had slept with Normy.

She looked at the phone. She wanted to hear his voice, the one on the answering machine. She dialed the number.

Suddenly she felt faint. He answered.

"You're not a machine?" she said, stupidly.

"Who is this?"

"Normy, it's Shel."

There was a pause.

"Shel! Is everything okay?"

He still cared. He still wanted her. She could tell. Laughing gaily, she said, "Just thinking of you, darling. My husband says we're a cold, distant family."

Barnard shut his eyes. What luck he had decided to answer the phone. "How are things, Shel?" He forced himself to be calm.

"Oh, Normy, I was just thinking. We've grown so apart. Maybe Victor is right. Why can't we be friendly? There's only you and I left now."

"But, Rochelle," he said sharply, "you wanted it this way."

They talked small talk, the weather, her boys, current events. But the tone in her voice . . . he had had conversations like that before with her, long ago. She wanted him.

"Wait a minute, Shel, I'll get a pencil." His hand was flapping stupidly like a fish as he knocked over the pencil case on his desk. Thank heaven he had answered the phone, he told himself again.

Rochelle smiled. "On second thought, don't bother, dear. I'd rather call *you*. You're not married. I am." He dropped the pencil. His hand was shaking. She was acting just like she did when they had discovered sex together.

"Okay, Shel," he said, not trying to hide the lazy seductiveness in his voice. "Have it your way, Shel. You always do."

She laughed deeply from the back of her throat. God, he loved her laugh. There was something wicked about it. "Right, Normy, I always do."

Hanging up, he started to pace around his air-conditioned study. His work on embryonization, the paper he was writing, was waiting for him, but he couldn't settle down to it. She had called. After all these years. It was an invitation to continue. He smiled. She thought she had the control. So she would call him. He would let her play her little game until he could gain control. Just like old times.

He sharpened a pencil and looked at his notes so far. Idly he wrote "Rochelle" on the top of the page in big block letters. She was his image, his first, the only woman he ever loved. But, as everyone knew . . . she was also his sister. He laughed.

Flora Butler sat in the kitchen, sewing and waiting for her family. She had eaten dinner and even topped it off with a piece of that good apple crumb pie Imogene had made for the church bake sale.

Her marker was in the middle of Luke when she closed her Bible. She checked the wall clock again. It was ten o'clock. Her family should have been home earlier, but traffic might have been heavy. At least the weather was clear. She stared at the wall clock, watching the little hand creep over to five minutes after ten.

She closed her eyes and breathed deeply. She'd best turn her attention back to her Bible. Not one minute later she heard the familiar sound of wheels on gravel. She looked up and smiled.

Chapter Twelve

The doorbell rang. Flora Butler's first thought was that it was a joke. The kids were feeling boisterous and merry, and it was way past their bedtime. She walked briskly to the front door. She was wearing a long summer bathrobe and scuffs. Her hair was braided and sat in coils on the top of her head. She was so happy her family had had a good time and that she had settled once and for all those secrets she had been harboring. With a big smile and a feeling that her life was in order, she opened the door.

In the dim light of the porch she saw a young man. He was holding a dark, dusty square in his hands.

"Ma'am?" he said politely. Then he took off his big hat.

Flora stared at him. It wouldn't be Christian to slam the door in his face. On the other hand, a woman alone couldn't be too careful. But she looked at him more closely and saw he was wearing a uniform of some sort.

The young man seemed to slither through the door, which Flora had left open about two inches. He smiled shyly. "Don't want to let the bugs in, do we?" Then she heard a soft groan escape through his lips, and again he whispered, "Ma'am?"

Flora's brain seemed to be frozen in the time space before she opened the door. Everything else seemed like a movie she was watching. The man cleared his throat. He pointed toward the kitchen with its warm glow of light. Flora's movements were quick and mechanical as she led the way. They stood in the kitchen. She looked closely at the man, seeing in the light how very young he was. So young she could see the soft downy hairs on his upper lip. He indicated a chair at the kitchen table and she shook her head, standing with one hand resting on the top of the chair. The state trooper swallowed. He had never done anything like this, but he had seen a lot of movies.

"I'll get my coat," Flora said in a falsetto voice, a bright dawn of understanding spreading over her face.

He put up his hand. "No, that won't be necessary."

Then he remembered. He reached in his pocket and pulled out his identification. At the same time Flora noticed the dusty metal square he was carrying was a license plate. Their license plate.

He looked at his hands. "We traced the license plate and came up with your address. It's registered under your name, Mrs. Ralph Butler."

Flora nodded. "What's your name?"

"Howard," he replied.

"How old are you, Howard?" Flora asked. The young man was beginning to feel spooked. There was a tinny, hysterical pitch to her voice. He wished they had sent someone else to do this job. He really didn't know what he was doing. It was his first time.

"I'm twenty-two, ma'am. This license plate we found. It was after the accident." Then he bit his lip. He had forgotten to tell her there was an accident. Flora stared at him holding the license plate as if receiving an award. "There were no survivors, ma'am. None. It was a three-car accident, and your van skidded off the road, rolled down the incline and fell headlong into the water. . . . I'm sorry, ma'am. I'll need you to help me with a report, because there are no bodies to identify." Then he added in a small voice, feeling as if every word pulled him down into quicksand, "Yet, I mean, they might wash up. But then, again, they might not be identifiable."

She didn't speak. In the silence Howard heard all the sounds of the house. He looked at the woman. She seemed to be listening for something. He hoped she would be all right. Maybe a more mature, more experienced man could have done it more tactfully. He didn't know what else to do.

"Ma'am," he said kindly, "maybe you better sit down." He was thinking she resembled a mannequin in a store window.

"When did it happen?" she asked. He had to lean in to hear her.

"A little before noon."

So they hadn't gone to the picnic. She had been asleep at the time.

The state trooper waited. She opened her mouth to speak and then closed it again. Her eyes were wide. Big, blue eyes. He wished she would blink.

Suddenly she stood up. "There must be some mistake."

He sucked in his chest. "You mean you're not Mrs. Ralph Butler of 527 Dane Avenue, Wananwa, New Jersey, owner of a brown and white Dodge van registered . . ."

"You see, Howard, they took the new van. *I* had the old van, the one with the brakes that keep slipping. That's the mistake." She held her hand over her mouth as if to hide a small belch, but he could see she was laughing softly.

"Mrs. Butler, ma'am, why don't you sit down? Can I get you a good stiff drink?" He couldn't figure out why she didn't react the way most women would be expected to. Cry, scream, wail, yell at him, even get drunk immediately. But nothing. She had to be in shock.

"We don't keep spirits in this house," Flora said primly. Then she smiled. "It's way past your bedtime, Howard. You run on home, now. I'll be up awhile. You see, I have to wait. Can't go to sleep until I know my family's home and, you see, Howard, they seem to be a little late tonight."

Amanda and the baby were supposed to meet Branch for lunch after his show. But Amanda had the baby dressed and in the car much earlier. There was something she had wanted to do for the last few months, and she knew that today was the perfect day. How many times had she seen one of the old secretaries or copywriters stop back to the agency wheeling a tiny stroller with an adorable baby in it?

How many times had she smiled and felt so envious she wanted to scream? She was going to stop in at the agency and show off her baby.

After she parked and carried Danielle on her hip, she took out the baby stroller. How long had it been? In January she had gone in, quickly and quietly, without fanfare, to clean out her office. Murray had hired a writer from New York. She hadn't met her. Or was it a he? Amanda felt a curious tingle of excitement and curiosity as she put Danielle, who was intent on squeezing a squeaky rubber toy, in the stroller.

Amanda felt nervous suddenly. She remembered she still had a key to the ladies' room on her key chain, and she quickly wheeled the baby in there. Just as she was taking the baby brush out of her bag, she heard a voice squealing, "Well, hi, little cutie pie! What a precious baby!" Amanda turned. The woman, who had just come out of the cubicle, screeched, "Amanda! That's your baby! What are you doing here?"

Amanda smiled and shrugged. "Oh, hello, Denise. I was in the neighborhood shopping and I thought I'd just stop in and say hello to everyone." Even as the words slid out she could picture Branch admonishing her. "Show-off. Don't make her perform so, Amanda."

Denise smiled. "Guess what? I'm not a secretary anymore. I'm in production. A raise and everything." Amanda gave her the required supportive hug and squeal. "Oh, Denise, that's terrific. I always knew you were going places."

"C'mon back. Everyone is going to want to see you and . . ."

"Danielle," Amanda supplied.

"Danielle. What a lovely name, and honestly, Amanda, she is the most gorgeous baby I have ever seen in my life. Those blond curls and those enormous blue eyes." Danielle looked up from her stroller and gave an exquisite, dimpled smile as Denise held the door for them. Denise was caught spellbound for a second. Amanda looked down lovingly at her baby.

She didn't recognize the receptionist, which disappointed Amanda somewhat. The old receptionist would have loved seeing the baby. Going into the inner agency, they all but bumped into Murray, who was coming out the door of the big conference room, finishing a conversation and leading a group from the client. Amanda didn't recognize any of them, to her amazement. The agency must have picked up a new account. "Amanda," he bellowed, and the whole entourage stopped behind him. "And this must be little . . ."

"Danielle," Amanda said.

"What an enchanting child. This is our new client," he waved his hand as if to introduce the uninterested group as one person. "Willoughby's Furniture chain. Wouldn't she be terrific for the print ads on the baby furniture. She's very appealing, Amanda."

Danielle's little face was turned up, and she was smiling at everyone. Amanda laughed. She didn't want the client to think she was any old housewife and mother. She was, after all, Amanda Whitney.

"Forget it, Mur. This kid doesn't have to work."

He smiled. "No, I guess she doesn't. Wait here. I'll be right back." Amanda watched as he showed the group of five people from Willoughby Furniture to the reception room. Seven, eight months ago, Murray would have said something like "But doesn't her mother want to work?" Amanda felt like an outsider. She had once been such an important part of the machinery. She looked down at Danielle, who was gleefully gnawing away on her rubber toy, and she came to her senses quickly. She was here to say hello to old friends, do some shopping and then meet her husband for lunch.

When Murray came back to her, she said quickly, "By the way, Mur, who'd you get to replace me?"

"Goodness, you really have been out of the gossip network. Irwin. Irwin Rosen. From New York. The Jerry Wald agency sent him. Good man. Creative director at J. Walter Thompson. Then president of his own little agency. One-man shop. It folded. Then he came here. Come meet him."

Amanda picked up Danielle. Everyone who was sitting at a desk or standing over one looked up as Amanda passed by them carrying the baby. There were some new faces. The old ones came up to her and kissed her and shook hands with the baby's dress.

Danielle was dressed in a pink and white checked pinafore dress with tiers of ruffles in the little skirt. On her feet were pink socks with white lace on the cuff and tiny, freshly polished white sandals. The curl on the top of her head was held by a pink barrette in the shape of a bow. Her bright blue eyes were wide open, framed by those long, inky lashes, and she was smiling happily at all the attention.

Irwin Rosen, a tall, trim man with a three-piece suit and a red hankie in his pocket, rose graciously to meet them. In a second Amanda saw how he had changed her office to suit his taste. It didn't even remind her of her old office. He chucked Danielle under the chin, and Amanda's ears turned pink as he said, "Kootchy-kootchy-koo." The baby looked for an instant as though she might want to cry, and pulled away from the man. Amanda marveled at the instinctive sense of her daughter. Danielle sensed Irwin didn't like her, probably had no use for children at all. Irwin, she suspected, had no use for women. Then she realized something. They had work to do. She was an outsider now. Actually, they were just humoring her; but they had things to do. Well, she remembered doing the same thing.

"I'll just make a quick stop by the secretarial pool and leave. I have to do some shopping, and then we're meeting Branch for lunch."

"Branch *Whitney?* Oh, I see," Irwin mumbled, making the connection in his head.

"You look just marvelous, Amanda," Murray said.

"Kootchy-kootchy-koo," Irwin said.

Amanda walked down the thickly carpeted hallway until she came to a huge room where she could eke the last precious drops of enjoyment from her morning. She was rewarded. The secretaries went mad over pretty little Danielle, who in turn loved being admired, petted and fondled. When the joy of watching everyone with her baby produced a lump in her throat she was having difficulty swallowing, she decided it was just the right time to leave. To cries of "Bye-bye, Danielle, wave bye-bye" and waves and kisses blown into the air, Amanda walked out of the agency, satisfied. It was only much later that she realized Murray hadn't even offered her free-lance. She had been forgotten.

Flora Butler sat stiffly in a folding chair in the corner of the room. Everyone had left. One woman had made her a tuna casserole and left it for her to heat up. She wasn't hungry.

Reverend Haver and his wife had suggested a memorial service. Everyone had agreed unanimously. Only she had objected. She would remember them in her own way, she had protested. But the real reason Flora Butler didn't want a memorial service was that she didn't trust herself. There were no graves. No coffins. No substance. It was like a dream. That was the awful finality of it. If there was a memorial service, she wouldn't just weep. She might lose control of herself.

She remembered what the young state trooper had said. He had been such a nice man. He had made her tea. What was it he had said? That the van had skidded through an oil slick on a highway that should have been repaired. There were too many potholes. It was a freak accident. Witnesses had seen the van plunge over the side of the road, tumbling out of sight until it splashed into the ocean. They must have drowned. But did they drown when they were unconscious? she wondered. She prayed then that they had been struck dumb by the impact of the fall. She could live with that. Getting up from her chair, she realized she had nowhere to go and sat down again.

"Forgive me, Ralph, Amy, Benjamin, Carl, Dennis. Forgive me. I can't go through with a memorial service. I'll pray for your souls." She shivered, though the breeze ruffling the curtains did little to move the hot air about in the house. The state trooper, Howard, had said the bodies might be washed up. That night he had cried. She couldn't.

On the dining-room table were piles of baked goods and gifts the company had brought. Homemade cakes and cookies, plants that she should repot and bunches of flowers. She was glad people had stopped by, but she was happier they had all left. She nibbled on some crumbs from a homemade zucchini cake. Why did the house seem full when it was empty?

She walked down the hall into her bedroom, their bedroom. To her surprise Ralph was there. He was pulling off his dirty T-shirt. It was wet. Above his belt she could see his belly sticking out over it. He was smiling. She stared, and he whispered, "Flora," though his lips didn't move. She reached for him, stumbling over the bed. "Ralph, oh, Ralph, I knew it wasn't true. Couldn't be!" But when she went to embrace him, she ended up hitting her arms. He wasn't there. Holding her hands over her ears, she ran from the room. She ducked into the little boys' room. They were sitting on the floor playing with blocks. They looked up at her, smiling. "Mommy," a faint whisper swirled around the room. She went toward them. They were wearing bright shorts and striped T-shirts, and then they disappeared. Running as if being chased, she went to the room with the bunk beds. "Amy? Benjamin?" she called out. But there was no sound. Nothing. Just an empty room. Then the front door slammed shut and she screamed—a terrifying, agonizing roar.

For the first time in her life, Flora felt fear. She was terrified to be in her own home. Woodenly she put one foot in front of the other and forced herself to walk into the living room. She realized she was laughing.

No one was there. The wind had forced the door open. It would rain soon. One of those flash New Jersey summer thundershowers. As she closed the door, she watched the shadows fall over patches of ground that had been rippled with sunshine.

Flora went back to her chair in the corner of the room and told herself she had acted like a silly woman. "Foolish," she scolded herself, as she would one of her children; but the sound of her own voice made her slide in closer to the chair. At first she thought it had started to rain. Then she realized she was crying, sobbing. Tears splashed onto her skirt. She jumped. It seemed the house had split in two. Thunder. She slumped to the floor, rocking and crying. A crack of lightning lit up the house for a fraction of a second, yet the gaudy neon-light effect lingered longer. She looked up. In the arched doorway to the hall were Ralph, Amy, Benjamin, Carl and Dennis. They were laughing. But they had no bodies.

She shut her eyes and prayed as it began to rain. She recited her favorite psalm. All during the long storm, she begged the Lord to forgive her for anything she might have done to have deserved this. She was frightened of her own home.

Then the rain stopped, and all that was left of it was the damage. A tree in her neighbor's property, a sapling she could see, had bent in two. The storm was silent now, like a baby who had cried fiercely for hours and was now spent, no tears left. The earth smelled fresh and new.

Flora Butler had talked to the Lord during those hideous hours when she was imprisoned in her own living room.

"Lord," she had asked finally, "I am a woman without a husband and children. What good can come of my life?"

She listened, trembling. And then she heard the whispered reply.

"You have one baby left, Flora Butler," the Lord said.

Chapter Thirteen

Flora felt stiff and her joints and muscles were tight. Her eyelids stung, and she felt as if she wasn't rested. She hadn't really slept. Just dozed for an hour or two. Her mind wouldn't let her sleep. And her bed wasn't too comfortable. The upper half of her body reclined on an armchair, and her legs shot straight out like a doll's lifeless limbs on another chair.

She scrambled some eggs for breakfast, but could hardly eat them. Scrubbing the frying pan, she began to feel the reassurance of her own personal order. The Brillo pad going steadily and determinedly over the pan. Elbow grease, she was fond of calling it. It felt good to get things clean. No plastic-tasting Teflon for her. She liked good, fresh butter, and she didn't mind cleaning a pot or a pan for it. She washed the pan in soapy water and then watched it rinse clean with clear water. She smiled. Her frying pan was clean. She put it in the drainer, paying no attention to the stack of dirty, food-encrusted dishes that lay all over the kitchen.

She dressed slowly, with her old sense of efficient precision. Her green cotton suit, the one she made for this season. She did such a good job on the buttonholes. She was proud of it. A white, cotton, sleeveless blouse she had picked up at Penney's. Old shoes, because there were puddles. The moccasins would do. And her umbrella. The plaid one. She could fix it along the way. They just didn't make things the way they used to.

All of her clothes were laid out neatly on the couch. The shoes were lined up. Her underwear was stacked in a neat pile. That was why she couldn't sleep on the sofa. She might wrinkle her clothes. And she couldn't stand people who looked unkempt. She didn't have to go toward the bedrooms again if she didn't want to. There was a toilet in the basement. She used that. She could wash in the kitchen or use the hose in the cellar.

She would have to call a cab. She didn't have much of a choice. She couldn't drive that old van. She shook her head. The old van. The brakes that didn't work. And they had taken the new van. A rush of panic made her shake and she ran out the door. She'd wait outside.

Some of Wananwa, New Jersey, was already on its way to work, and the rest were in various stages of waking up. It was 7:30. A lazy blanket of haze had cornered the small, lower-middle-class suburb. Flora wrinkled her perfect nose in the mist. Her house would have been awake with activity. Her children would be up and at their chores. She smiled. Oh, maybe she'd have to get after Amy and little Denny, precious little Denny, just two years old; he couldn't do much. She thought of him industriously trying to sweep with a child's broom. She looked toward the house cautiously. Had they come back again? Was Ralph at the factory? Maybe she should give back the big plant the company had sent.

She saw spots in front of her eyes. Had she been imagining things? Or had the good Lord brought them back for her? Or maybe their bodies were slow to join their souls in heaven.

Smitty's Cab Service pulled up, and the man waved. Turning back to look at the house she had loved and lived in, Flora Butler realized something about the one-level house that was her home. She was going to have to sell it.

Upstairs in the attic window of the third house to the left across the street, a little boy looked down and crossed himself quickly. He remembered only too well what he had done that night he had seen her big and naked through the window. He had thought she was a witch. Maybe it was his fault. Because her whole family had been killed. He looked down at her standing in front of her house. Her clothes were wet. It was still raining. He wondered why she didn't at least open her umbrella.

John, the driver, opened the door for Mrs. Butler. She didn't look quite right to him. A little green around the gills, he thought, and those deep, purple rings under her eyes. Well, he asked himself, how would you feel if one day everything was the same and the next day nothing was like it used to be? It wasn't John's way to speak of death or tragedy; so he said, "Bit of a rainy spell, ain't it, Mrs. Butler? Good for the reservoir," and left it like that. He drove in silence, and Flora sat stony-faced until he deposited her at the train station.

Amanda and Branch were having breakfast in the library. Branch looked at the rivulets of water pouring down the windowpanes. "If this storm doesn't let up, the power's going to go."

"The studio has a generator," Amanda said.

"Yes, but we don't."

"We have plenty of candles." Amanda smiled brightly. "And Mavis is here to help me take care of the baby. Don't worry."

Branch bent down to the floor to kiss Danielle good-bye. She was on her hands and knees, crawling on the blanket. When she got to the edge of the blanket, she grabbed the table legs and clutched them with all her might, causing Amanda to leap off the sofa and rescue an antique vase. She realized it would have to be transferred to the morning room if they planned to keep it in the family. Danielle smiled at them both, one of her diaper legs dragging, her two little front teeth surrounded by a backdrop of pink gums. They laughed proudly at her.

"I'm going to be late for that voice-over taping on the new restaurant, and then I have to go over some things with Jerry," Branch said, starting for the door.

"Branch?" she said in a small, almost desperate voice.

He turned. "Yeah, babe?"

"Do you think we're becoming a couple of old fogies?"

He studied her face, and said, finally, "No, you don't mean that, Amanda. You want to know if I find you attractive now that you're a housewife and mother, not the glamour lady of the Atlanta ad world. The answer is yes. Even more attractive."

He took her in his arms, but his eyes were out the window on the mudholes the rain was carving. Had she seen him getting up at night and walking around? Mooning about a woman he couldn't forget —who haunted him? A woman who, in reality, didn't even exist. His fantasy golden goddess. The mother of his child.

Amanda pulled out of his embrace. "Branch, what am I going to do when Danielle starts to go to school? She won't need me anymore."

Branch shook his head and laughed. "Honestly, Amanda, you look for things to worry about. She'll need you when she comes home from school. Do you want to go back to work? Is that what's behind all this? Your trip to the agency, that's it. Because we can afford all the help you want. You can work if you like, Amanda. You know I don't mind."

"No, don't be silly! I don't want to go back to work. I was just talking, that's all. It's just that, Branch, I'm afraid we're going to be like those typical married couples we never wanted to be like. Nothing is spontaneous anymore. We're falling into patterns. Oh, I don't know. Forget it. I sound like I'm unhappy when I'm not. You'll be late."

Branch followed her over to the couch, sat down with her and put his hands firmly on her shoulders. "Have Mavis stay tonight, get your hair done, buy a new dress. We're going out on the town, lady."

Amanda smiled at Branch, and they kissed. Amanda noted it was not the usual early-morning kiss. Danielle, watching from her blanket, was inching toward the couch leg. She grabbed it and then pulled herself up. She stood alone, her knees wobbling, for about ten seconds and then plopped down on her rear end.

Amanda was looking at the baby out of the corner of her eye all the time she was in Branch's arms. "Branch! You missed it. She stood alone. They're not supposed to do that until ten months."

Danielle looked up at them as they peered down at her. She had her finger in her mouth and was giggling, her tears having dried up. Branch laughed heartily, gazing down with adoring eyes at his daughter. Then he looked at his watch and saw he really was going to be late if he didn't hurry.

"Oh, daddy," Amanda said, winking. He stopped and looked back. "Have a good day." He waved good-bye. But, as he turned, he wondered if a simple night on the town would do it. Amanda seemed to be restless lately.

Getting off the PATH underground train, Flora Butler walked up the steps, mingling and jostling with the early-morning commuters, who traveled mechanically each morning and evening to work in a jungle so they could live where it was civilized. Verdant New Jersey. The crowd, carrying folded newspapers, little bags of coffee and rolls and brief-cases of all sizes and shapes, inched like one mass amoeba to the subways, which would distribute them to all corners of the city. Flora shook free of the stream and went up and outside to catch the cross-town bus. When she got off at Thirty-fourth Street and Madison Avenue, she wanted to walk. She would have about ten blocks to put her thoughts together.

But Flora Butler found she couldn't think. Her thoughts were disjointed, undisciplined, wispy associations that drifted into her mind at random. She remembered the very same route she took about this time last August. She was five months pregnant then. It was raining, but hot out; and her husband and babies weren't lying at the bottom of the Atlantic Ocean in a Dodge van that was just paid for. And they didn't even get to go to the picnic.

Flora swallowed so hard she heard it. She wished she had a mint, but she never kept such things in her bag. Bad for the teeth. Yet her mouth tasted bitter, her tongue, sour. Resolutely she kept walking up Madison Avenue, weaving in and out of the busy people who were walking in the opposite direction. They walked so quickly that umbrellas made people collide, muttering angrily at the invasion of their privacy. She passed a man who was barely visible underneath a cloud of black, shiny material that had been an umbrella not too long ago, but was now an angry weapon of protruding spokes. Still, he clung to it stubbornly. Flora closed her own umbrella and lowered it. She didn't mind the rain.

When she reached the big office building, she glided by the newsstand to the elevator bank. She punched the button that said nineteen when she stepped in the elevator. Other people pushed her to the back. As the elevator rode up, she stood smiling, arms folded across her chest, still not thinking of anything in particular, but feeling very calm and determined.

"How is she?" the man asked.

Even though he was perspiring in the heat, he wore his usual cardigan sweater. His white, curly hair looked almost powdered against his glistening black skin.

His wife sat in a chair by the bed. She weighed twice as much as her husband. "Ummmm-um," Ethel Williams sang. "This child is in a bad way. We should get a doctor."

"Maybe old Doc Holloway will have a look at her. But you just keep caring for her. She don't look like she's near death to me. She'll come around."

Ethel dabbed the girl's forehead with a damp, cold cloth.

"Don't look like she's from around here, do she?" he said, perplexed. "Can't understand it. Just lying under a tree. Now maybe she approached those woods from the highway. That makes sense."

Ethel studied the little girl's face. She was unconscious. But she wasn't peaceful. Pretty little girl.

Flora opened the door and walked down the hallway, stopping at the reception desk. The young girl was putting on her lipstick when she looked up and spotted Flora.

"Yes?" she said.

"I'd like to see Dr. Borg."

The receptionist's face was a study in recollection and confusion. Wondering what day it really was, she looked down at her big appointment book.

"The doctor's with a patient right now. You're . . . ?"

"Mrs. Flora Butler."

"Oh," she smiled, "you must have made a mistake. You have no appointment today. Your name's not in the book."

"I know I have no appointment with him, but I have to see him." There was something in the woman's voice that made the receptionist look up in alarm. Now she remembered. Flora Butler was one of those surrogate mothers. She excused herself and knocked on the door of the examining room. The door opened a crack, there were whisperings, and then the receptionist marched back to her desk. "Won't you have a seat in the waiting room, Mrs. Butler? Doctor will be with you as soon as he can."

Flora looked around the waiting room. She noticed a very pregnant woman who sat with her hands folded over her huge belly. She was chewing gum. Flora sat primly on the couch, her umbrella by her feet like a faithful dog. The other woman began leafing through a *Newsweek* magazine. Flora sat calmly and watched her.

In what seemed only seconds later, Dr. Borg appeared in his white coat at the doorway. The pregnant woman tried clumsily to rise. Like a conductor, he motioned her to sit and lifted his hand for Flora Butler. He did not kiss her hand. The expectant mother shrugged and pulled out a little plastic bag of raisins and nuts.

Briskly the two of them walked out of the waiting room, past the curious receptionist and into his office. He closed the door.

"Well, well, Mrs. Butler," he said benevolently. "What can we do for you? No trouble, I hope."

Flora found herself sunk into the same chair she had sat in for almost a year, looking up at that face. That face she had really never trusted.

"No trouble with my health," she said curtly, twisting her white plastic handbag in her hands.

Dr. Borg looked at his desk clock. His stomach contracted. No, it wasn't going to be an easy day.

"Well, what brings you here?" he asked patiently, a hint of cheerfulness in his voice. He felt like saying, "What brings you here without an appointment," but he didn't dare. These surrogate mothers. Risky. The very act they committed, getting pregnant for money, saying they did it because they wanted to help and enjoyed pregnancy, proved to him, without fail, that only a special personality type was a candidate. Slightly unstable, fanatically religious, sexually inhibited or in some other way emotionally disturbed.

He looked at the floor. He could guess what was coming. It had never happened to him. Not once. But he supposed it was the inevitable occupational hazard. As he heard it, he shut his eyes, as if getting a sudden headache.

"I want my baby back."

He nodded, his eyes still closed. "But, Mrs. Butler," he said slowly, "you signed a contract. Everything was done anonymously for the child's sake. It works like adoption. You can't just take the baby back."

"I'll pay $15,000 for her."

"You don't have that kind of money."

She sat up stiffly. "Don't tell me what I have!" she shouted. Then she relaxed back into her chair, trying to regain her control.

"The baby belongs to the adoptive parents," Dr. Borg said, trying not to raise his voice.

"But I am the natural mother," she said, as if that would end the conversation and bring him into agreement.

"Why now?" he said, throwing up his arms. "You willingly decided to be a surrogate mother and were paid." He squinted his eyes. "Did you spend all your money, is that it?"

Flora never blinked. "There was an accident," she said woodenly, mechanically. "My husband and four children were killed. I have no one." Then she bit her lip, as if she would allow no more words to escape. As if it were painful for her to confess to him something of herself.

"I'm sorry to hear that, Mrs. Butler," he said with a trained compassion in his voice. So, she was suffering from grief. That was it. At least he knew now how to manipulate her.

He leaned forward in his chair, almost touching his blond oak desk. "You *are* the natural mother."

She stared at him, then nodded.

"But," he said, raising his hand and pointing his finger up in the air, "the baby is with the natural father and is well provided for in a fine family setting. She has a good home. What can you, a recent widow, hope to give your child?"

Flora felt the bitter taste again in her mouth. She bit her lip and looked the tall blond man directly in the eyes. She heard a buzzing in her ears and it was hard to concentrate. "But . . . I'm the natural mother. A . . .a court would give the baby to *me*."

Dr. Borg waved her sentence away, as if it was irrelevant. "Maybe. Maybe not. In your case, the court might award the baby to the adoptive mother, who could give her the best home. I wouldn't even go to court on it, if I were you. That really eats up your money, Mrs. Butler. And then if you lose, which you probably will, what will you do about money?" She didn't answer. "Mrs. Butler, what will you do?"

She stood up, trembling with fury.

He stood up, too. "I can't give you any information on the whereabouts of your child, Mrs. Butler. Those were the terms of our agreement. Your child has been adopted by another woman and is in the custody of her natural father."

Flora's hands were clenched, as if ready for a boxing match. Her voice was low and strong; yet she was wondering in the back of her mind if she had the strength to go home. "I'll get the money. I have insurance, I'll sell the house, I'll . . . well, that's enough. And I'm going to use every penny I have to fight you in court. I don't think that contract means all that much. I can change my mind. I'm the natural mother. Any judge would agree to that. Your contract is just a piece of paper. Nothing more."

She turned to leave. He sat in his chair, letting her

make her own way out of his office. He noticed the umbrella she carried was dripping muddy water on his carpet. He twirled a pencil and then threw it across the room. She was going to ruin everything. Yes, a judge just might award the child to the natural mother. Especially a judge who thought poor Flora Butler was a victim.

Sonny Williams sat at the kitchen table. Ethel was scrambling eggs and turning pancakes over on the griddle. She had wanted to serve sausages or bacon, but she didn't have any. The prices were too high that week. Sonny was drinking his coffee. Ethel was humming a gospel tune.

She brought the food and a platter of hot biscuits to the table and sat down. They gave wordless thanks, only their lips moving, and then started eating, also wordlessly.

When they heard the noise, Sonny and Ethel looked up. They turned to the doorway. The little girl, her dirty blond hair hanging in her eyes, the pajama top down to her knees, stood and stared at them.

"She woke up," Sonny said in wonderment.

"Needs a bath," Ethel said, chuckling.

The little girl wasn't looking at them. She was staring at the table, which, from where she stood, appeared to be piled with heaps of food, all of which smelled delicious. She began gnawing on her knuckle.

"Here, girl, have a seat. You hungry?" Sonny said.

She nodded.

Ethel leaped up and took out two more eggs, which she quickly scrambled on the hot griddle. Sonny got her a chair and buttered her a biscuit. The girl watched the yellow butter melt into the soft, flaky dough, but she wouldn't eat. Ethel noticed her hands were dirty. "Want to wash up first?" she asked.

The little girl stared at the big black woman. Her eyes seemed never to blink.

"Maybe she's one of those deaf and dumb mutes," Sonny whispered. "That would explain everything."

Ethel laughed. "What are you whispering for? If she can't hear, that's not going to help."

Just then the little girl bowed her head and brought her two small hands together. Her lips moved in prayer. When she was through, she bit into a soft biscuit.

Ethel and Sonny exchanged knowing looks.

"Wish we could just keep her and not tell no one," Ethel said suddenly.

"Blacks don't keep whites," Sonny admonished her.

"Whites adopt blacks," she replied, stacking five pancakes on top of each other and drowning them in maple syrup.

"That's different. They don't live on food stamps when they do it."

"What's your name, little girl?" Ethel asked, serving her some eggs and some pancakes and pouring her a tall glass of cold milk. There was warmth and goodness in her voice. But the little girl, eating, still stared at her as if she was frightened.

Sonny said, "We just want to help you, child. If we knew your name, we could help find your people."

Ethel, in a universal maternal gesture, brushed the hair out of the girl's eyes and said, "Such pretty hair you have. I'm going to give you a bath, and wash that hair and put it in braids tied at the end with plaid satin ribbon. You're real pretty, girl. Now, don't be afraid of us, sugar, because we're your friends. What's your name?"

Amy Butler put down her fork and looked at the

woman. Her eyes were wide and filled with shame. "I don't know what my name is," she said.

Dr. Borg was just finishing up in one room with a patient and was ready to enter the next examining room, where another was waiting. His receptionist walked up and tapped him on the shoulder. "Your call on three," she said. The new patient would have to wait a little longer.

"I'll take it inside," he said calmly, and then almost knocked over the phone as he ran to his desk, after slamming the door behind him.

"Harve?" he said immediately, with a rush of relief.

"Yeah, Barn. I was in court. What's the problem? The message said urgent."

"Do you remember a Mrs. Flora Butler?"

"Vaguely. One of the surrogate mothers?"

"Right. A perfect baby girl around Christmas."

"Yes?" Harvey took off his glasses, breathed on them, waited for them to defog and put them back on. It was a nervous gesture.

"She wants her baby back."

There was a long silence.

"Give her her money," Harvey said quickly. "I thought you screened these women."

"I do. But she lost her whole family in an automobile accident. She has no one. She wants that baby. Bit of a religious fanatic, and she was very upset."

"Let me think for a second."

Harvey drummed his fingers on his desk. Barnard Borg ran his fingers through his blond hair.

Finally Harvey said, "You know, we have to keep this out of court at all costs. All costs."

Borg didn't say anything. He felt a wave of panic, thinking of the consequences.

"Does she have a contract?"

"They all do. You know that."

"We've got to get that contract. I can take care of it."

"She could still take us to court, Harvey," Borg said, beginning to get angry.

"Yes, but it's going to be hard to find an attorney to take her case. She has no family. You'll deny you were the doctor. And, as you said, she's a little unhinged, anyway."

"Very unhinged," Borg said, smiling.

"Above all, don't take her seriously. If she doesn't know where the baby is, she hasn't got a case, either."

"She doesn't. And she won't find out."

"This will blow over, Barn. Don't worry. Something was bound to happen. This is nothing. We'll handle it one day at a time."

When Barnard Borg hung up the phone, he felt a chill of fear pass over him for an instant. Harvey was right, of course. They could handle a woman like Flora Butler. Still, even the thought of going to court was enough to panic him. And one of his worst nightmares was going to prison. That would be a living hell.

Chapter Fourteen

Flora had moved the big fan from the bedroom to the living room. She switched it on almost as soon as she got in the door. Then she sat on the chair that was the upper half of her bed, and took off her damp shoes, her sticky pantyhose, her suit and blouse. That felt good. During the dusty, tedious ride back to Wananwa, New Jersey, the sun had come out and the temperature must have soared to ninety-five degrees, at least. She folded her things neatly and stacked them on the sofa. She thought of putting them in the dirty-clothes hamper in the bathroom, but decided to let them air out. It was easier that way, anyway. She just couldn't do as much as she was used to doing in this heat.

Lunch. That was what she would do next. She opened the refrigerator and found some lettuce, but it was soggy and brown. She tossed it in the trash can. There was a platter of fish cakes. She had just made them last week. Ralph and Amy and Benjamin and Carl and Dennis had had some. It was still fresh. She scraped it off the platter and threw it out.

She glanced at the big table in the dining room. She really should clean it off, put some things in the refrigerator, do something with the plants. And she would, just as soon as she figured out how to do it.

Pouring herself a glass of milk, she walked over to the table and ate two homemade chocolate-chip cookies. She brushed away cookie crumbs from her chin and looked down. Sinful of her. She was walking around in her cotton bra and nylon slip. She pulled the slip to the top of her bust line and then ran quickly to the couch to get something to wear. She picked up a sleeveless dress, smelled it under the arms and then slipped it on. She put on low-heeled, open-toed white sandals. When she was all dressed, she stood in the living room, perplexed. There was something else she wanted to do. What was it?

Oh, yes, sell the house. How would she do that? She found herself walking toward the stove. There was a drawer where she kept the potholder mitts and the Yellow Pages. Bending down to get the phone book, she felt weak, and saw those little dots, like tiny firecrackers, dance before her eyes again. She hoped she wasn't coming down with something. She had so much to do. Perhaps it was the heat.

Flipping through the pages, she sang the alphabet to get herself started. "L—M—N—O—P," her voice cracked, and she came down the scale with "Q—R—R." Real Estate Brokers. Her eyes scanned the page. She ran her finger over the column of names. And then she stopped. She had found it. Perfect. The Christian Lord Realty Agency, Ltd. That was it! Where the Lord wanted her to go. It was a sign. She slicked her fingers through her hair, shoving the stray blond hairs back into her bun, and then she grabbed her bag and ran out the door. She prayed the van wouldn't act up. Halfway to the van, she ran back inside. Quickly she snatched a piece of paper from a pad near the phone and wrote down the address of the realty agency.

Rochelle Vance had overslept. Lazily she went into the kitchen. She made herself a cup of coffee, drank a sip and then went out to the front of the house. Reaching into the mailbox, she pulled out a stack of envelopes. Maybe there would be a letter from Robert or Roger. The twins usually wrote their notes from camp at about the same time.

Back in the kitchen she finished her coffee and flipped through the mail. Bills she set aside for Victor. He took care of everything. Junk mail she usually tossed into the wastebasket, unopened. Then she stopped at something unusual. A letter from mother's maid. She poured herself some more coffee, slit the letter open and read with curiosity. She had suggested last August that Jenny take all of mother's furniture and things. Not that she actually gave them to her. It was understood to be a long-term loan. Normy didn't want to be bothered, and she had no desire to have her mother's things shipped to California. There was nothing she wanted, even as a keepsake. It just wouldn't fit in with the décor of her California ranch house. The old things from the house in Brooklyn meant little to her. She wasn't a sentimentalist. And the new things from Macy's. Well, that would be laughable. Besides, it was right that Jenny should have them.

But now Jenny was writing to say that all her children were married and gone and she had decided to sell her house. She was going to live with a sister in Detroit, and she didn't know what to do with all of Mrs. Tucker's furniture and things. She had called Dr. Borg's office, but he had never returned the call.

Rochelle nibbled on a corner of the letter absent-mindedly. She knew what should be done. She should tell Jenny, who had been so wonderful to her mother, to sell that stuff and pocket the money. But it was the daughter's place to take care of the mother's things. It was perfect. Victor would have no suspicions. Hadn't he accused her family of being cold, distant? And as for Normy . . . that was the best part of all. Wouldn't he be surprised when she called him after she got to New York? Which is what any sister would do.

Flora Butler locked the front door. Then she climbed up into the old van and marveled that it started right away. She drove out of the driveway and turned to the right.

An old car was parked not too far down the street. A Pontiac. Dirty white. It attracted no special attention in the neighborhood. When Flora's van disappeared, two men looked at each other and smiled at the unexpected good luck. They got out of the car and strolled over to the Butler residence. Then they disappeared around the back. They attracted no special attention. They were dressed in nondescript uniforms and looked like they knew what they were doing.

The men spotted a window open in the back. With a thud, they pushed in the screen and raised the window higher. One scrambled quickly into the window, springing from the shoulders of the other one. Then he ran through the house and opened the back door. They looked out. Bushes and hedges in the back. A wire fence separating property. No one had seen them. And, if someone did, there wasn't too much anyone could do. They were pros. They'd get what they were after, and in less than a half-hour their uniforms, fake mustaches and wigs would be buried somewhere in the woods of New Jersey. They would also peel the putty off their noses and take out the false teeth that altered their facial structures.

The men walked carefully into the living room. There was a bureau. They went through it carefully, finding only tablecloths, silverware, and odds and ends like bits of stationery and broken crayons. They looked around quickly when they closed it. Everything was left in exactly the same place.

Every second counted. Most people kept important papers carefully hidden away. They ruled out the kitchen from experience.

"Let's go to the back rooms," the first man said.

They stopped at the master bedroom. There was a piece of furniture that was a combination desk and bureau of drawers. Without a word they began their search. In the third drawer on the right-hand side were papers. The two men smiled simultaneously. Legal papers. A deed, four birth certificates, papers for a car, insurance policies, other unimportant papers and a piece of paper that stipulated Flora Butler had been paid $7,500 for conceiving by artificial insemination and would get the other $7,500 upon the birth of a baby, which she would turn over to an adoptive couple. The surrogate-mother contract.

"Piece a cake," the second one whispered.

The two men quietly and meticulously put everything back just the way they had found it. They replaced the screen in the window and made sure everything was exactly as it had been. Then they left the house in possession of the piece of paper they had come after. Carefully they crossed to the driveway and out to the sidewalk. They saw only one person at that time of day. He was stripped to the waist and mowing his lawn. He never even looked up at them. Without a word to each other, they got in the dusty white car and drove directly out of Wananwa.

Flora Butler drove the van confidently, forgetting about the sluggish brake. As she turned down the long street leading to her house, she felt almost optimistic. Her appointment with Mrs. Simmons at the Christian Lord Realty Agency had gone so well. A lovely woman. Soft, blue gray hair, hazel eyes and the sweetest smile.

At first she had hesitated a bit before going into

the little shingled house. There were photographs of grand houses, and the prices . . . $225,000 for a house! She almost turned around and left, but nice Mrs. Simmons insisted she come in. She was just returning from showing a house and invited Flora to have a cup of coffee.

She sat on the other side of Mrs. Simmons's desk and had her coffee in a real china mug. Mrs. Simmons seemed enthusiastic when she marked down the information. She said she could list the house at $100,000, but probably they'd get an offer of $85,000. Flora couldn't believe it. All that money. For their house.

"I have to sell the house immediately," she informed Mrs. Simmons. "My husband and four children were killed in an automobile accident over the Fourth of July, and I just can't live there."

Mrs. Simmons looked up, and Flora thought for a moment there were tears in her eyes. "Yes, I think I saw something like that on the news." She stared at Flora, and then said, "I'm a widow myself, dear." Then she said, firmly, motherly, "It would be best not to keep your house anymore."

It had all gone so smoothly. She had given a set of her house keys so they could show it immediately, even if she was out. One hundred thousand dollars. She and Ralph had bought it for . . . she couldn't remember offhand. It was ten years ago, when they got married. She was eighteen and he was twenty-three.

Her mother had never approved of Ralph. Daddy liked him. She turned into the driveway and flew up in the seat when the old van hit the curb and sailed into the gravel. Ralph would understand why she had to sell the house, wouldn't he? It was his house, too.

"Ralph," she whispered. The van was still and her head was bowed. "I have to. The walls are whispering." She wouldn't tell him about her baby. It wasn't his baby, after all. She pursed her lips, revealing a sly little smile. No, that would be her secret from him.

The fat little old lady who lived next door waddled to the bushes. Flora thought she was an old biddy. She didn't like the eager look on her fat face. Flora couldn't abide people who delighted in gossip and unpleasant thoughts.

"Everything okay, Mrs. Butler? Because I'll be glad to come over and pitch in and help. That's what neighbors are for." She clicked her tongue in her mouth. "Such a pity. And such a good-looking couple like you and your husband. Like I sez to my hubby, you've had your share, yes you have."

Flora managed a smile. "I'll be all right, Mrs. . . ." She smiled again. Odd. The woman's last name escaped her, and they had lived next door for nearly five years.

"See you got some repairs done. The men were quick about it," the woman said, but Flora wasn't really listening.

"Thank you. I'll call you if I need anything."

"You do that, honey," she chirped. Coming into the house, Flora was wondering what she had to do next . . . her mind was blank. If her family were there, she would be busy baking some banana bread or picking up after the kids or starting dinner. What day was it? She really couldn't recall. Oh, well, that wasn't important. It was a weekday. She'd figure it out soon. On Mondays they had fish. On Tuesdays, a meat dish. No, they had given up meat when they joined the church. On Wednesdays, pasta or a casserole, on Thursdays, chicken. . . . No, she had chicken every Sunday. Mama had chicken every Thursday.

She stood in the middle of the floor for a moment,

bewildered. Forcing herself to do something, she shut the front door and slipped out of her dress. She put on a pair of slacks and a scoop-necked, sleeveless jersey. She would clear off that table and dust, and then run the vacuum. Her dress was in a puddle on the floor. She folded it and put it on a chair. She felt guilty about not hanging it up, but that was just too bad.

There was something important she had to do. Oh, yes, the Yellow Pages. She had to find a lawyer to get that evil Dr. Borg into court.

There was a loud buzzing sound, and it startled her and made her angry. It took her a few seconds to figure out what it was. The phone. It was making demands on her, and she was thinking about something. It rang again and again, and she walked into the kitchen, not quite sure if she really wanted to answer it. She fingered it for a moment, and then she remembered the kindly Mrs. Simmons at Christian Lord and she picked it up.

"Hello?" she asked, and then she became startled. Her voice sounded hollow in the empty house, almost as if the sound came from another person, not her at all.

"Flora, baby, are you all right?"

Ralph! It was Ralph. Flora watched a fly settling on the kitchen chair and then taking off. She had never had flies in her house. Then she realized something and felt disappointed. It couldn't be Ralph. He was gone.

"Daddy," she said.

"Listen, Flora, your mother and I have been worried sick about you since we found out. We discussed it. We want you to sell that house and come and live with us. You can have your old room. Let us take care of you, Flora, until you get your life together."

"That's right, Flora, you come home." She winced when she heard the acid-tipped, gravelly voice of her mother. She wasn't even sixty-five yet, and she always managed to sound to Flora like an old witch of ninety. She wondered why Daddy had ever married her.

Ignoring her mother, she said evenly, "Thank you, daddy. But I can take care of myself. I am selling the house. I'll be okay." She wanted to tell him of the baby, about her new life, but she couldn't. Not yet.

There were a few seconds of silence on the other end. Flora spoke faster, in the voice of a dutiful child trying to please. Her voice was high and full of energy. "They say I can get as much as $100,000 for the house, and I'm going to get a little apartment and take a job and . . ."

Her mother's raspy voice interrupted her. "Get a job? What can *you* do? You got married right out of high school. Didn't listen to me. Didn't take the commercial course and learn some typing and short-hand. Miss High and Mighty. See where it gets you now. If you can't type in today's world, Flora, you're nothing."

Flora felt a sinking feeling. Her mother was right. She had married Ralph and then gotten pregnant with Amy on her honeymoon. She had had a baby every two years, and every once in a while Ralph would take a second job. That was really all she was good for. Having babies.

"I could learn to type, mama," she said, a note of challenge creeping into her voice.

She heard her mother's insulting snort, and then the phone was passed back to her father. "Baby, you do what you want. Just remember . . ." Then she heard her mother's voice say loud and clear, "She always *did* do what she wanted to. Why should

anything change?" When she was recovering from
the sting of that attack, her father said gently,
". . . that we're here for you. We'll do anything we
can to help. We'll send you your bus fare to come
back home."

"Thanks, daddy," she said.

"Now you take care of yourself, princess. Promise?"

"I promise, Daddy."

A tear started to trickle out of Flora's eye, but she
fought sobbing. Mustn't cry in front of daddy. He
would be able to tell, and it would make him feel
bad. Dear, dear daddy. She missed him, his warmth
and gentleness. A sad, defeated man. There were
nights when he would drink himself into an eerie
silence. But he loved her. No matter what she did or
where she was. Life in Madisonville, Vermont,
would have been unbearable without that tall, gaunt
man who had barely eked out a living for his family
in the pipe factory.

After he hung up, she held the phone in her arms
and cradled it to keep him with her just a little while
longer. They weren't much for long-distance calls in
her family. Births and deaths were about the only
time they made them. She didn't know when she'd
hear his voice again, and that made her sad. As for
coming back home to her mother's house—never.

There was a tight knot in her stomach, as though a
ball of acid had just formed. She looked down and
saw her fists were clenched, as if she were about to
box. She should have something to eat. She bent into
the refrigerator and noticed some cheese. It was
green around the edges. She left it there. Cake was
easier to eat. And a glass of milk would be soothing
to her stomach.

She cut out a slice of lemon cake with a dirty
spoon that was lying on the table. The frosting was

melty. She could type if she wanted to. Lots· of women learned after high school. She could take a course. Her mother was just jealous because Flora could have babies and she had only one. Her mother said it was because they could afford only one, but Flora saw through the lie. Hah! A cake crumb stuck in her throat and she started to choke, but she washed it down with gulps of milk. Her mother had always added that it was too bad one child should turn out to be such a disappointment.

Straightening up, she decided she had to forget about the phone call and try to remember something that had crossed her mind before. It was a question. Oh, yes, what had she and Ralph originally paid for the house? All the papers were in the bedroom. She couldn't go into the bedroom.

Struggling with herself, she said shakily, out loud, "Flora Butler, don't be a big baby. You go into that bedroom and you open that desk drawer."

On a run she turned the corner, almost bumped into the doorway and sprinted down the hallway to the master bedroom. In a panic she pulled open the drawer where the deed was. Nine years ago they had paid $40,000 for the house, with a $5,000 down payment. But then Ralph had added on a bedroom. One hundred thousand. She still couldn't get over it. Replacing the deed, she shuffled through the other papers to have a look at her surrogate-mother contract. She'd need that for the lawyer.

Funny, she couldn't find it. None of the kids were ever allowed in the desk. She took out all the papers and went over them again, one by one. Then she yanked out the whole drawer and dumped all the contents on the floor, getting down on her hands and knees, looking for it. She turned around sharply. A whisper. "It's gone, Flora. Taken."

She stood up and wiped her hands on her slacks. "Ralph? Where are you?" She waited, rooted, motionless for a minute or two, then ran out of the bedroom and arrived in the living room, breathless.

Then she remembered. "See you got some repairs done today. The men were quick about it." She looked around the room. Someone had broken in. Someone had stolen her contract. She started out the door to her neighbor's and then stopped. What was the use. She knew who it was. It was that Dr. Borg. That evil man. He had stolen her contract so she wouldn't be able to get her baby back.

Suddenly she felt as if her mind was free. All of her senses were heightened, as well. She had a new purpose in life. To get Dr. Borg. To destroy evil. " 'And the Lord shall deliver me from every evil work, and will preserve *me* into his heavenly kingdom: to whom *be* glory for ever and ever. Amen.' Second Timothy 4:18," she said to herself. She knew he had stolen her contract. And she knew she would make him give it back to her. Oh, no. No one put anything over on Flora Butler. She was too smart for that. In spite of what her mama thought.

Amy Butler sat curled up on a cushion that covered the window seat. Ethel was sitting with a book in her wide lap and rocking back and forth in an old rocker.

"Listen carefully, child, maybe something here will tickle your memory."

Amy wasn't really concentrating. Her yellow hair had been washed and dried and plaited into shiny braids. At the end of each was a starchy plaid taffeta ribbon. She sat playing with the tips of her braids, which reminded her of paintbrushes, and thought how nice the old black couple were who were taking care of her.

She still didn't know who she was or where she came from or what her family was like, but she wasn't worried. It was almost as if she didn't want to remember. But she'd remember one day. When it was important. Meanwhile, she wanted to stay just where she was. Ethel had baked an angel-food cake for supper, and she had licked the frosting bowl. She didn't really care that she didn't belong any special place, but she sure wished the nightmares would go away. It was always the same dream, but it came in different shapes and disguises. She was falling, tumbling, and she had to push something open. Something tough. But wet and slimy. With all her might, tears rolling down her face, she kept punching it. She felt the panic rise in her throat until she thought it would choke her. And then she burst free. It seemed very real in her dreams, but too silly to tell anyone about when she woke up. But she did feel as if she were being strangled in her sleep.

"This book is called *What to Name the Baby*, sugar. Now ain't that sweet?" The big black woman looked over at the girl, who scrunched up her face in mock concentration. "I'm going to read some names. One of them might be yours." The little girl nodded, but she had a headache.

"Is your name Abigail?" Ethel asked. "That's a nice name."

"I don't think so."

"Doesn't ring a bell? Okay, there's lots more names. What about Aileen?"

"Uh-uh."

"Alcea?"

"Nope. Ugh."

"Alice? Alison?"

"I don't think so, Aunt Ethel."

Just then Sonny strode into the room, heard what they were doing and snatched the book out of his wife's hands. "Don't be doing nothing like that. This here's dangerous stuff. Amnesia. You can't take any chances. When she remembers, it might be terrible for that poor little thing. You wouldn't wake up a sleepwalker, would you?"

Ethel looked puzzled. "Ain't never seen one."

"Well, I was just over to Doc Holloway's to fix his fence. He said we should bring the girl over to him. He'll examine her, and he won't charge us anything. Said it was interesting, but there are . . . certain procedures that have to be followed."

"C'mon," he said to the little white girl. He didn't know what to call her. Seemed silly to make up a nickname when she might recollect her real name. Ethel called her Sary privately, because she liked the name.

Ethel gave the little girl a big embrace, then held her away and looked at her. Skinny little thing. She knew Doc Holloway was the best person to look at her. They just couldn't do the right thing for her.

The little girl scampered out the door and climbed into the old car after Sonny opened the door for her. It was all so confusing and new; but she didn't have to do chores, she never got a licking and she didn't have to study the Bible. Her head started to throb a little when she thought of the last part, but Sonny opened the rickety old glove compartment and told her to reach inside. There was a raspberry Tootsie Pop, just for her. She clapped her hands in glee as they pulled out of the driveway. Ethel was looking out of the window, watching them. Her eyes were burning with tears. She knew she would never see that little girl again.

Rochelle and Victor sat opposite each other at the long shiny table in the dining room. There were two long white candles with twinkling flames and a basket of fresh-cut flowers for a centerpiece. Victor was thrilled and flattered that his wife had made dinner for the two of them.

Rochelle wished the twins were home. Without them she was forced to entertain her husband herself.

"I think you should go, Shel. Absolutely. That's what families are for," he was saying.

"Oh, I don't know," she protested, privately enjoying her little game. "How can I leave you? And to go to New York all alone and stay at a hotel?"

"What! Can't you stay with your brother, the doctor?"

Rochelle looked shocked.

"Okay, you said he lives in an apartment. But with what doctors charge, it must be big enough for his sister to stay there."

She looked up, sipping her wine and shaking her head demurely.

"Such a cold family," he was saying. He picked up his fork and used it as a pointer. A piece of chicken was wobbling on the end of it. "You know, Shel, that's where I think you get some of your problems from. That cold family life you had. Too bad you didn't grow up in California like I did. Where it's free."

Rochelle nodded. And when her husband finally looked down to retrieve the piece of chicken that had fallen off his fork, she had all she could do to stop grinning. Eventually she did intend to stay with her brother.

Chapter Fifteen

Amanda woke up. She looked at the luminous dial of the digital clock on the night table. Four o'clock in the morning. A dog barked mournfully somewhere. She turned to Branch and reached out for him. He wasn't there.

She sat up, frightened, disoriented. Then she saw his bare back and realized why she heard the dog barking so clearly. Branch was sitting at a chair with the window open, the moonlight grazing his body, just looking out. Amanda felt more frightened seeing him there.

"Branch," she whispered. "You all right, honey?"

He turned sharply. "Did I wake you up? Just wanted some fresh air. All that pâté at dinner. Didn't agree with me, or my stomach's not as strong as it used to be. You had the melon, didn't you?"

"Sweetheart, you're letting all the air conditioning go out the window."

"Sorry," he said, slamming the window shut, making the lacy curtains flutter.

"Can I get you anything?" she asked, concerned.

"No. I'll be okay. You go back to bed."

But he didn't join her. He passed by the bed and went into the marble bathroom connected to their room. Amanda wondered if she should go in. She felt nervous for some odd reason. But nothing bad could happen. Not now. Not to them. Everything was finally working out.

The night before, just a matter of hours, really, it had been as it used to be for them. The sexy patter during cocktails, the expensive food and wines, the gaiety and private jokes, the admiring stares, the waiters fussing over them. Only one thing had been slightly different: they pulled out pictures of their beautiful baby for everyone to exclaim over.

Then they had come home and made love. Now there was where it was a little different, now that she thought of it. She hadn't been able to figure it out, but now she knew what was off. Branch. He was detached, somehow. It was like making love to a person who was a million miles away. And, yet, if she accused him of it, he would say it was her imagination. She hoped it was.

In the all-white art-deco marble bathroom, Branch was gripping the sink and staring in the mirror at his hair. More gray hairs. Soon he wouldn't be a sophisticated salt-and-pepper anymore. He'd just be old. Maybe that was causing it. Middle age. Even sex felt different to him somehow. He felt he wasn't pleasing Amanda, and yet how could he ask if he was?

And how could he explain the golden-haired goddess that visited him in his dreams? It was stupid; yet he had no control over it. Amanda was Danielle's mother in every way, and he knew it. He opened the medicine cabinet. Maybe there was a pill he could take to get rid of this predawn insomnia. He looked around and then closed the cabinet. No, no pills. He would have a hangover in the morning. He'd somehow have to solve his problem.

"Branch?" Amanda called. "Are you okay?" There was no answer. She wasn't sure he had heard her. Then something came to mind, and she crossed her fingers under the covers. It couldn't be *that*. Was Branch playing around? Was that what she sensed?

Wasn't that how it was done? She'd seen enough of it. Hubby out and about and little wifey at home with the kid. *Oh, God,* she thought, *I couldn't take that.* Right then and there she promised herself she'd go on that little diet she'd been putting off. And she could drag herself away from Danielle one afternoon a week to spend it at the beauty parlor. She'd get a manicure and a facial and her eyebrows done. The works *every* week. She squeezed her eyes shut to blot out the pain.

The receptionist breathed a soft "oh, no" when she saw the determined woman march up the carpeted aisle. Dr. Borg had warned her, and now it was happening. One of the surrogate mothers. Very confused. To be humored kindly, but not taken seriously.

Flora Butler stopped at the front desk, gripping her white bag as if it were a weapon. One sandal heel was chipped off. She had tripped and stumbled on a curb. Walking up Madison Avenue, she had wondered why her scalp itched so and then couldn't remember the last time she had washed her hair. There were dark circles under her eyes. She hadn't slept the night before. She had been too furious for that.

"Mrs. Butler?" The receptionist asked and announced at the same time. She said all the syllables slowly, in a maddening, patronizing tone. "You do not have an appointment for today. Now, if you'd like to make one, I can . . ."

Flora shook her head. "No, I do not want an appointment with that evil man!"

Thelma, hearing the noise, stuck her head out the window. It was Mrs. Butler. But she looked distraught and disheveled. Such a lovely woman, and shouting like that. She wondered what had made her so upset. But inside Thelma knew. She had three children. She asked herself over and over if she could have another woman carry her baby or do it for another woman. No. It defied nature's intentions. She would rather be childless, much as she loved her kids and the grandchildren they had given her. She clucked her tongue and returned to the examining room. Poor woman. She wasn't exactly in love with this job or Dr. Borg. After the first of the year, she and Milton could retire to Phoenix. Until then they needed the money.

The receptionist found it hard to be even tempered. The whole situation made her angry, and she couldn't help it. When people signed contracts, they should be mature enough to stick to them. People like Mrs. Butler were pests. Besides, it made her nervous to have to be around emotionally unstable people. That's why she never took subways. She didn't want to see those people mumbling, singing, giving speeches or lying in the aisles. It made her feel strange. Threatened.

Flora Butler stood tall. She stamped her foot, the one with the chipped heel. "I'm going in there right now!" she said loudly, pointing to the big office in the corner.

The receptionist stood up and put her hands on her hips.

"I wouldn't do that if I were you, Mrs. Butler. Besides, he isn't even in his office."

Flora ignored her and rushed toward Borg's office. A strong, firm hand covered hers and stopped her from opening the door. She looked up into the dark brown eyes of Dr. Borg. He pried her hand off the knob and escorted her under the elbow into his office, shutting the door firmly.

"Mustn't barge in on the doctor, Flora," he said in a low, insulting voice that implied she was a mentally deranged, emotionally crippled individual. She wondered who he reminded her of. Oh, yes, her mother. That made her angry. So angry she wanted to strike out at him. It also made her dizzy. When they got inside his office, she put her hand on her head because the room seemed to swim around.

Immediately the tone of his voice changed into that of compassionate doctor.

"Can I get you some water?"

She shook her head, trying to shake out all the fuzziness. Why was her sleeveless blouse on the outside. She noticed it when she looked down. She had tucked it in, hadn't she? Stupid polyester material. She wouldn't make any more skirts like that. They stretched.

The door was closed. Dr. Borg was sitting behind his desk. She licked her lips. "You stole it," she announced.

Dr. Borg said nothing. He just stared at her. His heart was pounding. This was better than he had expected. The woman was acting more peculiar than usual. Almost berserk.

Flora saw the file cabinets behind her. She slid one drawer out. It had patients' names on file folders.

With an "aha!" to her wavering voice, she yelled, "Now, I'll have *your* copy of the contract, Dr. Borg. You can't fool me. You see, I *know* you took mine!"

She pulled open all the drawers, noisily, leaving some jutting out, slamming others shut, making the whole unit shake. Dr. Borg sat motionless, in silence, watching her. Flora yanked out a drawer midbottom to the carpet. "S," she hissed. But she wasn't really sure until she looked closer. "Yes, here it is! Surrogate mothers. You can't stop me now!" She sat down on the couch with the thin file and looked through it. He continued to study her as if she were a specimen under a microscope. Furiously, she pulled out the papers and ruffled through them. Then she pitched them on the floor. Just a stapled article on surrogate mothers. But she realized she was left holding an empty file folder. She picked up the article and started to rip it savagely. He sat at the desk, continuing to watch her silently. Then she heard long staccato screeches and realized that the noise was coming from within her. She closed her mouth and couldn't remember where she was. The couch and the doctor and the cabinet seemed painted onto the walls.

She looked up at him as if she were pleading. He looked down at her and nodded. He was smart to have moved the files out of his office.

"That's right, Mrs. Butler. There was no baby. The files don't lie. There never was a surrogate baby." He opened his hands from his body, palms upward, in a gesture of apology. "Will you let me help you?"

Flora Butler continued looking up at him, much as a dog regards his master. "But I had a husband and children, didn't I?" she said in a thin, shaky voice.

He nodded approvingly, as if she was beginning to catch on. But Flora stared at him and then shook her head. She got up slowly, brushed off her skirt and tried unsuccessfully to tuck in her blouse. If she had never had a baby, why did she know this place? She had no one to prove she had had a baby . . . for money. These people were all on his side. This man was the devil himself. She started screaming again and leaped at him, digging into his throat with her fingernails. Dr. Borg efficiently bound her two wrists together with his one hand, while with his free hand he buzzed his intercom.

"Yes," droned the machine.

"Call 911. Tell them to send a car. We have a very disturbed individual in our office. Immediately!"

Flora Butler, with superhuman strength born of anxiety, tried to wriggle free. When she did, she put her forefingers in her ears and screamed until the doctor again grabbed her wrists and held her so she couldn't move.

Amy Butler sat in the living room of Doc Holloway's house. She was sitting on a couch swinging her legs, which did not quite touch the floor, and twirling the ends of her fingers around her braids. She felt like crying. There was a lump of sadness in her throat, but her eyes were dry. So dry they burned. She couldn't cry.

Sonny was sitting on a chair, his hands folded and hanging between his lanky legs. "Listen, girl, we'll come and visit every Sunday. Maybe we'll bring you some of Ethel's chicken. How'd you like that?"

Amy could hear the voice of old Doc Holloway talking to someone on the phone. He had told her that her case of amnesia was very serious, that it wasn't normal not to remember the first eight years of her life, nor to land in Ethel and Sonny's house as if rescued from a spaceship. She didn't laugh at his supposed attempt at a joke. He said she should be put in a home with other children who needed care. Then she would find out who she was and where she belonged, and the authorities would take her there. The authorities. Would she go to an orphanage? That kindly, fatherly man Sonny thought so highly of was going to send her far away. Doc Holloway, with his gold-rimmed glasses slipping off his nose, his silly white hair that didn't stretch across his head. She hated him. She wished he would drop dead right then so she wouldn't have to go.

Flora Butler sat on a wooden bench with the policeman. He was slumped over, hands clasped between his knees. They were in the psychiatric admittance of Manhattan General. A man was sitting in a wheelchair, babbling about the overthrow of the pope, the lousy subway system and a planet from outer space that would attack any minute. Every once in a while he would rise, walk about and shout violently. Then someone would ease him back, and he would sob pitifully. People tried to pretend he didn't exist.

Flora clutched her handbag. She knew that wherever she was, she would find her baby. It was part of the Lord's master plan. The nice policeman sitting next to her had removed the handcuffs. He was in cahoots with a group of Christians, and that's the only way they could have saved her from that evil Dr. Borg. She knew who was on her side. The large black nurse, for one. She had smiled at Flora, and Flora had returned the smile. Yes, she was in on it. And there were others. Pretty soon she'd get her baby back, and she could go home.

When her name was called, she sat perfectly straight and motionless. The patrolman had to ask her to get up before she understood she was to go to the big desk and fill out some forms. At the desk she wrote her name. Under "next of kin," she wrote Ralph's name and her five children. Amy, Benjamin, Carl, Dennis and Emily. She filled in her address.

"Do you have insurance, Mrs. Butler?"

She stared at the woman, thought a moment and nodded yes. Of course there would be life insurance. Ralph had a policy. She didn't have anything with her, though. No card for the woman. She apologized.

Finally a nurse called her into a tiny room with a desk. Flora sat down in front of it.

"Are you going to give me my baby?" she asked,

whispering. The nurse looked up sharply. She was compiling a triage, or preliminary report, for a doctor to review. She looked closely at the form Flora had filled out. "Which baby, Mrs. Butler?" she asked.

"Emily. Because the others are all dead, you know. Just like Ralph, my husband." Flora's red-tinged eyes were wide open, as if she had just seen some horrible image.

"Mrs. Butler," the nurse said patiently, "you list Ralph Butler as next of kin. And then five children. Are they alive, or what?"

"He didn't really want me to have another man's baby, and I know it now," she said.

The nurse looked at Flora carefully. Flora didn't trust this nurse. She wasn't going to give anything away. *They* were trying to steal the baby away.

Unfortunately, the nurse never asked Flora the one question that might have helped the doctors with a diagnosis. The one question that might have helped Flora the most. No one asked Flora Butler how long it had been since she'd slept, really slept, since the state trooper had been there to tell her that her family was gone. In fact, no one knew that Flora had suffered this sudden grief and might still be in shock.

When Flora was finally seen by a resident, it was late in the morning. The young doctor had curly hair and a big mustache. He was very quick and perceptive because he was trained to be. He was also a person who hadn't slept much. He led Flora into a little room.

"Do you have my baby?" Flora asked.

Having seen the triage, the doctor said, in utter seriousness and simulated sadness, "No, I'm sorry, I don't."

She responded by quoting the Book of Job nonstop while he tried to ask her questions. Flora was tired. She didn't like this arrogant young man. She tuned him out and concentrated on a group of dusty tongue depressors. She wanted to clean them. Finally, getting no response, he said good-bye to her and walked out.

The next thing she knew she was riding down a long, long, underground corridor. She had been asked to undress and given a pair of pajamas. When the nurse had seized her handbag, she had screamed, then pulled out the only thing she could find, a kerchief. So she could diaper her baby when she found her. They had let her keep that. The nurse had said something silly. What was it? "You better not try to strangle yourself with that thing." Flora was shocked. "I would *never* do such a thing," she replied. "No, you won't," the nurse smiled. "It's too small. It's square, like a diaper." Flora beamed. The nurse was one of those on her side. And at the end of this long ride they would give her her baby.

Thelma stopped off at Macy's after work before taking the subway back to Brooklyn. She should have gotten a gift for her youngest grandchild's birthday on her lunch hour, but she hadn't had the energy. The way the police came and took out that poor woman. It was a disgrace. She had yelled, "I did have a baby. Get the files." Of course she had had a baby. A baby girl. It bothered her. That doctor was so cold. Cruel, really. And when she had asked him where the police were taking her, he had said, "Manhattan General."

Thelma wouldn't put a dog there. Such a lovely woman, Mrs. Butler. Surely there were other hospitals around the city that were nicer. She shrugged and stopped by a counter. A little sweater—that would do it. When they were installed in their new complex in Phoenix, she would be able to knit a sweater like this. She'd have the time. And she wouldn't have to take any more sweaty, crowded subways back to Brooklyn. If she could just hang on. She became immersed in the color of the sweater and promptly forgot about Flora Butler.

Flora walked slowly down the women's section of ward five. Her pajamas were loose and the pants were almost falling off. She had thought, because of the tunic effect, that she might be pregnant again. But she knew she wasn't. Her feet felt heavy, pulled down by weights. She was scuffing around in dirty white cotton flat-heeled mules that said "Manhattan General" on the side. All she wanted to do was go to her bed and sleep. But she couldn't. They might come with her baby any second.

There was a faint aroma of food on the floor. But she wasn't hungry. She walked into a big room at the back. An angled television set protruded from the ceiling. In another room there was a Ping-Pong table. There were no bright colors. Everything looked like a rainy day, though outside, through the dusty windows, she could see that the sun was shining.

People sat and smoked in the middle section, between the men's and women's wards. *Disgusting*, thought Flora. That was the dining room. There were bedrooms with two beds in them. But at the very end of the long hall was a room with many beds in it. One woman sat on a bed and rocked an imaginary baby. Flora thanked the Lord. She was sure the woman had been sent by someone. Flora sat next to her. The woman's cotton hospital pajamas were straining at her fat bulges. She was pulling a huge breast out of her top to feed the nonexistent baby.

"Is it a boy or a girl?" Flora asked sweetly.

The woman turned and smiled. She had a gold tooth right in the front of her mouth. She spat in Flora's face. Stunned, Flora got up off the bed and stumbled backward against another bed. A woman with a very short haircut that stood straight up, as if she had been electrocuted, put her arm around her and caught her.

"Listen, you don't look so good," she said. She didn't wait for an answer. Instead, she slipped her hand inside of Flora's braless top, pretending to check her heartbeat.

"You're real pretty," she said softly. "I bet when you get fixed up—you know, a little red lipstick, high heels, nylons—well, I bet you're a real sexy little bitch."

Flora stared at her for a few seconds and then removed the woman's hand from her breast. "No, no, you don't understand. I'm looking for my baby. I want my baby."

The woman nodded and closed her eyes sensuously. One of her legs was swinging over the other knee, so that her whole body rocked with the movement. Outside in the hall a man could be heard saying over and over, "Are you my doctor? Do you have a cigarette? Are you my doctor?"

"Listen," the rawboned woman said to Flora, leaning closer. "You're just about the prettiest little thing we've had here. Why don't you meet me in the bathroom when lights are out." She lowered her voice even more. "Don't swallow the medication they give you. Put it behind your tongue and then spit it out later."

Flora blinked several times. She was confused. She would never take any pills.

The woman laughed at her starry-eyed innocence. She bit her tongue so it stuck lewdly out the side of her mouth. She held out the middle finger of her hand and jabbed it into the air. "Listen, babe. I'm the best. Nobody does it like me. Ask any of the girls here."

Flora stood up abruptly. Her stomach hurt and she was doubled over in cramps. She staggered out of the bedroom and into the recreation room. Then she almost sobbed with relief. On the table in the corner was a Bible. She had never seen a torn, ragged Bible before. If she opened it at random to any page, would it give her a clue? Would it tell her who would have her baby and when she could get Emily and leave this dreadful place? She licked her finger and opened the Bible. It opened to the Book of Exodus.

Chapter Sixteen

Mavis sat Danielle upright on a hammock that was secured to two, perfectly spaced sweet-gum trees. Danielle looked tiny in the big stretch of canvas, and she sat blinking her eyes and looking around.

"You sure is a pretty little thing," Mavis said admiringly, her voice as gentle as warm milk, her soft touch like silk to the baby's skin. Danielle purred and smiled up at her.

Impulsively Mavis picked her up off the hammock and pressed her close to her breast. "You're going to be a heartbreaker, you wait and see." Danielle threw back her golden head and laughed, almost on cue, in that way she had of enchanting everyone. She laughed as if she knew exactly what her nanny was talking about.

Holding the baby away from her body so that her legs dangled, Mavis studied the little figure wearing a diaper and a tiny pink and rose tie-dyed T-shirt. Her hair looked like gold in the sunlight. Her pink barrette was clipped under the curl at the top of her head. Her big blue eyes were sparkling.

"Doll, you is gorgeous. The prettiest baby I ever did see."

Danielle missed her cue this time. She started to screech for no reason. Mavis pulled the baby to her breast and rocked her, but the baby still screamed.

Mavis smiled and began to sing:

> *"Hush little baby,*
> *Rock-a-bye,*
> *Mavis gonna sing you a lullaby*
> *and if Danielle don*
> *like that lullaby*
> *Mavis gonna sit right*
> *down and cry. . . ."*

Mavis looked down. The baby was quiet now, resting on her shoulder. Mavis started to sing again but realized the baby had fallen asleep. She smiled knowingly and whispered, "Lordy! You're a good little baby. Except when you gets them dark spells. I think it's because you got birthed strange. Oh, yes, I knows all about it." She rocked the baby gently. "Mavis believes what folks tell her until she can get quiet and figure it out for herself. But you is a fourth-generation Whitney, and I'll protect you with my life. Yes, I will."

Out in the front of the large lawn that circled the house, Amanda jumped up. "I thought I heard the baby crying," she said.

"So did I, but she's stopped. Besides, don't get up every time for her, Amanda. You'll spoil her," Joyce Hirsch said. "My God, you're always making fun of all those Junior League ladies. You're grooming one right there."

Amanda sat down again and smiled wryly. "One thing I love about you, Joyce, is that you're not timid. You get things right out into the open." She sighed. "You're right, too. If we don't stop, we'll turn out a monster."

"Don't worry about it. She gets a lot of good old-fashioned love, too."

The two women were sitting on white wrought-iron chairs. On a matching table with a glass top was a tray with a pitcher of iced tea and a plate of homemade sugar cookies. Sprigs of fresh mint from the herb garden floated in the iced tea. Not one cookie on the plate had been touched.

"I started my diet," Amanda announced.

"Oh, I was hoping you would," Joyce replied languidly. "You're really getting obese." Joyce laughed. Weight was a constant hassle for her. "Wait until Danielle gets older. The Milky Ways and peanut butter and ice cream. It will be harder to nibble on carrots and celery. Oh, it's just so nice to spend an afternoon like this. Two kids in day camp, one kid farmed out. I feel free."

Amanda looked at her toes. She realized self-consciously that she had torn up clumps of fresh, dark green grass with her toes. She slipped back into her thong sandals.

"Joyce? Did you ever think Justin was playing around?"

Joyce looked across at the perfectly chiseled face of her friend. Her mouth dropped open. She laughed, but it sounded brittle, even to her own ears. "Wow, talk about timid; talk about changing the subject drastically. Why is it, Amanda, when two women get together, it always sounds like a soap opera? What brought this on? Do *you* think Branch is playing around?"

"I asked you first," Amanda replied, seriously. She looked into her eyes, but squinted because the sun was behind Joyce's head. "Well," Joyce said, after realizing that this meant something to Amanda, "this means being honest. Telling you something I've never told anybody." Joyce thought a moment. "Okay, yes. I did and I didn't only think he was, I knew he was. It was with his secretary. Just recently as a matter of fact. I never said anything."

"Why?"

"Because it wouldn't have helped. He's almost forty-six. He's in good shape and he knows it. But forty-six is not twenty-three. His secretary, however, was twenty-three. I knew he would never leave me, Amanda. The secretary left for another job. I'm sure it's over. But I knew all along, and I think it would have been worse for our marriage if I would have made an issue out of it. As it is, I think it may have helped us."

Amanda put her face in her hands and rested her elbows on the glass top of the table. "I see," she said simply. "But Branch doesn't have a secretary."

In a loud, staccato voice, a nurse's aide called off the names. Visitors formed a line outside the closed doors of the ward and were let in one at a time. Behind them was the forensic psychiatric ward. Many famous criminals had been incarcerated in that dangerous ward of Manhattan General for psychiatric evaluation. Flora Butler watched the visitors being let in. She didn't expect anyone to visit her. There was no one now except her baby.

When the voice shouted, "Flora Butler," she didn't hear it. She was standing, but she was half-asleep. They had given her a pill the night before.

Flora had said she wouldn't take it, but the nurse had said it was just an M&M. A patient laughed after she swallowed it. "Thorazine," she had called the M&M. It had made her sleep deeply, and when she got up she bumped into a wall. Then the nurse had given her another one in a little white cup. Her fingers felt like they were curling into claws, and her words seemed to retreat back somewhere inside of her. Her nose was stuffed. But she didn't feel that painful, pinched tiredness.

"Flora Butler!" the voice shouted again. Flora stood straight and raised her hand. Then she looked at it and pulled it down to her side stiffly and self-consciously. A woman emerged from the throng of visitors.

Flora squinted.

The woman was carrying a box of candy and came toward Flora holding out her hand. Flora stepped aside to let her pass. She thought it was a mistake.

"Mrs. Butler?" the woman inquired.

Flora nodded.

The woman had gray hair and looked vaguely familiar. "Can we sit down?" Flora looked around. There were groups of folding chairs. They sat down. The woman gave her the box of candy. "I'm Mrs. Schneider. Thelma Schneider. You remember me, don't you, Mrs. Butler?"

Flora nodded. She didn't want to offend the kind woman. It was just that she felt so woozy and foggy and thirsty.

"Mrs. Butler," the woman said firmly, "I heard about what happened. I came here to help you."

"Why?" Flora heard herself asking.

"Because I like people," the woman answered. She looked around the tables and chairs at the patients drugged and sad eyed. It was a dismal cage. She had done the right thing. This was no place for a woman like Flora Butler.

"Here," she said, "I brought you some candy." Flora opened the cellophane and began eating a piece of chocolate hungrily. "I took a pill . . . ," she began, and then started to choke.

Thelma thought her heart would break. When it came time to tell Milton that she lost her job because of this, she knew he'd agree she was right. She'd tell him all about this poor woman and what Dr. Borg had done to her.

Thelma looked at her watch. She had an appointment with a nurse's temporary agency.

"Mrs. Butler, I brought you the name and address of the couple who have your baby. The Whitneys. They live in Atlanta." She handed Flora the piece of paper. Flora looked at it.

"What baby? Did I have a baby?"

A chill ran down Thelma's side and her mouth quivered. She gulped. "Yes," she said firmly. "You had a baby girl. I was there in the examining room with you during all of your visits. Don't you remember?"

"Oh, yes," Flora said, smiling thinly.

Thelma reached over and seized her arm. "Look, Mrs. Butler. Try and pull yourself together. I heard about the strain you've been under. You always seemed like such a composed young woman to me. Look, comb your hair a little and . . ." She reached inside her bag and gave Flora a lipstick and a comb. "Maybe if you looked neater, they'd let you out."

Then Thelma pulled another piece of paper out of her bag. "Now, look, take good care of this," she said carefully to Flora, smiling. "It's the doctor's copy of your contract. There's no doubt now, Mrs. Butler."

Flora looked up at her as she stood and smiled. Thelma sighed and took her hand. There was a little of the old brightness in her face. Maybe she'd be all right. Yes, Flora Butler probably would, she hoped. And she had eased her conscience. Wishing her good luck and kissing her, Thelma left by the double door in front.

As she went down on the jammed elevator, Thelma smiled to herself. Hot stuff, Dr. Borg. Well, not to Thelma. She had gone to him and said, "That poor woman. You've made her go crazy."

He had said, "Impossible. She was disturbed when she came here."

"Dr. Borg, everyone could hear what she was screaming as the police dragged her out like some public nuisance. She wasn't sure she had a baby or not," she had protested.

"That happens to women who are emotionally disturbed, Mrs. Schneider," he had said coldly.

"Well, I don't like it," she had countered.

"Well, if you don't like it, leave," he had countered back.

Just like that. He was young enough to be her son. Stay and be miserable. Or leave and not even collect unemployment. It took Thelma two seconds to get her hat and coat and put her uniforms in a shopping bag. When she was sure he was up front, she went into an empty, unused, small office in the back. There, as she suspected, was the surrogate-mother file cabinet. Hands shaking, mouth dry, she had lifted Flora Butler's contract and stuffed it in her bag. Then she called Manhattan General from a pay phone and found out when visiting hours were. Well, that poor woman. Someone had to do something. She just couldn't live with herself if she didn't. She and Milton would manage. Sometimes a temp agency had work for months.

On the fifth floor Flora Butler walked around and around. She had combed her hair and put on some lipstick. In the pocket of her pajamas were the precious pieces of paper. She didn't know yet what she could ever do with them, but she would protect them with her life.

Rochelle Vance sat in a sticky upholstered chair in her hotel room. The air conditioner was on high, and still she was sweltering. It must be the humidity. She had walked around for a while, had lunch in a coffee shop and staggered back to the hotel. In all the years of marriage to Victor, she had never cheated. She looked at the bed again and then took off every stitch of clothing. It was easier to sleep than to think, especially when she was feeling anxious.

Dr. Borg always reserved half an hour between 1:00 and 1:30 for his private time. In the summer he would have a salad ordered. In winter it would be a soup and sandwich. He rarely left his office, preferring instead to sit and think.

On that day it took him exactly ten minutes to eat his lunch in his office. He sat alone with his door closed, watching the drapes blow in the breeze of the air conditioner. His hands were clasped behind his neck, and he leaned back in his chair.

Someday, he thought complacently, his practice would be devoted to genetics. First, the transfer of embryos. It would not be just breeding, but selective breeding. That was the cure for America. And the salvation, too. Then the world would improve, because he and others like him would breed a superior human race. The day would come soon. He needed research facilities, though. The kind that cost a lot of money—money that would come from a lot of surrogate-mother deals.

Funny he had chosen genetics as his ultimate career. Especially with his background. It would amuse his colleagues in the field to know the truth.

But they never would. He would never tell them what he found out when he was fourteen, when Nana died. Again his mind reworked the painful scene.

Nana had patted the covers, and he had sat down on her bed. "Normy," she whispered, and he had to lean in to hear her more clearly, "I haven't got much time left." She rubbed his arm lovingly with an almost skeletal hand. "I left you most of my money, you know." His heart skipped a beat. Nana was rich. She was his father's mother. His dad had been killed in World War II. He didn't remember him. He was two when he went away. He always felt special with Nana. She had class. He liked to pretend she was his real mother.

"I want you to use the money for medical school," she said. "You'll be a doctor, yes, like Nana wants you to be?" He nodded. She always wanted him to be somebody important. She cared. He liked that. Then she tapped him on the shoulder again. He shivered at her touch. "Something else, darling. Someone should tell you. She won't. Ever. And I hate to do it this way, but there's so little time."

He remembered that moment. They say the past gets colored because memories become distorted by emotion. But he recalled exactly the way it had happened. His stomach seemed to flip over, warning him something awful was about to happen. He was about to have something taken away from him. She motioned for him to come in closer. He did and was almost inches away from her paper-thin yellowish lips. The pungent smell of her illness repulsed him. Out of the corner of his eye he could see his mother and Shel waiting respectfully in the hall, while Nana said her good-byes. "The man who was her husband," she said in a low, rumbling voice. "My dear son . . . the man you think was your father . . ."

She shook her head with all the energy she had left. "Not so. You were adopted because your parents thought they couldn't have children. She made my son think it was his fault," she said bitterly. "Sweetheart, that's the truth. No one knows who your real parents are. You're not even my grandson, but I have always loved you and thought of you as mine. That's why I left you all that money, you poor orphan. Don't have any hard feelings. Love your mother and sister." She smiled up at him, parting her lips painfully so that the effect was almost grotesque. Then she shut her eyes. Those were Nana's last words. She died within the hour.

For a while he couldn't accept the harshness of it. It was like a turning point in his life, though. The picture of the man on the piano. The decorated war hero. Not his father? It was like a bad joke. And if Nana had died sooner, he never would have known. He felt betrayed. Most of all by Nana, who wasn't his grandmother. Not his real grandmother. He had loved her, and now he would have to forget her. She had pitied him; that was all. And that word. He knew it. Orphan. She had said it. He had no real parents. What a dirty trick. But then he realized that . . . Rochelle wasn't his real sister. Which meant what they were doing wasn't as bad. It wasn't quite as forbidden. Of course, it didn't make any difference to him. Shel was his friend and enemy at the same time. It was the enemy that excited him. But if she knew, it might ruin the excitement for her. She must never know.

His "mother" was a stupid woman who was constantly overweight, always trying to boss him around. He was ashamed of her. That night, after Nana's funeral, he approached her in the kitchen when Shel was upstairs doing her homework.

"Shel isn't my sister," he said.

"Of course she is, and I want you two to stop

fighting." All he could see was her fat rear end as she cleaned the kitchen counter.

On impulse he picked up a kitchen knife, so that when she turned around she saw it pointed at her. "Nana told me the truth. I know I'm not Shel's brother."

He saw her Adam's apple slide down as she gulped. He came up close and held the knife to her throat. "Nana says I'm an orphan. That means I'm not Rochelle's brother." His mother blinked and tears rolled down her cheeks. He didn't need an answer. That was enough.

He brought the knife close to her throat. "Don't ever tell Shel that I'm not her real brother or I'll kill you."

"Please . . ." she whispered, terrified.

Finally he lowered his arm. She looked at him sadly and shook her head. "I'll never understand you, Normy."

"Just don't ever tell her," he snarled.

His mother never gave away the secret. And she never caused him any trouble again. He simply treated the cow like a piece of furniture. Except to browbeat her. That was fun. Shel never knew that they were not brother and sister. Every time they made love, she would giggle and say, "What if people knew? All the girls in school talk about their boyfriends touching their boobs. I'm doing *it* with my own brother!"

He had decided to become his own father. And he had made himself strong and superior. Before college he picked a new name and had his old one legally changed. It didn't matter what he was like genetically, because he was superior. He had crafted himself to be the person he wanted.

Barnard stared straight ahead, and his gaze took in the wall clock. It was almost 1:30 and time for his next patient. Yet, untypically, lazily, he let himself think of the lavish research and development facilities he planned to have. A whole building, possibly in New Jersey somewhere. It would come. Oh, yes.

People were willing to pay a lot for babies. He had twenty-five surrogate deals so far. With inflation, he could raise his price. Flora Butler. A dot, a speck. She would present no obstacle to his scheme. No, the woman wouldn't be a problem. After Manhattan General transferred her to a state institution, that would shut her up.

Mrs. Simmons sat at her desk. No one was in the office, so she decided to eat her lunch. She tried Mrs. Butler's number once again. A little blob of egg salad fell onto the napkin she had spread out. She had the keys, but it seemed Mrs. Butler had disappeared. The woman was always out. Or perhaps she had taken a little trip.

Still, she had to know. It had been the easiest sale she had ever seen. A couple from Hoboken had seen the home and wanted it immediately. Eighty-five thousand dollars. Mrs. Simmons sighed. Well, the woman would have to show up sooner or later. Meanwhile, she'd have to tell the young, eager couple to sit tight. She knew they wouldn't lose interest. They'd never find another house like that in their price range. If she could just find Mrs. Butler.

Chapter Seventeen

Rochelle Vance dressed very carefully. Her makeup was flawless, though a bit smoky, her dark hair was tied at the nape of her neck with a black ribbon, and her large gold hoop earrings set off her heart-shaped face. She wore no stockings but had smoothed hand lotion all over her legs to give them a sheen. She wore a black and white patterned dress with black and white sandals made of leather circles. She wore only black and white in the summer in New York. Colors were for California.

When she had waked up, refreshed from her nap, she had made a decision. She couldn't very well go barging into his office. She would go to his apartment and just wait for him there. It was better than waiting in the hotel.

Amanda was spooning strained apricots to Danielle, who was kicking her arms and legs happily. When the phone rang, Amanda yelled absentmindedly, "I'll get it," then remembered she and the baby were alone. Branch was filming a hardware store commercial, and Mavis had taken the day off to take all her children to the dentist.

She was surprised to hear Murray's voice.

"Amanda, how are you?"

"Just fine. And you?"

All the time she was talking, she was keeping her eye on Danielle, who was getting restless sitting in her highchair with nothing to do. She was hardly giving Murray her full attention. Obviously he had called because he hadn't had much time to give her when she had stopped in.

She was wrong.

"Amanda, come back, please."

"Murray, you saw my baby. I don't want to go back to work. I don't need to. What on earth for?"

"Because we need you."

"C'mon," she laughed. "You have what's-his-face." She couldn't remember her replacement's name for the life of her.

"What's-his-face isn't working out," he said flatly.

"I thought you thought he was terrific."

"For New York. Not for Atlanta."

Amanda chastised herself for even getting involved in the conversation. "I don't want to work, Mur. I'm happy. My place is at home with my child."

Danielle was making spitting noises with her mouth. Amanda looked over and saw she was trying to blow "raspberries." She had never done that before. Amanda smiled. It was cute.

"Amanda, please consider it."

Why did she feel she was talking to someone in another world? Okay, she was flattered he had called. But she had left the rat race forever, and it was hard to comprehend a full-time job.

"Amanda, please," Murray whined. "You can have a four-day week."

"Thanks, Mur. But find someone else," she replied.

"I guess I'll have to. But if you come back, I'll make you creative director."

Amanda was touched. That was Murray's title. Though the associate creative director really did all the work.

"Never," she said lightly.

"Never say never," he parried.

"Murray, I'll never ski in the Olympics, sing at the Met or be twenty again."

"Touché." He laughed, but it sounded hollow to Amanda. "Well, you can't blame me for trying. Remember, if you ever . . . but then you won't ever change your mind, I guess."

"I'm flattered you asked. Listen, a housewife and mother like me. You made my day."

Murray hung up the phone and crossed Amanda's name off the top of his list. Then he picked up the phone again and dialed.

Rochelle Vance looked up briefly from the long aqua velvet couch in the lobby and recrossed her legs. She was waiting for Normy in his apartment building. It would be a dramatic surprise. One he would go for. She wondered, though, if the doorman didn't think it odd. She had been sitting there for two hours, pretending to read from *Vogue* magazine. It was 6:30 in the evening. What if she was wrong? What if he didn't come home after work?

Danielle was sitting in her highchair, crumbling bits of crackers into mush on the tray. Amanda was fixing Branch a late lunch.

"Hey," he said expansively. "I like this. The three of us together like this. You fixing my lunch. A family, that's what we are."

Amanda laughed and placed a tuna-fish-salad plate in front of him. "Don't take me for granted. I'll have you know Murray called today to give me my old job back."

"Did you . . ."

"Don't be a silly. Of course I said no. That's all behind me now. Still, it made me feel glamorous again."

As Amanda passed by Branch to go to the sink, he

grabbed her arm firmly and rolled her into him. His head in her stomach, he looked up adoringly and said, "Hey, you are glamorous."

She laughed. She was wearing one of his old shirts, with the sleeves rolled up, and an old pair of jeans.

He nodded, though nothing was said. "You're still glamorous. To me you are."

Amanda wriggled free and continued on to the sink. Branch started to eat but watched his wife very carefully. Was Amanda really happy? She didn't still blame him for . . . no, she loved the life he had given her and the baby. Still, he wondered if she was entirely satisfied. Maybe she should work. A little free-lance or something. She had been acting funny for a while.

Amanda almost let a dish slip out of her hands before she reached over, rinsed it off and put it into the dishwasher. The way he had pulled her toward him like that. She had felt the same old catch of desire in the back of her throat. Yet even in the intimacy she knew she was studying him. Were there lipstick marks on his shirt? Blond or red hairs stuck to the jacket he had flung on the chair? Was his shirt too wrinkled? And then she hated herself for it. For being jealous of someone she didn't even know existed. But Amanda knew one thing. If it was true and Branch was playing around, she could never be a Joyce. She could never ignore it.

Chapter Eighteen

Flora was standing in the hall, wondering where to walk next, when she heard her name being called out sharply. She turned around. Her face was clean, her hair had been parted and combed and the lilac lipstick was applied very carefully to her lips.

"Visitor!" an aide barked at her.

Flora looked around.

"Visitor," the aide said again, and Flora snapped to attention. Why would anyone visit her? Could it be that nurse again? Must be. The woman brought Flora to a closed door, and then she opened it. Flora clapped her hands and let out a childish squeal.

"Oh, Lordy, Lordy!" she cried, not trusting herself to talk anymore.

They hugged. She could tell he had changed. He seemed thinner and his hair was almost completely gray.

"Daddy!" she cried. "What are you doing here?"

As they sat down on the hard-backed chairs, Flora thought her father was still one of the handsomest men she had ever seen. Ralph hadn't looked like him at all. Ralph had been short and beefy, whereas her daddy was tall and slender. It would take her a while to get used to the hair that used to be salt and pepper.

"The hospital called your mother and me, honey. They said you were sick. I got right in the car and drove down." He looked around the room as if to give an estimate. Then he looked her in the eye and said, "This place. I don't like it."

Flora nodded, then jumped up nervously.

"What's wrong, baby?"

"Oh, nothing. I'm just so thirsty, that's all. I need some water."

She rushed out of the room and stopped at the water fountain. Then she came back into the room, announcing, "I'm still thirsty."

He patted his daughter on the shoulder. "Everything's going to be all right, princess. Your mother wants to have you transferred to Lakeside Hospital, near us."

Flora's mouth dropped in shock. "But, daddy, that's a mental hospital. There are crazy people there." Then she felt the old anger.

Bill Nash looked down and shook his head in despair. "I just don't know why you and your mother never seemed to get along. But, honey, your mother just wants the best for you. We could visit you during the weekends. I have to drive a long way to be back at work on Monday, you see."

"My God, daddy. She wants to put me away in a mental institution!"

He looked sad then. "Flora, that's where you are now."

They were both quiet. He added calmly, "But they don't let you stay here beyond a few weeks. They'll send you to a state hospital. Your mother thought you might like to be closer to home."

"*She* didn't come!" Flora whined.

"Well, she has a little cold."

Flora sat tensely, her body curling inward, as she comprehended the reality of it. She clenched her fists. "I'm not crazy, daddy. You don't understand!" She saw her torn scuffs, the pajamas tied with gauze and the pillowcase she carried around to keep her things in. Her finger accidentally brushed against her teeth and came back with a lilac smudge. She probably had a violet streak across her teeth.

Then Flora Butler stood up, turned her back on her father and sobbed. Bill Nash didn't stand up and go to his daughter to comfort her. He sat rigid, at attention, as if he were to receive a beating. Bill Nash didn't like to see women cry. He had no idea what to do. To his knowledge, his wife had never done it.

When she finished, Flora took the tail of the gauze belt and wiped her eyes. She was ashamed of herself. Then angrily she ripped off the belt and threw it in the wastebasket. She turned to face her father, and said slowly and meticulously, "I am not crazy, daddy. And I won't let you have me transferred to that horrible hospital near the woods. I'll get out of here. It's not really a mental hospital, is it?"

He nodded sadly. "It's called Manhattan General and it's on First Avenue. A big, old hospital. You're in a psychiatric ward. Didn't anyone tell you?"

"No," she said simply. "Not that I recall. You see, I was so upset after Ralph . . . no, that's not it, I don't let things get to me. . . . I mean that doctor wouldn't let me have my baby back, and then he stole my contract. . . . And . . . you don't believe me, either, do you?" she said, watching him closely, starting to shake. He said nothing. She threw up her arms. "Good Lord!" she cried indignantly. "Have I ever told a lie? Even though everyone's accusing me of being crazy, I'm still a good Christian."

Bill Nash looked at his lovely daughter. Those sapphire eyes were asking him if he trusted her. He thought his heart would break right then and there.

"I believe you, Flora. I never said you were crazy. Come to think of it, you don't seem . . . mentally ill. Just a little upset, that's all. Not quite yourself."

Flora kissed him on the cheek. "Oh, thank you,

daddy. That means so much to me. I just *have* to get out of here. Because I . . . put the house up for sale."

He looked at her face carefully. "You sure you want to do that, honey?"

She nodded. "Yes, daddy. I just have to get out of here and settle my affairs. Sell the house. Get my baby back."

He held up his hand like a stop sign. "I don't know nothin' about that baby you had. That's your business. But I stopped over at your house, and I found a note pasted to the door."

He reached down into his pocket and handed Flora a three-by-five index card. Flora read it aloud. "Flora Butler. Please contact Mrs. Simmons. Important." It sounded as if she had just read off a telegram.

"I called her," Mr. Nash said. "She says she sold your house."

"What did you say? You didn't tell her where I was? That the deal was off?"

He leaned back in his chair. "Well, I felt I should consult your mother." Flora made a face. "She thinks we should take over and handle it for you. That you're incapable. Not in your right mind. You know your mother," he chuckled conspiratorially.

Flora stood up and balled her fists. A light bulb of anger turned on inside of her. "Why, she can't! That's illegal."

"Not if you're declared legally insane, honey. But," he said as if wheeling out a big surprise, "I told Mrs. Simmons that you had gone away unexpectedly and couldn't be reached."

Flora clapped her hands. "That's true, that's true."

"And that you would call her as soon as possible. I figured you would want the deal to go through, so I gave her permission."

Flora couldn't decide to sit or stand. Her face was lit up, and her father could see her vagueness give way to brightness. The worry lines faded with her natural beauty.

"You get yourself out of here, Flora Nash Butler. I know you can do it." His voice was almost a growl.

There was a reverent silence from Flora. "If it weren't for you . . . ," Flora began. But she wasn't sure she could finish without embarrassing herself again.

"I checked your mailbox," he said. He reached inside his jacket and pulled out a crumpled envelope. "Looks like something from Ralph's company."

Flora ripped the large envelope open and noticed that her fingernails were dirty. She looked up at her father as if she had solved the clue to a mystery. "Insurance forms. I'll be able to sell the house, plus collect on the insurance. That's enough money, isn't it?"

"Seems like enough to me," her father said softly. Then, more cautiously, "Except you could bank it and live with us, honey. Your mother and I could put you up for as long as you like."

"No!" Flora started to scream, and then lowered her voice. She was looking over his shoulder through the window. She could see some lights winking through the purple backdrop. Almost hypnotized by the scene, she said firmly, still staring, "I want my baby back. I have the money to do it."

Bill Nash looked at his daughter and slapped his thigh respectfully. "You know, Flora girl, there's a lot of your mother in you. You two are a lot alike. I guess that's why you don't get along." He stood up suddenly and stuffed his hands in his trouser pockets. A nurse was coming into view in front of the half-open door. "You'll do whatever you set your mind to do. Like always," he said matter-of-factly.

"Now, I'll just stay overnight in Wananwa. Went in through the back window. Now I want to seal up that screen. Anyone could break in. Then I'll stop in tomorrow for a quick visit, and it's straight through to home."

Flora's hands reached urgently into her pockets. There were the papers. As she watched her father walk away, she opened her mouth to shout, "Wait." But nothing came out. She had forgotten to show him the papers. But he knew she had had a baby. The contract. She should have shown him the contract. Her fists clutched the prizes in her pockets. But she had told him that doctor stole her contract. Best not to call him back. Mama wanted to put her in a nut house. She looked around her. Every once in a while, one of the patients caught her eye and held it. She wanted to run for the door, but it was locked from the inside. Frustrated, she walked to her room. She had to get out of this place. She knew that. And at the same time she knew no one was going to help her.

Rochelle Vance felt the numbing prickliness of her leg. It had fallen asleep. She stood up and shook out her foot. Then she looked up at the ornate turquoise- and gold-framed clock in the apartment lobby. Just a minute later than it was the last time she had looked. One minute past 8:30.

She was hungry and tired and discouraged. What a stupid, impulsive idea of hers. To think that she could just wait for him to come home to her. It was better to call. She walked toward the big glass doors. Not really aware of anybody, she pressed her palm against the revolving door and pushed. Then she jerked her head back. She saw him as if he were in a mirror. It was like a mirage. Unable to stop, she kept going around the circle until she was standing outside before the curb to the winding sidewalk and he stood inside the lobby staring out at her, shocked. Then he shoved his way out to where she was.

He put his hand under her elbow and they walked wordlessly nowhere for a minute or two. Then he raised his arm, and a cab came to a breathless halt two inches in front of them.

"Where are you staying?" he asked.

"The Summit," she said, as they climbed into the cab.

She looked at him, half-surprised, half-knowing. He loved that look. She was thinking how Normy always took command. It felt so natural to be with him, though they had hardly communicated in over twenty years. She felt as if every fiber, every nerve, all her senses were deliciously alive. Something like being on a roller coaster that kept going up and up and never came down.

His hand rested on her knee. "Let's get your things out of that hotel and bring them to my place. Then we'll have dinner. Have you had dinner?" He didn't wait for her to answer. "I have a couch in my living room that opens up into a comfortable bed. There's a second bedroom, but I turned that into a study. You can have my bed, and I'll sleep on the couch and . . ."

Rochelle wasn't even listening anymore. She leaned her head back on the back of the cab seat, smiling dreamily, her eyes closed. It was so nice to have him taking care of her. Making the decisions. They were like soul mates. Still. How simple everything was, really. She should have come back to him years ago.

Flora stared at the closed door where her father had just exited. She tried to wash down the lump in her throat by finding something on the table for evening nourishment. The only thing left was a hard, crusty piece of brown bread smeared with melted margarine. The paper cups filled with Tang were emptied, and there was nothing to wash it down with. She left it there. Everyone was beginning to line up for evening medication. The nurse was holding the pitcher. Suddenly she knew. There was only one way to get out of that place. If not, her mother would take control of her life forever. It was risky, but it was worth it.

She smiled at the nurse, a young woman with an engagement ring. In return, she was met with the same hardened look she had seen on the faces of the staff. If eyes could smirk with pity and repulsion, this young nurse's did. For some odd reason that fortified Flora with courage. When it was her turn, she took the little paper cup and held it while it was being filled with water. Then she took the pill and plunked it behind the top of her tongue. Looking directly at the nurse, she swallowed the water slowly, emphasizing a gulp. Then she tossed the paper cup in the trash can, smiled and walked slowly to her bedroom.

Once down the hall, she swerved unnoticed into the lavatory and quickly retrieved the almost-mushy pill she had been hiding behind her tongue. She sat down on the toilet and reached behind her. When she got up and had flushed, she knew the pill would fall apart and disappear before it reached the sewer system of New York City. She had done it successfully. Just the way she had heard the other patients bragging about how they had done it. Another pill would have made her more foggy, more thirsty, more unsure of herself.

It was not even nine o'clock when she went into the big room with all the beds. But almost all the women who slept there had fallen asleep. Some were snoring. Flora got into bed. It was hot and airless in the ward. There was a tall floor fan, but unless you stood directly under it, it didn't help. She flung her

arm across her eyes and shielded them from the light
in the hallway. It was going to be hard to fall asleep
without that pill. She had to fall asleep. If she didn't,
she might make a mistake, and she couldn't afford
that. She shut her eyes tightly, praying for sleep to
come. But her mind had one after the other worri-
some thing to pick at. The panic started. She
wouldn't fall asleep. And if she couldn't sleep, she
would get confused and people would treat her as if
she were crazy. She felt for the papers under her
pillow. Then she prayed that she would sleep.

"Did you really think of me often?" he asked. "I
thought you hated me."

"I could never hate you," she replied. She rolled
over on her back. "I thought of you always. For
years." She was pensive for a moment. Then she
asked, "Mind if I smoke?"

"No, of course not," he found himself saying.
Barnard Borg detested the odor of cigarette smoke,
especially in the room where he slept.

He disappeared into the bathroom, and when he
returned and Rochelle looked up at his beautifully
formed body, she couldn't help but laugh. He was
gingerly carrying a portable pink soap dish shaped
like a fish. She motioned toward the chair, and he
brought her her black and white bag. She dug inside
for her package of Newports, and he took her gold
lighter out of her hands and lit it for her. While she
blew smoke toward his face, he studied every inch of
her naked body and twisted a strand of her long,
dark hair in his fingertips.

"Tell me," he said simply, smiling.

She smiled back at him. "Tell you about what?"
She took a deep drag.

"About you."

She looked at his straight, perfect nose, his silky
blond hair that never seemed too thin and his

exquisite amber eyes. How could she tell him that she had no life story until this moment? It was somebody else's. That she only wanted to be part of him? That when her mother had passed away she had been confronted with death for the first time and had realized that life lasted about a minute? She wanted to live hers. She couldn't tell him all that. It would need the right words, and she was never good at that sort of thing.

He took the cigarette from her hands, crushed it out in the soap dish and put it on the dresser. "You wanted to hate me. Because of what we did. Because I'm your brother." Even as he said it, he could feel the excitement rising inside him, making him want her again.

"I hate the thought of it. I can't help myself. But I've always wanted you, Normy. Always. It was never the same with Victor."

"When you came here tonight, you never thought for a moment that I would sleep on the couch, did you?" he asked playfully. She could feel his hardness skimming the top of her thigh, and she became instantly excited.

"I—I didn't know." He was stroking her tantalizingly with his nails on the inside of her sticky thighs. She couldn't talk, much less think, intelligently. Yes, he had changed. He knew just what to do and when. If she didn't know he loved her, she might think he was just some Casanova.

She could never go back to Victor after this kind of lovemaking. It would be like being condemned to a prison. She shut her eyes and gave in to the sensations.

Barnard Borg always kept his eyes open, even when he was kissing. He explored Shel's ecstatic face. He wondered if those long-lashed eyes would fly open if he told her the truth right then. But after all these years?

He would have to think it over. If he did, the magic might evaporate. Shutting his eyes, he pretended it was years ago. When her body was young and supple and her chest was almost flat. And their mother might have walked in at any time.

Flora opened her eyes and felt immediate joy. It was morning. She congratulated herself. She had slept and felt good. And it was real sleep, not drugged sleep. She felt proud of herself for something she had taken for granted almost every night of her life.

Everyone was still asleep. Even the nurses' aide dozing in a chair in the hall. She was in charge at night. The place looked different. Not like a mysterious chamber of horrors. Just a drab old hospital with people whose minds were sick. They wouldn't be in such a bad way if they prayed to the good Lord a little more often, Flora thought. Flora Butler clasped her hands under her neck. Yes, she felt her old self again. There was no telling what she might do.

Rochelle Vance and Barnard Borg woke up at dawn and made love again. Then they poured bubble bath in the bath water and took turns scrubbing each other.

"When are you going to call Jenny?" he asked, locking toes the way they used to do.

"When do you leave me?" she asked, impishly.

"Monday morning. I go to my office. But that's years away. We have the rest of the weekend to play in bed. I have a file of excellent take-out places for food."

"Sounds like a lovely way to spend the weekend," she said contentedly, laughing. He heard a thousand tinkling mobiles singing in the breeze. Without taking a breath, she asked, "How is it you never

married? I would have privately died a thousand
deaths, but just out of curiosity—why?"

He smiled slowly and positioned his body on top
of her, pinning her down under the water. "Because
I was waiting for you."

Amanda and Branch showered together in the
white marble bathroom with the oversized shower
fixture. "They should stage a murder mystery in this
house," Amanda joked. "This spooky old bathroom. Picture it with spurts of blood inching across
the snowy marble. Or the ravine! That would be a
nice setting for a murder." She was washing
Branch's back, making circles out of the soap.

"Amanda, why don't you write a book?"

"You mean another *Gone with the Wind* or something?"

"Whatever. I think you could do it."

"Maybe," she shrugged. "When she goes off to
school. Yes, maybe that's the answer," she said
again, humming happily.

They put on white terry-cloth bathrobes, which
they had had specially made up. Amanda's breast
pocket was embroidered with a navy "HIS."
Branch's identical robe said, "HERS." They both
automatically walked in the same direction. When
they reached the baby's room, they found her wide
awake and playing with a pink stuffed dog Amanda
had placed in her crib the night before.

Branch diapered her, picked her up, and they all
went into the big master bedroom and got back into
bed. Danielle lay on the pillow, her toes in the air,
smiling up at them both.

"Look at her little feet; they're so perfectly
formed," Amanda said. "This little piggy . . . ," she
sang, and tickled Danielle's pink-pajamaed stomach
until she giggled. "God, she's so beautiful, Branch,

isn't she? I never saw such a beautiful baby in my life. Everyone says so."

Branch looked down at his daughter and watched her heart-shaped little face become the face of the lovely lady who haunted his dreams. He blinked. The blond silky hair swept up on top of the head, the clear blue eyes, the sculpted rosebud mouth. He blinked again, and then he saw only Danielle challenging him with one of her merry stare-downs.

Amanda reached over and lovingly punched his shoulder. "She wants you to do something, daddy. Go ahead. Laugh or make a face."

Branch tickled Danielle under her dimpled chin, but he was looking past her and into the tree branches that crisscrossed their second-story bedroom. He had looked at his daughter and seen his lady. She was his daughter, or what she would look like in years to come. He watched Amanda, who was playing peekaboo with her head behind a pillow. He couldn't let this sickness or whatever had happened to his mind get control. Amanda was his wife. She was the mother of his child. He didn't know which was more disturbing: to see the woman in his dreams when he was asleep, or when he was wide awake.

By the time the women in the big dorm were coaxed to get up and face a day that held no more meaning for them than the last, Flora was sitting in the middle section. Her blond hair was up in a perfect bun, a skillful job of hairdressing using no pins, but bits of gauze braided and weaved in. Her smooth complexion was scrubbed clean and glowing; and she had found that if she dabbed on the lilac lipstick gently, she looked more like herself than a violet-streaked crazy lady. The Puerto Rican mopping the floors looked up at her admiringly, but she gave him such a mean look he muttered something under his breath and wore the expression of a naughty schoolboy.

Patients scrambled and pushed each other to the kitchen, where they picked up their plates of lukewarm oatmeal and hard-boiled eggs. Flora waited tensely on a bench seat, her back straight, apart from the rest. When everyone was seated, she got up quietly and walked gracefully into the kitchen area. She got a plate of food and a cup of coffee, and sat down on an end, two seats away from the noisy group of patients. She ate quietly; and when everyone started to bargain, beg or trade favors with the controllers who had the cigarettes, she went into the kitchen and cleaned off her plate over the trash can. Then she walked down the hall. Making sure she was seen by at least one nurse, she started to straighten out her bed. She was seen by a nurse, who jotted down the striking change in Flora Butler.

At nine o'clock, her name was called out. She had been pretending to read a book, curled up on a chair in the middle section, trying not to gag on the cigarette smoke. A bundle was presented to her. She accepted it. Then she saw it was a sack containing her clothes, her purse, everything she had worn when she had come to the place.

She searched the nurse's face. "Can I go home? Does this mean I can go home?"

The nurse smiled. She had never realized it, but Mrs. Butler was actually a very pretty woman in an old-fashioned way. She must be feeling better, because it showed. "Well," she replied. "I'm not so sure of that. However, I will try to get a doctor to speak with you." Flora set her jaw and ground her teeth together. Then she covered it quickly with a smile. Trying wasn't good enough. She was impatient. Out of the corner of her eye she saw the nurse wheeling in the medication cart. Medication. She had to go through that again. What if she accidentally swallowed it? She couldn't take that risk.

"Mrs. Butler, please?" said the nurse beckoning her with a little white paper cup, while her eyes were on her wristwatch.

Flora Butler stood up as straight as she could. She cradled her bundle of clothes. "I'm not taking any medication. I don't believe in it. I don't need it. I want to go home."

The nurse smiled slyly. She had been trained for these people who might charm you one day and then try to commit suicide the next. "Mrs. Butler, we discussed this before. It's not going to go against your religion. Look, it looks just like an M&M. Think of it that way, and it will go down smoothly and you'll get better faster." She paused, and the smile she was propping up became the stern look it really was. She was confronted with Flora's pursed lips. "Are you going to swallow it like a . . . helpful patient, or will we have to send for a doctor?"

They stared at each other. Flora had seen an hysterical patient get an injection, but she was quiet and calm. She was winning.

"Okay, then," the nurse said, a whine edging her voice, "I'll have to call a doctor."

Flora tried not to look bemused. The nurse who had been observing the changes in Mrs. Butler saw the scene and stepped in. "There should be a doctor on the floor soon, Mrs. Butler," she said pleasantly.

Holding her bundle close, Flora went into the lavatory. The lady with the hair that shot straight up stood near the wall, her arms folded, waiting. Flora felt like screaming, "Go away. Don't bother me." But she didn't want to start a scene. It might ruin it for her. Instead, she walked out and stood behind the door in the bedroom.

She shrugged out of the foul-smelling pajamas she

had been wearing. Then she shook out her blue and white striped Dacron sleeveless dress and put it on. It was too hot to wear her pantyhose; so she tucked them in her bag. Her slip stuck to her. She was ashamed of the missing heel on one of her shoes, but there was nothing she could do except try to walk straight so she didn't appear to be limping. A careful inspection of her bag revealed her hairpins, which she sorely needed, were missing. Also her ball-point pen and a compact with a mirror. Someone had taken her belongings, and that made her angry.

Walking over to the nurses' station, she knocked on the frame of the open door. She stepped in and said crisply, "Besides holding me here against my will, you have stolen items from my purse." The nurse looked up, confused. She thought for a second it was a visitor. Then she understood and shook her head. "No, those things which are considered sharp objects are kept in an envelope for you. You see, Mrs. Butler, a lot of people here might try to harm themselves or others with anything sharp. Be very careful with that belt on your dress. They shouldn't have let you have it, but I'm going to trust you. But turn it into the office when you're not wearing it."

Just then a doctor approached her. "Flora Butler?" the young resident asked.

Flora Butler stood up and said, "That's me."

She followed him into a small makeshift office. The doctor pointed to two chairs and then sat with his finger under his chin, scrutinizing her carefully. Flora sat opposite him, wanting to scream but forcing herself to speak slowly and distinctly. She didn't know what to do with her hands; so she clasped them together loosely and made sure they stayed in her lap.

When she had told her story, she wet her lips with her tongue and inquired softly, "Wouldn't it be possible for me to go home now? I have so many things to attend to. I'm putting my house up for sale, you see."

The doctor dropped his statuelike pose of finger resting under chin. He had absorbed all of her that he needed to know for evaluation. He cleared his throat. Between his thumb and forefinger was a low-tar cigarette he was dying to light but was trying to put off. "We would require that you follow up at the outpatient clinic," he explained, looking at her sternly.

"Of course, no problem. I can drive in," Flora said cheerfully and obediently, begging the Lord to forgive one more lie.

The doctor leaned over, making Flora press her back into the chair she was sitting on to escape his bad breath. "Every once in a while," he whispered, "Manhattan General makes a mistake. I think that's what happened here, and I apologize."

He stood up, looking down at her. "On the other hand, you were in an extremely stressful shock situation; and at least you got a chance to recover." He laughed thinly. "Though I admit this isn't exactly a fancy sanitarium." Flora looked up. She didn't understand the joke.

As she came out of the room and the doctor walked away, signifying he had already forgotten her case, she saw him. His face lit up, too, when he saw her.

"Daddy! I can go home now," Flora said happily. He was reminded of her holding her graduation diploma in the air.

"Good girl," he said, patting her on the head.

"Give my love to mama," she said, dutifully, her stomach churning.

Her father smiled. "Now I know you're feeling better, princess. That's nice. Real nice. You keep your faith, you hear?" He kissed her on the forehead and left. Flora wondered if he suspected she had been lying. No, that was impossible. Well, she would be more faithful to the Good Book as soon as she found her baby. And she would make sure that the baby learned it just as well as Amy, Benjamin, Carl and even little Dennis had. May their precious souls rest in heaven.

As the train chugged out of the station, she thought it would take her less than two weeks to straighten out the disorder and do what had to be done. She relaxed against the seat. Where would she sleep? In the living room, of course. But with the lights on. And it would be good to go home again. She missed Ralph and the kids.

Chapter Nineteen

"Yes, darling, I know I've been here two weeks; but it's not easy to sell furniture . . . in the summer."

Rochelle was alone in Barnard's study when she made her call.

"Try to wrap it up by next week, would you, Shel? I've been eating out every night. The maid comes by, but it doesn't look the same as when you're here to supervise. And you have to write letters to the boys. You know I'm no good at that. And I miss you, honey."

Rochelle was unconsciously pulling at the skin on her throat with her thumb and forefinger. She felt as if she were drowning. It was so difficult to stall for time. Pretty soon Victor would begin to get suspicious, though the last thing he would suspect was an affair with her brother.

She heard his loud phone kiss smack into her eardrums; but try as she might, she couldn't return it. "Good-bye, Victor, dear," she said, trying to brighten up her voice. "I'll call you soon."

"Don't call! Come home! Surprise me. Listen, give my regards to your brother. Tell him we expect him here for a visit. God, I've never even met him."

Rochelle closed her eyes. "Good-bye, Victor," she said softly.

When she hung up, the receiver clattered to the phone. One more week. Was it possible to squeeze in one more week of heaven before she went back to that half-life?

Slowly she walked back to the living room and collapsed on the couch, folding into Barnard's chest. He handed her a gin and tonic; and they sat quietly, listening to the steady hum of the air conditioner, looking out at the city, its blinking lights flooding the room romantically.

"I'm going to miss this view," she said sadly.

"Why leave?" he asked simply, looking straight ahead.

"Did I tell you what I finally did with mother's things?" she asked, choosing to ignore his question.

"I assumed you and Jenny sold everything."

"No, I gave them away. To people in the neighborhood. I have so much, you see, and they seem to work so hard." Then she added defensively, "Well, it was my money to do what I wanted with." She looked up into his face. "Unless you disagree. I suppose it was also your money."

He laughed as one would at a child. "No. It's okay. But why didn't you tell me this before?"

She shrugged and wiped her chin with the frosty drink. "I don't know."

He pulled her closer to him, stroking her hair. "What did you do today?"

"Oh, I went shopping and walking in the crowds. I watched all the people rushing around. Afterward I sat in the park and had a hot dog, and then I came back here and took a little nap."

"And you weren't bored?" he asked incredulously.

"Oh, no. I love New York."

They fell into silence. She wished he would say something, anything, to stop the aching depression that was coming on. "I guess I better make my plane reservations. Victor isn't too thrilled," she finally said with a sigh.

Gently, he cupped her chin in his hand and tilted her face up to his. She watched him curiously while his perfect features seemed to contort. His mouth twisted, and it looked as if he might say something. His lips parted, but no sound came out. She looked into his rust-colored eyes, searching.

"Normy, I . . ."

But he put his finger over her mouth and said, "Shhhh." There were butterflies in her stomach. He was going to ask her to stay. Her mouth fell into a pathetic "oh" when he said, "Shel, I'm not your real brother. I never have been."

Flora Butler brought her knees closer to her chest and rested her head on a rolled-up jacket. In the back she heard a baby cry and the mother trying to make it hush while the other passengers grumbled about the noise. She could quiet that baby. She was good at that. Finally, she sat up straight. It was no good trying to sleep. The bus had become blazing hot.

Just two more hours and they'd be in Atlanta, Georgia. She had started from Port Authority in New York City at six in the evening the night before. She had two old suitcases filled with clothes. Everything else had been packed in cardboard boxes and placed in storage with her furniture. She had saved no snapshots of Ralph or the children.

As the bus rolled down the highway, Flora shifted her weight and rummaged in a big shopping bag until she found an orange. She looked out at the blur of scenery whizzing by. Emily was the only baby she had left, really. When she dealt with those Whitneys, she'd have to be firm. She had no understanding now for the poor barren woman she had given a gift of love to. She wanted it back. If they wouldn't give the baby to her, she'd look in the Yellow Pages for a good lawyer and take them to court. She thought sadly that, when Ralph was alive, they barely had enough money from one cavity to another outgrown shoe to a brake that needed to be repaired on the old van. Now she had the insurance money and the money coming in from the house. She would use it to start a family.

When the bus finally reached the Atlanta bus station at two o'clock in the afternoon in mid-August, Flora was smiling for the first time in a long time. The other passengers looked wilted and sweaty. Flora felt fresh and confident.

Stepping off the bus, she bent her head back and looked up. So this was Atlanta, Georgia. She had never been beyond the Northeast. Squinting in the sun, she gazed high at the shimmering towers and spires and thought how like New York City the skyline was. Only it was cleaner, shinier.

The bus driver opened the bottom hatch and handed her the two old valises that were held together with straps. A young boy ran up immediately to grab them, but Flora wouldn't give them up. "I can carry them," she said sternly. She began to walk without knowing where she was going.

Directly across the street was a green and orange stucco hotel. Putting her bags down for a moment to catch her breath, she walked without another stop until she made it up the steps and into the lobby. It was a welcome relief to stand under the two tall fans. She set her cases down. She was rather shocked to see a film of dust on the big desk. No one was behind the desk.

Picking up her suitcases about an inch, she let them drop with a thud. A heavyset black man with a mustache emerged from a little room behind the desk.

"How much are your rooms?" Flora demanded.

The man eyed the woman. "This isn't your kind of hotel. This here's a hotel for black folks."

"I don't mind. Heirs of God, and joint heirs with Christ." She added, "That's from Romans."

He smiled back at her from half-closed eyes. "Madam, this isn't your type of hotel, believe me."

Flora glared at him. "I'm tired and hot, and I've come to this hotel to rest."

"Not going to get any rest with folks screaming and banging all night long. Our clients come and go, you might say. Most of them are hookers." He smiled at her, knowing she would pick up her bags and run indignantly out of the hotel. Flora stood up straight. After a few seconds she smiled back.

"A single room, please," she said firmly.

The man sighed. "Okay, lady, have it your way. We don't discriminate." He handed her a key with a number on it. Flora saw the "16" and looked around for an elevator. There was none. The man smiled at her.

"One flight up," he said, pointing. She paid in advance for a room for one night and then hiked up the chipped marble steps to her room. When she kicked it open, she felt a tide of homesickness. She longed for her orderly house in New Jersey. The room had a drab green cloth bedspread over a double bed, a chair upholstered in plastic and a ceiling fan that buzzed as if a mosquito were trapped in it.

She tried the bed. It was soft, lumpy. There was a telephone on the night table. And a Bible. Flora examined it and found coffee stains on it.

It was time to begin. The Whitneys didn't live in this part of Atlanta. That much she knew. This was the downtown area. She sat down on the bed. She had to decide the best way to let them know she was in Atlanta and that she intended to take her baby.

Danielle was stark naked except for the little pink clip in her hair. Mavis was holding her under the armpits while the baby kicked her legs. She was dangling about six inches from the child's pool in the backyard.

"Oh, go ahead. Plunge her in. It's warm. It will seem like a big bath to her."

Mavis laughed heartily and lowered the baby into the pool. She immediately started splashing around. Amanda laughed. "She likes it. Good, I want her to be a swimmer. You know, Mavis," she said, not taking her adoring eyes off the baby, "they can teach infants to swim. I read it in an article. After all, it's natural to them. They started their life swimming."

After the words were out, Amanda thought about how talking like that just didn't bother her anymore. She finally believed what people had been telling her all along: that the woman who raises the child is the true mother.

Mavis couldn't help but smile at Amanda, who was on her knees with her elbows draped over the sides of the baby pool. Mrs. Whitney was finally relaxed with Danielle. Mavis remembered how Mrs. Whitney had fussed and fretted over that child. It was good that those unhappy times were over.

The baby was splashing, kicking, and clapping her little hands in delight. Mavis held her firmly in the middle. Danielle squealed at Amanda and tried to bob her head in the water. Just then the phone rang. Amanda hopped up and brushed the grass off her knees.

"I'll get it." She ran quickly up the little porch steps through the enclosed patio and picked up the wall phone in the kitchen.

"Hello?" she said.

There was no answer.

"Hello?" Amanda waited, and then demanded. "Who is this?"

Silence. Amanda could hear faint breathing. Then she crashed the phone down into the receiver. Probably one of Branch's fans. A slightly befuddled lady who was bored with her middle-aged husband and had wangled the unlisted number from someone. It happened occasionally. Occupational hazard. She hated it. Never failed to give her the creeps. She went to the sink, filled up a glass with cold tap water, drank it and went back outside to be with her baby. There was a touch of anger at having been interrupted for such nonsense, but as soon as she had gone out the back door she had forgotten about it.

Flora sat on the bed by the phone. Her hands were trembling. That must have been the woman who had her baby. That voice. She didn't like that voice. It sounded like she was singing. Flora had wanted to tell her she was coming for the baby, but at the last minute she hadn't been able to open her mouth. The only way to do it was to go to their door.

Rochelle was using the phone in Barnard's study. Looking at the big, wooden-rimmed oval mirror, she saw a fleck of mascara on her cheek and brushed it away. Then she turned sharply. It was hard to look at herself in the mirror when she was talking to her husband.

"Rochelle," Victor demanded, "I would like to know when you are booking a flight home. Or shall I make it for you? I need you back here. The boys will be coming home from camp soon."

"I sent the boys postcards of New York," she replied, as if defending herself. "I think I'll stay on until the end of August."

"But, why . . . ?" Victor moaned, and Rochelle noticed that he whined just like Robert and Roger.

"Because my brother needs me." She clenched her fist and shut her eyes. "Honestly, Victor, you're right. Families should stick together, and now I'm beginning to realize that for the first time. Especially with mama gone."

"What do you mean, he needs you?"

Rochelle cut him off. "He has . . . ," she stalled for effect, "the big C." She heard the gasp on the other end of the line. "That's right, Victor, he may be dying."

"I understand."

"I think I should be with him during his treatments."

There was a silence.

Then, finally, he said, "Well, maybe I could take some time off and come there." She said nothing in reply. If he did that, she would be forced to tell him the truth before she was ready. She just couldn't face it, though. She said softly, "Wait a bit, Victor, dear. He's too depressed for company." When she hung up, she knew she was on borrowed time. Eventually she would have to go home.

* * *

Flora Butler gave the black man behind the hotel desk a piece of paper with the name of the street printed carefully in big letters.

He shot her a dirty look that seemed to say, "I can read." Then he nodded. "Yeah, that street's in the Buckhead area. You drive?"

She made no reply.

"Well, best way around that section is with a car."

Flora turned away from the man. His smile was like a snarl. There were some souls that would never be saved.

An hour later Flora was sitting in a rented car, studying a map of Atlanta. She had never driven in a strange city before, and she had never rented a car. But it was obviously the best way to keep track of the Whitneys. She was still trying to recover from the shock. The neighborhood. It was rich. The houses, some of them, were mansions.

Finally, she stopped in front of the address and parked across the street, folding her map of Atlanta neatly and putting it in the glove compartment. West Paces Ferry Road. She sat looking at a white mansion with stately columns in the front, a double stairway ending in a semicircle, and a long, winding driveway. It was almost hidden from view by tall trees that shielded it from the road. It was a strange-looking house to Flora. Very old, historic. She had never seen anything like it in New Jersey. But then she had never spent all day pleasure-riding through ritzy neighborhoods. She was becoming angry. She thought the adoptive parents were regular people. Now she saw they were sinfully rich. All that money. Surely they were out of touch with the Lord. While waves of outrage and impatience washed over her, she thought of something else.

Maybe it was the Lord's plan. She was being called to take her baby away from a life of sin and indulgence. And whatever way the Lord had to do it, that's how it would be done. Even if it did put Ralph, Amy, Benjy, Carl and Denny in heaven. She rolled her window down and stared at the house. Waiting.

The woman sat in her chair, playing nervously with the strap to her shoulder bag. Dr. Borg wished she would stop. He loathed petty, nervous habits.

"After all, Mrs. Frommer, it is nine months out of your life, and you'll only get to see your baby once, when it's born," he said, as he had said so many times. "But then you do have the satisfaction of giving a gift of life and love to a childless couple who, without you, wouldn't be able to have this miracle baby. Think of the poor adoptive mother who has tried everything to have a child. Who wants more than anything what God can never give her, but what comes so naturally to you to give her. *You* can give her that child and make some money for your family at the same time. Just by doing what you do so beautifully, having babies. Think of the good feeling it will give you."

"It sounds so wonderful, Dr. Borg; it really does," she replied. "And I want to but . . . it's just that . . . people will talk and I don't know if . . ."

He had the perfect inspirational answer when the phone rang. He tried to ignore it, but it wouldn't stop. He had asked the receptionist to put a hold on his calls. The ringing wouldn't go away. Finally, he picked it up.

"It's Mrs. Vance on three, Dr. Borg. She says it's urgent."

He punched the button. "Yes, what is it?"

"Normy, honey. It's me."

"I know that. What's wrong?"

"Wrong? Nothing's wrong," Rochelle said.

"My receptionist said it was urgent."

"Well, yes, it is, honeybun. I want to know if we're eating in or out."

"Rochelle, not now," he said curtly.

There was a second's silence. "Well, I'm sorry," she replied softly, hurt.

"I mean, I have a patient."

"Oh, Borgy, why didn't you say so. I'll get off right now."

Dr. Borg felt a pressure headache begin to thump against his right temple. He looked at the woman carefully. He had lost her, he knew. Just in a matter of seconds. Everything was in the timing.

"I'll let you know," Mrs. Fromme said in a weak voice. "The idea of this I love. And I do make beautiful babies. With my husband. It's just that I don't know if I have the guts."

His head was throbbing as he watched her go. He'd never see the woman again. He could tell. What was the use? He missed the moment when he could have sold her, and he couldn't go back now. Of course, it wouldn't be fair to be angry at Shel. He picked up his silver paperweight and flung it across the room.

He loved her, yes; he had always loved her. But when did her breasts get so full? And her hips? When had they grown so wide? He shook his head. What was he thinking of? Shel was a slim woman. She had the figure of the fashion models he used to date. She had just grown up. That was it. Suddenly he felt inconsolably sad. The walls were closing in. He couldn't breathe.

For two days, since she had first positioned herself outside the house, Flora had spent all her time following the Whitneys. She had screamed with joy when she saw her baby for the first time, though no one heard her or saw her. Doggedly she trailed the family.

Yes, she had been duped by that doctor, all right. She couldn't trust these people to mind her baby. Not with their fancy cars and fine clothes. Too many things. She was sure they never would take her Emily to church on Sunday.

Around four o'clock on the second day of her vigil, the red Porsche came rolling down that long driveway. She could see little Emily's head from the baby seat. Flora was parked in front of the house. At a safe distance, she turned the key in the ignition, started her car and followed them down the street.

They turned into the parking lot of a shopping center. Flora parked nearby and watched every detail obsessively. The pink ruffled romper suit and matching bonnet. The woman with all that makeup, wearing red short shorts and a white T-shirt that said, "Love & Kisses," and had some radio station's letters beneath it. She didn't know her, but she knew she didn't like her. All the fussy clothes on her child. Poppycock. In this sweltering Southern heat, she needed only a diaper and a little shirt to protect her. A bonnet, yes, but not something that looked like it belonged in the Easter parade.

Once inside the supermarket, she stalked the aisles until she found the woman with her cart. Then she was careful to keep a distance and look as if she were shopping. The baby was sitting on the top part of the cart. She was kicking her legs. Flora noticed the little pink socks with lace around the cuffs and the tiny sandals. Ridiculous. The child would be more comfortable barefoot. She couldn't walk yet. The woman was at the meat counter, picking out steaks.

When she had gone on, Flora checked out the price of steak. She couldn't believe it. And the woman had bought two large ones, too. Now where was she? Oh, Lordy, in the frozen-food section. Flora would never buy anything frozen. She was getting a clear picture of that frivolous woman and what would happen to her baby if she, Flora, didn't take her away and raise her like a good Christian. The woman and child had disappeared when Flora heard the loud screeching.

Rushing to the front, she found it was coming from the checkout counter. And from Emily. Shocked, she saw there was a bin of packaged chocolate-chip cookies on sale. Emily was kicking up a fuss, screeching, pointing to pictures of the cookies on the front. Apparently she knew the cookies. The woman was ignoring her. And then Flora watched in horror as the baby's squawking got louder and more piercing and as the woman grabbed a package of those cheap cookies, ripped the paper and shoved one in the baby's mouth. The shrill, nerve-racking screeching stopped. Flora kept watching, clutching her cart. That woman was wrong to pacify her that way. And she was making a spoiled monster out of her child.

Flora was so furious that, in her haste to unload her cart, she put everything in the wrong places. When she finally got outside, she saw their car was gone.

It was then she realized the charade had come to an end. She got into her rented car and drove to the Whitney mansion. She parked outside, walked up the stone path, climbed the steps and stood in front of the door. She punched the doorbell.

Amanda was unloading the frozen vegetables into the freezer when she heard the front doorbell chime. It was Wednesday and Mavis's day off. Sometimes she felt like a one-armed paperhanger, but she didn't mind. It was fun.

Danielle was safe in her playpen, investigating a new baby doll Branch had brought home. Yelling, "Be there in a sec," Amanda ran to answer the door. When she opened it, she stared at the face and thought for an instant it was terribly familiar looking.

"Yes?" she said politely.

The blond woman said, "Mrs. Whitney? Mrs. Branch Whitney?"

"Yes," said Amanda a little impatiently, squinting into the harsh, dying rays of the sun she was facing.

"I'm Mrs. Flora Butler. The surrogate mother who gave birth. I've come for my baby, Mrs. Whitney."

Amanda stared into the familiar blue eyes she had been looking at for seven months. Then she shook her head, clenched her fists and screamed, "No!" so loud and long the baby began to cry in the distance.

Chapter Twenty

Branch let himself in the side door and walked into the kitchen. He stopped, frozen. He saw the back of her head first. She turned and looked at him, her deep blue eyes piercing, her silky blond hair piled on top of her head, her skin like the petal of a flower. He scanned her exquisitely sculpted form without moving his eyes. It was the woman in his dreams. The woman Danielle would look like when she grew up.

"Branch," Amanda said, in a cracked, bitter voice. "This is Mrs. Flora Butler, who's come all the way from New Jersey to get . . . to take . . ." She couldn't say it.

"I've come for my baby," Flora said.

"It must be a joke. Say it's a joke, Branch," Amanda pleaded.

Branch shook his head. "No, I would never do anything like this to you. You know that," he said, his voice starting to crack.

Amanda choked on a sob. "Then it's a nightmare. The one I was always afraid of. Except I had forgotten about it."

He went to her and took her in his arms. "Where's the baby?"

"Upstairs," she answered, her teeth chattering. "I—I couldn't have her here while we were talking. Mrs. Butler insists on calling her Emily. Oh, Branch," she cried into his shoulder, "please don't let her take my baby away." He patted her on the back and shushed her.

He glanced quickly over at the woman. She was scowling at the words Amanda had used, *my baby.* He had a strange feeling. That he was expected to act as a judge. Some kind of Biblical prophet who would decide which woman was the real mother. He tried not to stare at the woman. But she was lovely. Just as he knew she'd be.

Then he remembered this wasn't any baby. There was that will. There would be complications. And it *was* his child. Maybe Justin . . . my God, what was he thinking of? And at a time like this. It was his daughter they were debating, not a piece of real estate. Nobody would take her away. He would never allow Danielle to be separated from him.

"Mrs. . . ."

"Butler," Amanda and Flora said together.

"You cannot just come for your baby. It's not your baby. There was a contract and you signed it. The baby belongs to my wife and me. Surely you understand this."

"I don't think that contract is worth much," she

said, startling them both. "You see, I'm the natural mother."

"Stop saying that," Amanda almost screamed. "I swear, if she says that one more time I'll have a fit."

Branch held up his hands. "Let's be calm about this. Now we were assured nothing like this would ever happen. How did you find out who we were? Amanda, get Dr. Borg's number. Call him immediately. This is absurd."

Amanda started to leave for the library, as Flora said in sure, precise vowels and consonants, "I am the natural mother. Any judge and jury would give me my baby."

Amanda stood rooted, a knuckle stuffed into her mouth.

"Is it money you want?" she said, finally. "Is that what this is . . . blackmail? Name your price, just go away."

"I've come for my baby," Flora said, not acknowledging the insult, not smiling, not frowning.

"How can we know you're the natural mother? Maybe it's all a hoax." But as they looked at each other, they could see the evidence was in the woman's face. Danielle was a mirror image of her.

Branch let his eyes travel down the delicate curve of her throat and the fine line of her lips. He had never seen a woman like that. Her lips and cheeks were rosy, yet it was clear she used no makeup whatsoever. Her eyebrows were dark, and her lashes were dewy and black as if she had bathed them in mascara. But he could tell she hadn't. He stood up straight and forced himself to take command.

"Mrs. Butler, I'm going to have to ask you to leave our home. You are upsetting my wife. We can't settle anything this way. And . . ." He allowed himself to look at the woman for a second and forgot what he was saying. He gulped. Those eyes. Dan-

ielle's eyes. But so determined. It chilled and titillat-
ed him at the same time.

"Where's your husband?" Amanda interrupted,
her voice shrewish. "And you were supposed to
have your *own* children."

Flora looked away. "Dead. They're all dead. I lost
them in an auto accident. That's why I've come for
my baby."

Amanda groaned.

Flora stood up, and Branch looked away once
again. "Okay, I'll leave," she announced. "But I'm
coming back the first thing tomorrow morning. If
you won't give me my baby, I'll get her. I'm the
natural mother."

She spun around and left. Neither Branch nor
Amanda made any move to let her out. Upstairs
they could hear Danielle crying. Flora stopped at the
door and looked up the stairway. Amanda rushed
past her and ran up the steps. Branch had followed
Amanda, and he felt a shiver when he accidentally
met the eyes of the woman.

Barnard was sitting in his office. The staff had left.
He was clipping his nails. It had been a good day. He
had signed another surrogate mother. A woman who
had once had an abortion and felt, since she had
taken a life, she must replace a life. He chuckled to
himself. They were all the same. Whatever the
reason, they did get paid for it. Just then the phone
rang. He pressed down the lit button and answered,
thinking it was Shel. He wasn't prepared for the
furious voice on the other end of the phone.

"Borg, this is Branch Whitney calling from Atlanta and I would like to know what kind of racket you
are pulling, because when we paid to get a surrogate
mother . . ."

Dr. Borg held the receiver about an inch away
from his battered eardrum and interrupted him.

"Mr. Whitney, I do remember you. However, I have no idea what you're talking about."

"She's here! The surrogate mother!"

He heard a woman's voice on what he guessed to be an extension. "Mrs. Flora Butler," Amanda Whitney said loudly and clearly. "And she wants *her* baby back. You have to do something. We signed a contract. All that money we paid you."

Flora Butler. She had escaped from Manhattan General. They had a lunatic on their hands. He couldn't admit anything. They could sue him. Perfectly healthy mothers were what he was supposed to be selling. "It must be a mistake," he said, and then stopped, realizing how idiotic that must sound.

"I don't think it's a mistake," Amanda replied, getting more angry with his weak response.

"Well, let's not jump to any conclusions yet," he said in his best syrupy bedside voice. The doctors at Manhattan General. He would have to find out first why they had double-crossed him. And Harv. They would have to confer immediately. Just as he heard Mrs. Whitney sucking in her breath to release more of her wrath on him, he said hastily, "I'll have to get back to you. Let me make a few phone calls."

Shakily he dialed the numbers he had for the psychiatrists at Manhattan General whom he considered colleagues. If he had tried to dial the main number for the hospital, he would have been there all week trying. But even with his list of numbers, he found out, one by one, they were nowhere to be found in the hospital. Probably they had all left for their private practices.

It was not possible for Dr. Barnard Borg to become confused. He was unflappable. Not like ordinary people. But he found himself dialing the same digits over and over, or so he thought, but continually getting wrong numbers. Finally, a Dr. Tipton answered his phone.

Keeping his voice low, steady and beautifully modified, he explained the case he was after, trying skillfully not to explain why. The resident thought for a moment, and then replied, "I remember her."

"She's in Atlanta!" Borg said impatiently.

"Oh, well, they never do come back for the outpatient," he muttered. "Yeah, I remember her."

"Did you release her?" Borg said.

"Yes, it was a mistake. She shouldn't have been admitted. She was in shock. Found out she lost all of her family. She was functioning when we released her. What was I supposed to do? Put her in a state hospital?"

"But she tried to kill me!"

The resident psychiatrist thought to himself what a pain in the ass board-of-director doctors were. What was he supposed to do? he asked himself again. When he had a cushy practice and taught at Bellevue, he'd be sure to bother a harassed resident just to get even.

He said calmly, trying to keep the sarcasm out of his voice, "You say she's in Atlanta? Well, as long as she stays there, you're safe."

Borg sensed that he had to appear very cool. "Well, it's reassuring to know the case is closed and she's been released. However, I did get a strange phone call from her and I wondered if she had, well, escaped."

"No dogs combing the woods, doctor. It's only Manhattan General. By the way, if I remember correctly, she was very contrite about you. She told me she had never had a surrogate baby. Made it up. Happened to be in your building. That's the kind of loss she had, Dr. Borg. Quite a case of shock," the resident said smugly. He had a million things to do.

"Yes, well, thank you very much."

Borg hung up, trying not to slam the phone down hard. Dumb, arrogant resident. Hopefully he wouldn't do too much damage when he became a full-fledged psychiatrist. Right now he couldn't tell a loony tune from a chair. He hated psychiatrists. Always had. Never even had a surrogate baby? He hadn't realized she was that smart. Now she was down in Atlanta trying to get the baby. How the hell she had figured that out was something he'd get to later. Right now he was aware of only one thing. He swiveled in his chair to look down over Manhattan. If the Flora Butler thing wasn't handled right, it could go to court. And if it went to court, it would get lots of publicity. One of the big landmark genetic lawsuits with a lot of complications. And investigations. He didn't think the law would look kindly upon the buying and selling of babies. That's why he was so careful. He slammed his fist down on the table. Goddamn that woman. He knew she was a nut from the very beginning. He felt immobilized. When the phone rang again, he was tempted not to pick it up. Finally, curiosity won out. For a second he wondered whom the naggy whine belonged to.

"Sweetheart? What *are* you doing? Come home. The chicken's cold. I'll have to reheat it and make more sauce, because it's shrinking. Maybe we could go to a movie later?"

Dr. Borg sighed and started to bite the edge of his thumbnail. "I've got a little problem, here, Shel. I'll be home as soon as possible. Reheat the dinner. Or, if you want, we can go out to eat."

"You know something, Normy? You work much, much too hard. There's a name for people like you. It's *workaholic*. I'm going to help you with all that. You'll see."

"For godsakes, will you stop calling me Normy!" he screamed at her. "My name is Barnard. Barnard Borg. I haven't been Normy Tucker for years!"

There was a pause that lasted a second too long.

"Shel?" he said cautiously.

Then he heard the loud sob. He chewed his nails. He hadn't wanted to hurt her. He was taking everything out on poor, helpless little Shel.

"Shel?" he whispered. He heard some sniffling. "C'mon, Shel. I'm sorry. You know how I get, and I'm under terrible pressure. Shel? Please say you'll forget it." He held his breath.

"Can I think up another name, like a nickname that I can call you?" she asked in a small voice. "I just never liked Barnard." She started to cry again.

"Okay, Shel, yes, I understand. Now why don't you read your fashion magazines and don't worry about food. I'll be home as soon as I can. Whoops, see I have to hang up. My other phone is ringing."

The voice on the other end was no surprise. There was no fury. Mr. Whitney just sounded tired and sad. Barnard told him the grim news: "Keep it out of court. It will be time consuming, costly and . . ."

"And what if we decide to go to court, anyway?" Mr. Whitney asked tensely. "Maybe we could win."

"Your lives would be shattered by cheap publicity," he answered matter-of-factly. "You see, you would be very famous, but obviously for all the wrong reasons."

"My career . . ." Branch whispered.

"No, Mr. Whitney, it wouldn't be possible to continue your career in the same way. Or your life, for that matter. You would be like a circus freak. The child would suffer the most. Five years later they would still be hounding you for a story. And she would know, from someone, because the world would know, that she was a surrogate child. Do anything, but don't go to court. Because, unfortunately, if you do that, you're going to lose your baby, anyway."

"Are you suggesting that we give *our* baby to this strange woman who has no right to it!" Dr. Borg recognized Mrs. Whitney's voice and realized she had been listening in. The anger again. Women were always trouble.

"You promised us anonymity! What is this, anyway? Why should we have to go through this? We paid you in full and then the surrogate mother shows up. She's *our* child. Do something!"

Dr. Borg clenched his fist. He couldn't get angry at the woman, no matter how he felt. She was, of course, right.

"Give me some time," he pleaded. "Nothing can be done overnight. I can refund your money, but it might take me months to do something about this. Just don't make plans to go to court."

She interrupted him. "I *would* go to court to keep my baby. We want her. What are we supposed to do? Just give her away?"

Dr. Borg sank physically, from the middle, into his chair. He massaged the space between his eyebrows with his thumb, digging deep and rotating in tiny circles. He wasn't hearing a word the woman was saying.

"How did she get our name and address?" Amanda screamed, not able to stop herself.

"Not from me, Mrs. Whitney," he said wearily. "I assure you, not from me. I did not give Mrs. Butler your address. Why would I? She probably hired a private detective. I think the key to keeping you all out of court may be the contract. She doesn't have one." Of course, that was the solution.

What Mrs. Whitney said next came as such a shock he had trouble breathing. It would have been easier to take, he thought momentarily, had he been beaten up by thugs in the middle of the night. It was the final shock.

Mrs. Whitney said, crisply, "We've seen her contract. She received $15,000 for having our baby. Quite a business you're running. We ought to sue you!"

Borg vaguely heard Branch Whitney's murmured "Now, Amanda . . ."

There was a long pause. The three of them seemed to be waiting for someone to say something. Finally, Borg said, "Look, stall for time. I'll think of something. Perhaps Mrs. Butler can be persuaded to leave Atlanta."

He heard the silence.

Hastily, he said, "It might take awhile. Call me if you want. I'm going to call my lawyer now. Just don't go to court immediately."

The Whitneys hung on the phone, hoping for more. Finally they hung up, unsatisfied, thinking some kind of out-of-court settlement or arrangement would be made. When Dr. Borg picked up the phone to call Harvey Nathan, he had something very different in mind.

"Honey, come to bed."

Amanda didn't answer him. She was sitting in her boudoir chair, wearing a long cream-colored satin nightgown and looking out the window at absolutely nothing.

"Look, do you want a valium? I'll get you a valium." Branch got out of bed and went into the bathroom. He opened the medicine cabinet and located the little plastic vial of pills. Quickly he swallowed a valium, then took a pill and a glass of water into the bedroom.

Amanda was still sitting exactly the way he had left her, her face ashen, her expression unchanged. "We're going to lose her, Branch," she said in a small voice without turning.

Branch handed her the pill and the glass of water. "Take this. We won't lose her. Honestly, Amanda, I've never seen you give in like this. I need your fighting spirit, your spark. What's wrong, honey?"

"First we tried and tried, and then we got a

surrogate mother to do it for us; and I hated that, hated it," she said tonelessly. "After that, the baby didn't like me very much, and I don't blame her. But we got to know each other, and I'm her mother now." She stopped to brush away the tears that were spilling lightly. "Danielle loves me and I know it, and I would give my life for her. And now this woman comes to the door and wants to take her away from me forever because she gave birth to her. Don't let her do that, Branch. Please? What did I do wrong? I've always tried to be a nice person. Why am I being punished like this?"

He knelt down, putting his head on her breasts and feeling her tears fall on his face, wishing they were his. Wishing he could cry out the sad feelings that were eating at him. "It will be okay, honey. You're not being punished. It just happened, that's all." He wished he could say, "I promise you'll keep your baby," or, "Just let me handle everything," but he couldn't. Instead he said, trying to be strong for her, "Look, we've rehearsed what we have to say over and over. When she comes over tomorrow . . ."

"I don't think she wants money, Branch," Amanda said softly.

"Well, we'll say the other things."

"Welfare of the child, honoring the contract, the bond between the baby and myself . . ." Amanda stopped and shook her head. "No good. Even if we convince her to leave us alone, she'll come back again and again. We'll never be able to leave Danielle alone. She might kidnap her."

Branch patted her shoulder. "Now, now. Let's not get dramatic. It's not like you, Amanda."

"And that woman," she kept on, not paying any attention to him, her eyes growing wide. "She's so strange. Something about her frightens me. I would never let my baby go away with a woman like that."

They were both silent. *"I'm* the natural mother," Amanda said firmly. "Danielle knows me. She's used to me."

"I know you are, honey. Now let's go to bed. We could do this all night. I need you in the morning. Go to sleep and try to rest your mind for a while. You're going to make yourself sick if you don't."

Amanda nodded and let Branch help her into bed. They held each other for a few minutes, and then Branch rolled over on his left side, his best sleeping position. Amanda turned the other way, and their backs touched slightly. She tried to fall asleep, but she knew if she got an hour or two she would be lucky. Branch pretended he was asleep. But his mind kept reworking the problem. What if none of their arguments worked? And that's when the idea came to him. Or had it always been there waiting to be beckoned? Of course, it wasn't perfect; but it was a temporary solution. It might keep everyone happy for a while. He fell promptly asleep.

Barnard and Rochelle kept the hanging lamps on while they talked. It was late. From the bedroom they could see an exquisite view of the city.

Barnard Borg couldn't fall asleep. How had the Butler woman gotten the contract from his office?

Rochelle made sympathetic clucking sounds with her tongue. "I didn't know you did that, Barnard. Surrogate mothers. Why would they want to do that? God, if it wasn't all my own baby I'd rather not have it at all. Those women are like human incubators. That's all they are." Then she giggled. "Hey, that was clever."

Barnard wasn't listening. Thelma. It could have been her. He had checked the little storage room and his copy was missing. Yes, he was sure Thelma had taken it. How could Mrs. Butler have done it? Well, it didn't really make any difference now.

Not losing a beat, he turned to Rochelle. "You don't understand. The women who become surrogate mothers enjoy the experience of pregnancy. The money is really secondary for most. In fact, some women do it for no money at all. Sometimes they know each other." He frowned. Not a good idea, he felt. The thought of the Butler woman meeting the Whitneys made his stomach churn. There was a psychology to surrogate motherhood. It didn't work to meet the other partners. Emotions couldn't be trusted.

"Of course. It must be lovely. Look, I don't want you to think I have anything against motherhood." She slid down underneath the covers and tucked the sheet in under her chin, pouting. "I mean, I'm really a good mother. The boys and I have lots of fun when . . ." Then she was shocked into silence as a tear trickled down her face.

Barnard squeezed her hand. Damn. She was feeling guilty about walking out on her twin boys again. He hated when she did that. He wanted to believe she had never married, never even grown up. She was his.

Rochelle, though, had stopped thinking of her boys for a second. She had returned to a thought she had had for a long time. If she and Normy . . . or whatever she would call him . . . could get married, she could fight legally to get visitation rights or something like that. Maybe he could check with that lawyer of his he was always talking to. It would be hard, judging from the way Victor had taken the news that she wasn't coming home. Especially that the man she was living with wasn't her real brother.

Barnard knew the easiest way to shut her up was to start making love. "Poor Borgy, you have so many problems," she said, running her hands through his hair. Then she shot straight up in bed; so he slipped off her, astonished.

"That's it. Borgy! I'll call you Borgy!" Barnard rubbed his forehead. What the hell was she talking about? And then, he remembered, he had forbidden her to call him Normy. And now he didn't feel the urge anymore. Honestly, Rochelle was becoming a pain in the neck lately.

Amanda had bundled up the baby and given Mavis instructions to take her for a long, long walk in the stroller. Before they left, Mavis saw the blond woman come into the house. She was a pretty woman, but she knew how to give dirty looks. Maybe she didn't like blacks. The woman kept staring after her and the baby. Mavis hoped she never ran into that one again.

Pushing the stroller, she saw the kitchen lights go on before she turned her head. In the kitchen the three sat around the table. The coffee was untouched. So was the slab of coffee cake Amanda had set out, more out of habit than anything else. Flora looked at the sugary confection dotted with glazed walnuts and shuddered. It was store-bought.

"If you're not going to give me my baby . . . ," Flora began, sounding arrogant but feeling insecure in this big house with these rich people so unlike herself.

"Of course we're not. You act like I've just been taking care of her until you were ready to pick her up. It isn't your natural right to claim her. I've been her mother for almost seven months to the day." Branch looked over at Amanda and nodded. She had stopped crying, though he could see her eyes were still puffy. She would be okay. Talking more as he hoped she would. Her voice was stronger.

"Then I'm going to have to take you to court," Flora said firmly. She had spoken to a young lawyer just yesterday. Picked him out of the phone book because his office was near her hotel. Oh, yes, he would take on the case. But it would take time. Lots of time. It was good that she had that contract so he could believe her. But he didn't know how it would stand up in a court of law. The buying and selling of babies *is* illegal, he kept repeating. And the Whitneys would put up a big show. After all, this was Atlanta. The Whitneys were powerful. On the other hand, she did stand a good chance of getting the baby.

When she asked him if he would take the case, he nodded enthusiastically. "Something like this could *make* my career. It would mean headlines." But that had offended Flora, and she gave no number to be reached. Besides, she needed a lawyer who would tell her she could have her baby in a few days.

"Now look here, Mrs. Butler," Branch said, still not able to look her in the eye. "We have one of the finest lawyers in the South. We have the money to win. We can pull out everything in your past, if there is something. Everyone has something, Mrs. Butler. We can hire witnesses. Money means nothing when it comes to Danielle." Branch shuddered. The last thing he wanted was a highly publicized trial. It was a natural for the news. He noticed Mrs. Butler grimacing at what he had just said. Maybe he was making headway. "The thing is, Mrs. Butler," he said, almost pleading, though trying to keep an upper hand, "money is very powerful, and you don't have one-tenth what we do."

Flora's face was controlled. But there was Manhattan General. She didn't tell the lawyer that they had put her in the nut house for a while. But that was a mistake, the doctor had said. She was getting angry. Money, money. These people. They kept bringing up the fact that they were rich. "I've got the Lord on my side, Mr. Whitney," she said finally, triumphantly, feeling a quick spurt of joy in the knowledge. "I don't suppose you know this quote— 'I am come that they might have life, and that they might have it more abundantly.' It's John 10:10."

Amanda stared. She didn't really understand the quote. She had never cared for people who had to quote things. "But what can you *give* Danielle? You're a widow. You have to go out to work," she tried, pleading.

"Well, first, I can give her a mother's love," Flora said smugly. "Instead of things. I have enough money, too. The life insurance from my late . . . Ralph. And the money from the sale of our house."

"But surely that won't add up to much. Not enough to raise a child. There's clothes and medical bills and . . . college! And with inflation rising every day. You'll have to pay someone to look after her, because you'll need to work," Amanda said, knowing in her heart that they were winning.

Then Flora responded with, "Oh, I can make money last. As for college, she won't have to go. Girls just need some sort of vocation and Bible study. She'll marry. You folks spoil her too much." Flora spread her arms. "She has too much. The good Lord didn't want this for her."

Amanda swallowed with her mouth open. "I don't think a judge would want to hear that," she said.

Afraid that the two women would upset each other and everything would end in an impasse, Branch shifted the conversation. "Would you have come for her had your family not been killed that way?"

"No," Flora replied simply. Then she added, "But I think this was meant to be."

Amanda buried her head in her arm on the back of the chair.

"How much money do you want?" Branch said,

finally, beginning the bargaining he thought was inevitable.

"I just want my baby, Mr. Whitney."

"It's our baby," said Amanda.

Flora stood up angrily, almost knocking over her full cup of coffee. She didn't like the way these rich people were talking to her. "I'll see you in court," she said grandly. Branch watched her. Suddenly he saw her lawyer. Bright, young, eager to score. It would be a case where the lawyers would be stars. Even Justin, a personal friend, who was the godfather of the baby, would get swept away with the glamour of the trial. Then he recalled, somewhat reluctantly, what had come to mind the night before.

"I might have a plan for all of us," he blurted. "Don't forget it takes time and money to go to court." He stopped, not able to look at Amanda. "Look, what about this? Why don't you become Danielle's baby sitter, or nanny, for a while? Stay here."

Branch looked down. At least if she was under their roof, they could watch her. Until a better plan was devised, it was a stall. Besides, where would the woman stay in Atlanta? And how much money did she have? It was a harebrained idea, and he should have consulted Amanda; but he didn't want to upset her. He stole a look at her.

Amanda's eyes narrowed. It was a shrewd move. They'd have the woman right where they wanted her. But it wasn't going to be easy; she sensed that. Maybe for Branch, but not for her. Amanda managed to smile when the woman looked at her. What she really wanted to do was take every pin out of the woman's sensible topknot of exquisite blond hair and pull it down. Then she wanted to take the ends of hair that would fall on either side of her face, and tie a neat little knot under her chin. So tight she would choke to death. Still smiling, encouragingly, and not thinking, Amanda took the cake knife and sliced off a walnut dripping with white icing. Then she cleaned the rest of the knife with a flick of her tongue.

Flora looked at the woman across the table from her. She didn't like her. Didn't like anything about her. Most of all, the way she spoiled her baby. But she didn't have that much money. And what could she do in Atlanta? Take some kind of job and come back to a lonely hotel room. Her place, as always, was with her baby. It went against her grain to stay in such a house, to be sure, but she would have her baby. Suddenly she had a brilliant idea. Maybe she could take the baby. At the right time. It wasn't kidnapping. It was her baby. She gave birth to it. She smiled at Mrs. Whitney to throw her off guard. She had wondered lately which of the people she met could read her mind. Yes, she could take her own baby. And when she did, they'd never find her.

Chapter Twenty-one

"Don't touch that child!"

"But I was just putting her little pink clip in. She always wears that. Ever since she got hair!"

Danielle was crawling across the kitchen floor after the dropped pink barrette. Mavis was clutching onto her dustrag, her body shaking with anger. Flora was facing her, hands on hips.

"It's silly and foolish for her to wear such things."

"Mrs. Butler, you're a good-looking woman. When you were a girl, didn't you like to be pretty and foolish?"

"Not when I was a baby," she said woodenly.

"And Mrs. Whitney has such pretty things for her. Why do you have to dress her like this when she's not here?"

Danielle had found the pretty clip and was sucking on it. Flora yanked it out of her mouth and gave her a tap on her rear, which was encased in worn cotton overalls over a plain white T-shirt.

Mavis looked down, and she ached to pick up that baby as freely as she always had. "Why don't you find yourself some man and make more babies?" she said sharply. "You're still a young woman." Then she turned back to her dusting, muttering to herself. She didn't notice in her anger that Flora was holding the baby and standing behind her.

"If you would fold your dustcloth up in a triangle and grip it in the palm of your hand, I believe you would find you did a better job. You see, the way you're doing it, you're actually blowing the dust back into the room. Also, I don't believe you shake out the dustcloth often enough. And you should do it outside," Flora said kindly.

Mavis stood a few seconds with her back to the woman, fighting hard for self-control. When she spun around, Flora took a step back. "Look, woman, before you came, I took care of that baby, the house *and* the Whitneys just fine." Mavis's breathing was heavy, and she was so furious she couldn't locate the right words to tell the Butler woman what she thought of her. "Why don't you go where you belong? No one wants you here. You're not like them. The Whitneys is quality folk."

Flora's mouth dropped open. She had never heard

such hatred. "'Do not forget to entertain strangers, for thereby some have entertained angels unawares.' That's from Hebrews!"

"'The very hairs of your head are all numbered.' Figure it out," fired back Mavis. "I know my Bible, too, missy."

Then she turned and stomped out the back door, running toward the ravine. She stared down into the muddy waters. Oh, yes, she knew that the Whitneys hadn't adopted that poor baby. But that woman who said she was the mother didn't deserve to have a child. She was bloodless, heartless and would deny her Danielle even a drop of motherly warmth, if she had any in her soul to give. She didn't even call her Danielle. Not when the folks weren't around, she didn't. She called her . . . Emily. She had tried to tell Mrs. Whitney, but all she had said was, "We must try and make her happy here." Happy? Hah! That woman could never be happy!

Mavis didn't realize she had begun talking out loud. "All my friends say I should leave my job. Just a maid—that's all I am. The colored maid. Old Mavis. They don't talk to me nice like they used to. But I can't leave, because I have to protect that baby. If I wasn't here, Lord knows what Mrs. Butler would be doing with all her preaching and carrying on. Reading to that baby from the Bible when she's sleeping. I see Mrs. Whitney when she comes home from work. So pale. Must be about ten pounds she's dropped. But it's Mr. Whitney I fret about most. It's about a month and a half now, and the change has come over him. I catch the looks he gives that woman. It's not right. Uh-uh. I don't like this at all."

Mavis searched the muddy waters of the ravine. Her eyes rested on a gnarled old tree, and she said, "Something tells me I better stay nights. Someone has to protect this family from that woman."

* * *

"Are you a Jew?" she asked.

The young bearded man looked down at the little blond girl placing a jigsaw-puzzle part tentatively into the puzzle. He shifted in his tiny child's chair at the low table.

"Yes, I am. Does that bother you?"

"No, sir, it doesn't bother me," the little girl said. "But it's un-Christian."

"And what does that mean?" he prodded, smiling.

"It means I can't play with you no more."

"Who told you that?" Dr. Resnick asked quickly.

The little girl screwed up her face, then shook out her head like a wet dog. "I dunno."

"I think you do," the psychologist said softly. "Let's talk about your dream. Last week you said you woke up in the middle of the night; and it was like punching through something that's tough and hard, but you have to break through or you won't be able to breathe."

She shrugged. "Something like that. I don't like this place, doc. How come they all call me Number Six?"

"I told them to. I don't want you to pick out a new name and get used to it. I know it's hard and it hurts your head, but we want to remember your real name, don't we?"

The little girl thought for a moment and then tested another piece of the puzzle.

Dr. Resnick had worked with all types of youngsters at the Hillcrest Home, but he had never, in his whole career, encountered an amnesia victim like this little girl he saw one afternoon a week. It was a fascinating challenge. Again, he had lost her to whatever ran through her blocked little mind.

"You know," he said gently, "what we have to do

is a little like putting together a jigsaw puzzle. But I
can't do it unless you want to help. I think you don't
want to go home."

"I do! I do!" the little girl shouted. "Anything
would be better than this place. All those girls
sleeping in the same big room."

"Did you have your own room before, Six?"

"Bunk beds," she said, without thinking.

The doctor hunched his shoulders and bent lower.
"You shared it with your sister?"

"Don't have no sisters," she said freely.

"Then with your brothers?"

"Don't have no brothers," she said fiercely, and
then suddenly started to cry. Dr. Resnick reached in
his briefcase and handed her a vivid yellow Kleenex.
He always carried a supply of bright multicolored
tissues whenever he visited the home.

Looking at his watch, he frowned. "I have to leave
now, Six. We'll get together next week." She stood
up and took his hand, clutching it so that he found it
hard to leave. He looked down into her pleading,
glistening eyes. "Look, you can't go home unless
you *remember*. I think you're afraid to do that. But it
may not be so bad. Anything you remember we can
talk over together and figure out. Sometimes we
become ashamed of what we've done and we're
afraid of being punished. . . ."

The little girl gasped, holding her hand over her
mouth, and then started to giggle.

Dr. Resnick studied the play of emotions on her
face.

"Once you remember, those nightmares should
stop," he said, smiling at her.

She walked him down the long corridor that
smelled as if the windows had never been opened,
though they were. He held her hand.

"Sonny and Ethel never come. But I knew they
wouldn't. . . ."

That part was in the records, though it wasn't of much help. He had already interviewed the couple.

He stood in the hallway before the big double doors that opened onto a circular driveway. He held both of her hands. "You know what, Six? I'm beginning to think you love them more than the people who might be worrying about you."

Amy Butler hung her head and let her hands drop.

"I've got it!"

He looked up, his magic marker poised, waiting.

Then she said smugly, "Make Willoughby's your one-stop shopping center for fine furniture."

"Amanda! Stop joking around. It was funny the first day. We always do that. But this is the tenth day on this goddamn campaign, and you're not making it easier for me."

"Sorry, I couldn't resist it," she said brightly. "Okay, I've got it! Willoughby's Year-Long Furniture Sale." Brad stared at her. "That's what we go with, kiddo. Nice concept. They're not looking for a class image, anyway. And I think the visual should be this peepshow-type thing of the inside of a doll house. I mean the warehouse with all the rooms filled with furniture." She stopped, as if seeing her art director for the first time. "Don't you think, Brad?"

Brad was running his tongue around his teeth, but his mouth was closed. They had always worked so well together in the past. And now she was acting like every clichéd, bitchy woman in the business that men just loved to hate.

He said softly, "Oh, I think we can still come up with something a little more original for Willoughby. Though, yes, they can probably sell that to the client. You don't mind if I think up my own visual, do you, Amanda?"

"Brad! Of course not! It was just a suggestion."

She smiled radiantly. "I think this should be the introductory ad. Later, we'll move that headline down to a slogan in the logo, and we'll headline the furniture featured."

"The Amanda Whitney way," Brad said with a touch of sarcasm. "Never fails, does it?" There was nothing he could do. She was the boss lady of the team. It wasn't equal anymore. She was a creative director. When she left his office, he didn't start a new layout; he called a head-hunter.

When Amanda closed the door in her office, her smile had vanished. She picked up the phone and punched the buttons. Mavis answered. "The Whitney residence," she said crisply.

Amanda sighed. "Mavis, you don't have to say that. A simple hello is fine."

Mavis had been acting awfully huffy lately. She should have a talk with her to clear the air; but whenever she came home from work, Mavis was dashing out.

"Where's Mrs. Butler?" Amanda asked.

"In the baby's room, Mrs. Whitney."

Amanda thought longingly of the white rocker with the pink heart-shaped pillow. She pictured Danielle taking her afternoon nap. And then she wondered what the hell *that woman* did in the baby's room all the time. Branch promised her daily everything would be over soon. If she would just have patience. Justin was studying all the angles. If they had to, they'd go to court, but only if they were sure they could win. After a week of watching Flora Butler take care of her baby, Amanda thought she would go out of her mind. She had called Murray, who was delighted to have her back. She didn't tell him it would only be for a little while.

"What did she have for breakfast?"

"Cereal, I think, Mrs. Whitney?"

"And lunch?"

"Chopped scrambled eggs and some junior vegetable. She did very well. Though I wasn't standing real close." The last was said sarcastically.

It escaped Amanda. "And what about her toilet training?"

"Well, I don't know if I should say, Mrs. Whitney; but I think you ought to know she ain't tried that in a long time. Mrs. Butler, she says she doesn't believe in anything that doesn't come naturally."

Amanda could feel her face getting hot. Behind her back. Well, she would have to confront Mrs. Butler. The pediatrician she used believed in toilet training as early as six months. It made for healthier babies. And well-adjusted adults.

Mavis paused a second and made a fist of her hand. Then she let it spring open. There were so many things she wanted to tell Mrs. Whitney. Like the fact that when she came home from work Danielle was dressed in one of her little pink dresses with her little pink clip in her blond curls, but during the day she ran around no better than her own children had. Worse, in fact. During the day something different and frightening happened. Like what went on in that room. The chanting from the Bible and the praying. But Mavis was too afraid of losing her job. The Butler woman might accuse her of lying. She couldn't bear being separated from the family she loved more than anything else in the world.

Amanda said good-bye and hung up. She wrapped her arms around herself. Sitting hunched over, she rocked as if in pain. Only a month and it was like a living nightmare. Every day it got more confused, more sick and twisted. If she let herself be sucked into it, she wasn't sure she could keep from having a nervous breakdown. And so she kept a mental distance, though she wondered what it would be like to live without the constant heartache. The only rock that sustained her was Branch. It was his strength that kept them going without trying to murder the woman. His patience, his diplomacy. His reminding her that they would get to keep Danielle. It would just take time to work out. Amanda didn't feel she could really talk out her feelings to anyone about the situation. Not even Joyce. Though she obviously knew what was happening.

Getting through the days was the hard part. She couldn't really concentrate. Their agreement was Mrs. Butler would take care of the baby only until she got home from work. Five o'clock was the best time of the day for her, because she knew she could drive home in a half-hour and there would be her own precious baby girl dressed in pink. She hugged and cuddled her and fussed over her, and bought her presents almost every day. But all too soon she would have to feed her and put her to bed.

After her dinner with Branch and Mrs. Butler, she would disappear into the baby's room for blissful moments when she could just rock and watch her sleep. Just the two of them. She liked to feel the closeness between them.

It would work out. Lots of mothers worked. And this was just temporary.

Amanda stared out the window as the September sunshine lazily splashed the buildings. *Who are you kidding, Amanda Whitney? You know damn well you'd rather be home with your baby*. Angrily, she took a piece of yellow copy paper from her desk and lowered it into the typewriter. The ideas didn't come as fast as they used to. Mainly, she supposed, it was because she didn't care. But she had to focus her mind on something or they'd have to lock her up. Slowly, she started typing:

Dear Danielle . . . just because I'm
not home all day doesn't mean mommy
doesn't love you . . . maybe one day I
can explain that . . . Willoughby's
Warehouse is more than just a furniture store . . . you can furnish your
whole home in just one day . . . your
mother   loves   you   very   much,
Danielle . . .

The baby was sound asleep upstairs. Flora put on
a sweater over her housedress and went out the side
door. It was cool for September in Atlanta. Atlanta.
She hated it. She was drowning in loneliness. She
walked up the long street. She had never seen streets
like this. Mansions on every block.

She wondered if any one of the rich people in any
one of those huge houses filled with things ever read
the Good Book. She read it every night.

She was crossing over to the other side of the
street when Ralph warned her, "Watch out for that
car." Thank heaven for his voice, or she could have
been killed. A big car came speeding down the
almost-empty road. Flora was the only one walking.
Rich people never walked and used the two legs that
the Lord blessed them with. They drove.

When she stepped back to the curb and out of its
way, she stumbled. If it wasn't for a tree to hang on
to, she would have fallen. It almost seemed like the
car was aimed at her. She squinted her eyes and
looked after it. But she couldn't see the license
plates. That was the trouble with these people. In
her old neighborhood someone would have come to
help her, or at least chased the car.

Emily would grow up like this. With a fancy name
like Danielle. A foreign word. Danielle, with her
frilly pink dresses and spoiled ways. But when the

Whitneys weren't looking, she became Emily. And she was raising her as she had all her other children. But the girl was too pretty for her own good. She wondered, too, if Emily would behave better when she brought her back north. That's what was delaying their trip. She wanted to take the Whitney out of her baby. She wanted her pure, the way she was born. And, dear Lord, it was so hard. Discouraged suddenly, Flora started walking back toward the big white Whitney mansion, which gleamed in the early autumn sunshine.

"Mind your manners, Benjy, and don't hit your sister." They were all up in heaven. But she could see them clearly sometimes. As she had seen them in the old house. They were probably still there.

Just as Flora was going up the long driveway, the same car screeched around the corner and came up the long street at headlong speed. Flora didn't hear or see. She was lost in her voices.

The driver of the speeding car was muttering angrily to himself and beating his fist against the seat, while one hand clutched the wheel. "Son of a bitch. I could have had her. One second off."

He'd have to try again. The doctor in New York was anxious to have the job done quickly. Trouble was, the woman hardly ever came out of the house. Well, he didn't have time to waste. It would have to be something else. Closer to home. He leaned over and spat out the window. He wasn't used to making mistakes. Next time he wouldn't miss.

"Scooby-dooby-doo," Branch sang, along with the Sinatra record.

"Scooby-dooby-doo," Jerry mimicked from the engineer's booth. Branch dialed the phone while the record played. "Yes?" Mavis answered. Branch felt like asking her if it would be too much trouble to just say hello, but she had been acting testy lately. "How's our baby doing?" he asked instead.

"She's doing fine, Mr. Whitney. Cereal for breakfast, chopped eggs for lunch, and she made a nice doo-doo."

Branch laughed, keeping his eyes on Jerry. "And Mrs. Butler? Is she around?"

"I don't believe she's available right this moment," Mavis said stiffly.

Branch didn't notice the tone of her voice. His mind was on Jerry's cue. He hung up, mumbling, "Thanks, Mavis." As he put another mellow record on, he thought, with satisfaction, that it had all worked out after all. His household was running smoothly. Amanda was working. She didn't complain about not appearing glamorous to him and she seemed busy and active. Danielle was flourishing under the love she was getting from everyone. And Flora. He had almost physically bumped into her this morning. She was wearing a plain navy bathrobe tied in the middle. She was slipping into the baby's room. He saw her cleavage, just a little of those large, perfect breasts he had dreamed about. But it was her hair that made him stop and catch his breath. Her long ash blond hair had been unwound from that tight little bun. It was tied in back, but fell over one shoulder. He had stared at her. She noticed, and then rushed back into the baby's room.

Justin had warned him that the law took a dim view of baby selling. And this wasn't just the ordinary surrogate-mother case, not with the kind of inheritance arrangement they had. Branch had been firm. There could be no losing. They must get the baby. He knew Amanda would go over the edge if the baby was awarded to Mrs. Butler. And so would he. But Justin was still tangled in a web of research.

So, in the meantime, they were forced to wait it out.
But he thought at times Amanda complained a bit
too much. It wasn't all that bad.

Flora Butler sat rocking in the white chair. She
would have to remember to bring in a good, sturdy,
straight-backed chair. She distrusted rocking chairs.
Danielle was taking her nap. Flora had been reading
Proverbs to the baby, even while she slept. There
was so much work to do with the child and so little
time to do it. Looking around, she knew she would
be forced to redecorate her baby's room, even if
Mrs. Whitney didn't agree. She positively couldn't
allow a child of hers to live in such a gaudy display of
greed. She had already taken half the toys and
stuffed animals and piled them in the closet. What
she really wanted to do was give them away to needy
children who had no toys; but they weren't hers to
give out, so it really wasn't right.

Pretty soon it would be time to dress the child in
one of those flouncy dresses that lined her little
closets. All to please Mrs. Whitney. Not to rock the
boat. As soon as possible she'd stop doing that, that
was for sure. Looking at her sleeping baby with pity,
she whispered, "Don't worry, Emily. I'll take you
away from these people. You won't grow up like
them."

Though Mr. Whitney never said much to her, she
knew with every nerve in her body, when she
chanced to look at him, that they were the real
parents of that child. She didn't like standing close to
him or sitting near him. It made her feel awkward.
Because they both knew the truth.

Flora permitted herself to rest her eyes for a
moment. Eyelids closed, she saw herself taking
Emily triumphantly up north. The baby stirred then
and woke up, her big eyes blinking and looking

around. Flora reached to pick her up, but the baby screwed up her face for a cry and started kicking and pounding her fists furiously. Danielle screeched when Flora tried to calm her. When Flora finally succeeded in picking her up, Danielle arched her back and hissed like a cat, yelling as if she were being beaten. Flora gave her a little smack on her rear, which made her wail even louder. "That's enough, Emily," Flora said sternly. But Danielle never heard her. She kept right on squealing, even when Flora gave her some firm smacks on her little hands.

Mavis, who was polishing the intricate woodwork on the downstairs banister, could hear the baby even down there. She stopped. "Mmmmm-mmmm, that one's going to last awhile," she said to herself, picturing their precious baby, her hair in damp ringlets, her eyes bloodshot red, her face purple with rage. If she were upstairs, she'd rock her and sing to her.

The screeching increased. Well, who could blame the child for crying? Being around that sour-pussed old witch all the time. She sighed. It wasn't her business, she supposed. But this Flora Butler better not harm her baby.

Chapter Twenty-two

It was Indian summer in October, and the little girl and Dr. Resnick decided to spend their afternoon session walking through the crunchy yellow orange leaves in the woods surrounding the home.

"I hear you haven't been eating well," Dr. Resnick said.

"I don't like the food here."

"Maybe you're used to eating a different kind of food. French? Norwegian? Maybe German? Or Italian?"

"Nope," she said in that husky voice he had grown accustomed to.

"Why don't you like the food?" he persisted.

"It tastes like plastic," she said abruptly. There was a long silence. They sat down on a log.

"You know," he said, "after you remember, we can still be friends. If you live far away, we can even write to each other."

"We can," she said, with an animation she hadn't shown for a while. He noticed her face light up. Then it fell again.

Dr. Resnick pulled out a large box of Raisinets from his pants pocket. "Well, look what I almost sat on. Have some, Six?"

The little girl shook her head, horrified. "I'm not allowed to eat candy."

"Don't be silly. The home gives parties, and they

have little baskets of candies donated by the volunteer ladies. I understand you never have any."

Her headache was starting. Moving from her forehead to the middle of her head. "I can't have candy," she said, mechanically.

The psychiatrist sat rigid, afraid to move. "Who said so, Six?" he asked. "All children have a little candy. Sometimes."

The little girl looked all around like a trapped animal ready to dart. "Please don't call me that. Six, I mean."

"When you remember your name, I will call you by it," he said, using what sounded to her like his teacher's voice.

She started to sob.

He handed her a bright pink tissue from his pocket. "I think you know your name," he said soothingly. "And I think you know where you live. You have for some time. You're afraid to go home, aren't you?"

The little girl dropped the last Raisinet she was letting melt in her hand, and started to run away. But the young psychiatrist was faster and stronger from his daily jogging. He caught her and bound her small hands in his big ones. "What's your name?" he screamed.

Sobbing and shaking her head wildly, she shut her eyes. He could see the veins in her forehead. "My . . . my . . ."

"What's your name, Six?" he demanded. He knew her amnesia was going to be a thing of the past soon. He knew she knew.

"My name," she screamed back, unable to hold back the fact that she finally remembered any longer, "is . . . Amy Butler. And I live at 527 Dane Road in Wananwa, New Jersey. And I was in . . . in . . . the van when it went over the side and fell into the water. I forced my way out when the door swung open. I pushed my brothers aside and I jumped over them and I swam to the top, and then I couldn't remember. And those people found me." She held her head together with her hands. "And my mama is going to punish me. And I hate her. Please let me live with you. Or Sonny and Ethel. Please."

She slid down his legs as if they were a tree trunk and fell in a heap among the dead leaves and scattered twigs lying in the dirt. Dr. Resnick waited until she was cried out. He picked her up, stood her on her feet and held on to her, putting her thin arms around his middle.

"It's all right, Amy Butler. We're going to find your mother, and she's going to be happy to see you. No one's going to hurt you. Everything's going to be fine from now on."

Amy looked up through the spaces in the branches of the trees, where the white sun winked at her like diamonds. She was Amy again. Really Amy. And she remembered everything. Even that today was October 3 and her birthday, and that she was nine years old. She had known all this for a few days, but now she could tell. She was free again. Just then she shuddered. What if her mama knew she had eaten all those Raisinets?

When he walked to the door, he frowned. Something was cooking. The odor wafted out to meet him. He wasn't used to all this cloying domesticity. He preferred to snack or eat out. But Rochelle was intent on making him a home. He didn't have the heart to tell her she was a lousy cook.

She came out of the kitchen, beaming. "Hungry, honey?" she said. He looked at her. There was no way of stopping the sinking feeling. She had begun to bore him at times. Ever since he had told her the truth and washed away years of delicious guilt. It was hard to make love to her, and she was always wanting it. Lately, he had felt trapped.

Then he wondered, What was wrong? It was Shel. Shel. After all those years. He should consider himself lucky to even have her there.

The table was set with a centerpiece of fresh-cut flowers, a kelly green tablecloth and silver napkin rings. She was carrying a lopsided pan of rolls, freshly baked. His heart ached with love in spite of himself. Rochelle was so pathetically stupid. He wanted to go up and kiss her, but he wasn't capable of that kind of display of affection. He could kiss her in bed. That was different.

"Borgy," she sang out, passing him a dish of something or other.

"Shel, wouldn't you rather call me Barnard?"

She giggled and scooped the salad into bowls. "You know, I'm always afraid it will come out . . . Barnyard."

He didn't laugh.

"Borgy, I spoke to my lawyer today. . . ."

He was buttering a roll that was mushy on the inside. He must insist they eat out more often. If there was one thing he hated, it was indigestion.

"Oh, yes?"

"He said my divorce would be finalized in the summer. Of course, I won't get any alimony and Victor will have the house; but I can see the boys if I go there."

"Fine," he said. He wondered who was going to pay for those trips.

Rochelle swallowed hard and looked at this gorgeous man she always thought was beyond her reach. Instead of thinking of him as her brother, a miracle had happened. And now she thought so much better of herself. All those years they had done those things with each other, it wasn't sin. It was true love.

"I want us to get married right after the divorce. The day after. I don't care about a ceremony, of course; but I do . . ."

Borgy, Barnard, Normy stood up suddenly, toppling his salad bowl. "I can't get married. You don't understand."

Rochelle looked at him, stunned. "But you said we weren't brother and sister. That it wasn't really . . ." After all these years she still couldn't get it out.

"Yes. But I can't get married."

"But there could be no children. Why not? We love each other. I left my family for you. I don't understand. . . ." She rushed over to throw her arms around his waist and rest her head on his chest.

He pushed her away.

"I said no!" he screamed.

Rochelle blinked. He looked like a kid of twelve again. Although he had never been vulnerable at that age. She studied him. All these years he had never married. Maybe that was it. He had said it was because he loved her. But he must be afraid now. Still, she was hurt. He had pushed her away. He'd just been a bachelor too long. That was it. He'd marry her. She had faith in their love, which had lasted all these years. It would be a dirty trick to be disappointed now. She'd wait awhile, until he got used to the idea. He'd come around. And then her boys could visit them.

Branch had finished his day early and come home to rest and take a shower. He and Amanda had been invited to a dinner party. Some important friend of Justin's. As Branch went up the steps, Flora was going into the baby's room. She didn't see him, but he saw her. What a beautiful, sensuous woman. Just enough distance to excite a man. He wondered if she was attracted to him.

He liked to fantasize about her. He couldn't help it. Then, as usual, he scrubbed up vigorously with soap, as if the thoughts had made him unclean. Then he tried to channel his thinking. He would wear his navy sports jacket and gray flannel pants. He could taste his first drink, which would be a scotch and soda. All the people at the party would be lawyers and real-estate people. He would be treated like a celebrity. He liked that.

Putting on a silk bathrobe, he went into the bedroom. He looked at the bed, but then decided he wanted to see his daughter before she went to bed. As he lifted his hand to knock on the door, Flora came out of the room. She was wearing a light-colored sleeveless blouse. As she lifted her arm to fix a hairpin, he found himself fascinated by the little rim of white bra and the hair under her armpits. It had been years since he had seen that. Most women shaved. For some reason it excited him.

"I guess I'll go in and see the baby," he said, smiling, feeling awkward as a schoolboy.

She nodded, then slipped out of the room. "Make it quick," she said to him.

Then Flora grimaced. Mrs. Whitney, carrying an armful of boxes, came dashing up the stairs. She shouldn't have let him in. She had been training the baby to go to bed earlier. She had been staying up way too late. Besides, the earlier she fell asleep, the easier it would be to take her back up north. By the time they got out of the house, she would be in a deep sleep. She wasn't a fussy sleeper, thank the Lord.

Amanda rushed into the room, brushing past Flora. Danielle was sitting on Branch's lap, playing with his nose. Amanda swooped over and lifted the baby up, pressing her close to her fur coat. Danielle laughed.

"How is mother's precious?" Amanda cooed,

kissing her over and over, as if she hadn't seen her for a week. And it felt to her as if it had been that long.

"Here, sweetheart. . . ." She juggled Danielle while she shrugged off her raccoon coat and placed it on a huge toy chest. Then, with Branch laughing at the two of them, she hoisted the baby high on her hip and leaned over to get a box. "See, love, mommy bought you something."

Flora stood in the doorway scowling, knowing no one noticed her. But she saw the whole disgusting scene. Another toy. A bright pink panda. The child had fourteen stuffed animals at last count. Who was that woman buying it for, the baby or herself? Or was she buying the baby? It wouldn't do her any good.

She watched as Amanda opened another box. A little white organdy dress with a red sash and little pink bows all over it. Must have cost a fortune. You could feed a family of four for a month on the money that woman spent on things for the child. She watched as Amanda changed Danielle into the dress. Then she and the husband cooed over the child, who reminded Flora of a fussed-over French poodle, complete with a diamond-studded leash.

She coughed loudly. No one paid any attention to her. Amanda was showing Danielle a new baby doll. Finally, Flora said, "It's getting past her bedtime."

"Oh, it's only six o'clock," Amanda whined, hugging the baby.

"She's tired and she may be getting a little cold," Flora said.

"Maybe we should go, honey," Branch said to Amanda.

"But we just got here," Amanda protested. Branch picked up her fur coat and guided her out of the room.

"We'll stop in and take a look at her later tonight."

The two of them left the baby's room, Amanda almost walking backward, blowing kisses to Danielle. As soon as they left, Flora yanked the doll away from Danielle and took off the frilly little dress. Danielle immediately began to scream. Flora gave her a little smack on her fanny. She screamed harder, holding out her arms to be picked up. Flora picked her up and plopped her in her crib. Danielle screeched louder, her breaths coming in staccato gasps. She was so furious she began to grab fistfuls of her baby blanket.

Flora was shocked. She had never seen the baby so willful. Worse than Amy, she thought to herself. "I apologize," she said to her daughter, who might have been watching from above. Discouraged, she sat in the white rocker and watched the baby cry harder until her amazement turned to anger and then disillusionment.

When Branch and Amanda reached the bedroom, Amanda fell face down on the enormous double bed and began to cry.

"Amanda, sweetheart, what's the matter? Something go wrong at work?"

Amanda started to weep louder. Then angrily she got up and mimicked him, "Something go wrong at work? Branch, something's going wrong in that room. The baby's crying."

"Flora's with her. It'll be okay."

"Floooora? Since when is it Flora?"

Then they stared at each other. Amanda wiped her face with her hand.

"You know," she said softly, "this is getting dumb. The only thing we ever fight over."

"You're right, honey. Okay, tonight I'll speak to Justin."

"You mean, go to court, anyway?"

Branch sighed. He nodded. Yes, he would talk to Justin. They talked every day. But it was he, Branch, who wouldn't give the go-ahead to start a case. It would ruin his career, for one thing. It would harm his daughter, for another thing. He was biding his time until the subject of surrogate motherhood wasn't so sensational or until Flora got tired and left. Flora. The mother of his child. He was a weak man, he supposed. But he liked looking at her. If it weren't for Amanda's impatience, he would be perfectly content to continue this way for a while. In fact, that was what they were going to do.

"We almost there?" said Amy, starting to fidget in the front seat of the old station wagon.

"Almost," said Dr. Resnick.

"How come we couldn't wait till tomorrow?"

"This is called going over and above the call of duty. Tomorrow is Saturday. Quite frankly, my wife would kill me. That's the time I spend with my family."

"Oh," Amy said, not wanting to know about his other life away from her. Then she began to see familiar landmarks. "Oh, look!" She clapped her hands. "There's my house. Pull into the driveway." But it was empty and the drapes were drawn. "She got new drapes," Amy said seriously. "We needed them." She sighed the sigh of an old woman.

"We could knock on the door," Dr. Resnick said cheerfully, "but it looks like no one's home, doesn't it?" He looked down at the bright little girl who had fascinated him for so many months.

"My mama never goes out around dinnertime," Amy said knowingly. "She only goes shopping once a week. Never forgets anything. Buys everything she needs according to what's on sale."

Dr. Resnick didn't want to make any jarring suggestions. He had to be careful that he didn't imply that the mother had altered her lifestyle in any way since the girl had last seen her.

"C'mon, let's get out and stretch our legs," he said.

Amy scampered out of the car, smoothing down her faded olive green dress. They walked up the street, and a boy on a bike came whizzing past and then crashed into a tree behind them. Dr. Resnick turned around and ran back to help the boy, who was entangled in his bike.

"I'm okay," the boy said. "My bike's a mess, though." He pointed at the girl. "You're Amy Butler," he said accusingly.

"What of it?" she said sassily.

"You're a ghost!" he said, his voice quivering.

"No, I'm not. I'm a human being." There was no mistaking her voice. Low. Husky and breathy, with a faint hint of a baby lisp. He had hated Amy Butler's voice as much as he had hated her when she was alive.

Dr. Resnick stepped in. "Amy survived the automobile accident, but then she lost all her memory. She lives in an orphanage in upstate New York, and we'd like to find her mother. Can you help?"

"Wow!" said the boy, scratching his reddish hair. It always excited him when he could play a real part in the drama he watched constantly from his attic window. Mrs. Butler. Wow, he'd never forget her.

"New people living in your house," he said, imitating his dad.

"Where's my mama?" Amy asked, her legs apart, hands on hips.

"No one in the neighborhood really knows for sure. She just up and left. End of July. Didn't tell no one where she was going. Christian Lord was the ones who sold her house. Sign up in the front lawn for a little while."

Dr. Resnick glanced at Amy, whose mouth had sagged open at the corners. She was gazing jealously over at her house and trying to adjust to the hard reality that it wasn't hers anymore. And if she didn't live there, where did she belong?

"How about we see if the people who sold your house know where your mother is, Amy?" Dr. Resnick said cheerfully.

Amy didn't budge, still staring at the house. "I hope I never find my mama," she said, tears rolling down her face. "I want somebody nice to adopt me."

"Now, Amy," Dr. Resnick said patiently. "You know you don't mean that. We've talked this over before. Your mother will be happy to see you."

Amy shrugged, still staring at the house. Her back to the doctor, she stuck out her tongue, put her thumb on her nose and wiggled her fingers.

The smartly dressed woman sat in the small office. She faced her supervisor. "I turned it over to the IRS for an audit," he said. "You say he offered you $7,500 for the conception and the same for the delivery?"

The woman reached in her bag and pulled out a tiny cassette tape.

"A simple case. We'll get him on income-tax evasion. His books must be a work of art."

"I would guess so," the woman replied.

"Do you think he suspected anything?" her boss asked her.

"No, not really. I told him I was answering the ad in the personals section of that newspaper. A New Jersey lady who was interested. And if he calls, I'll tell him I'm not interested, but thank you. I don't think Dr. Barnard Borg has the slightest inkling that

I'm a widow." She chuckled. "Or that the plain Mrs. Fromme is an agent for the FBI."

Amanda shifted her weight. Her feet hurt in her new pewter high heels, and she was searching for a chair in the crowded living room. She felt too warm in her mauve wool dress, though she enjoyed knowing she looked good. Branch was on the other side of the room, chatting with Justin. She crossed her fingers. Joyce was sitting with a group of women, discussing, she supposed, their children.

"Well, if it isn't the only female creative director in Atlanta's ad world," a male voice said behind her. She turned. It was a friend of Justin's. She had met him once before. He was a presentable alcoholic. "Oh, this is my wife, Marion."

A small-boned blonde with streaks in her hair laughed and shrugged at the same time. "How do you do," Marion said coolly. "I'm his nonworking wife and the mother of his two children. All I do is take care of all of them and the house. But I don't work."

Amanda ignored the obvious sarcasm and smiled genuinely. "I envy you. That's the best life of all when you can stay home with your children. I'd like to do it more often. I have a little girl."

The woman thought it was considerate of the great Amanda Whitney to say such a thing when she obviously couldn't mean it. When the group went into the other room for dinner, she asked what her daughter's name was.

"Danielle," Amanda replied.

"Such a lovely name," Marion said. "And how old is she?"

"Nine months."

"So is my baby. When was she born?"

"A little before Christmas. Well, December 19, to be exact."

The other woman's hands shot to her face. "Oh, you're kidding! What hospital were you in? My son was born the same day."

Amanda looked at the woman, and her mouth simply refused to work. She thought everyone knew. Did she have to say that Danielle was adopted? Amanda tried to swallow and couldn't. Looking around frantically, she excused herself. Then she ran for a bathroom. She found one downstairs and was grateful it wasn't wallpapered. It felt so good to press her forehead against the cool tiles; and when she was able, she sat on the seat, bent over and put her head between her ankles to keep from fainting. The dizziness had come over her like ocean waves.

How long could she lie to herself? She hated her life, hated Mrs. Butler. It wasn't fair. It made her physically sick every time she realized the truth. Mrs. Butler was the mother of her baby.

Amy and Dr. Resnick were eating hamburgers and drinking Cokes in a MacDonald's in New Jersey.

"We'd better step on it, kid. We have a lot of driving to do. You can sleep in the car."

"We had a van, too," Amy said wistfully.

"It will be all right, Amy," Dr. Resnick assured her. "At least we know your mother is in Atlanta."

Amy frowned. Her mother had found the girl baby. The pretty one.

"Tell me what my Grandpa Nash said again," Amy said.

The doctor had called him from a pay phone and been chilled. "Both your grandparents were happy you were alive," he said. Actually, the woman had said they couldn't care for the girl. To give her back to the orphanage. Her husband seemed kind. But the old woman had taken over. He had suggested getting Amy to Atlanta without telling Flora. She just might not be too happy about it. No one seemed to care about the child.

The whole thing made him angry. Slurping the last of his Coke and dipping a last french fry in a pool of ketchup, he studied the little girl he had grown so fond of. No wonder she had chosen to forget. What was he sending her back to? As he paid the check, he thought, Well, what the hell can I do? He had gotten her memory back. He had brought her to Wananwa to find her mother. What more could he do? He wondered who was going to take her to Atlanta and who was going to pay for it.

It was after midnight. Flora knew that the Whitneys would be coming home any minute and she should leave the baby. But tonight was a special night. She realized her decision had been brewing on the back burners of her mind, as she always put it. Even though Amy and Benjamin and Carl and Denny had all nodded their joyous approval, it was still her decision. And one she couldn't make lightly. Though she knew from this evening on there was no hope of saving Danielle from this sinful, indulgent, rich family.

The child was ruined. Her only hope was to join her brothers and sisters in heaven. The ravine. That was the place for Danielle. Because she would never be Emily in this life. But, first, before the baptismal ritual, her soul would have to leave her body and go up toward heaven. That was the way to make sure she was saved. Flora smiled at the peacefully sleeping baby. She would have to kill her. To release her poor tortured soul. To save her from a life of ruin. Not now. But soon.

Flora sighed. For the first time since she had come to this awful house, she felt relaxed. It was the Lord's way.

Chapter Twenty-three

Barnard Borg put the phone down and stared straight ahead. He had gone to his study to talk in private. He wondered for the first time about Harvey Nathan, the man who was his attorney, his accountant and his business manager. Barnard Borg still opened his own mail. And the envelope sitting on his desk had panicked him. He never felt panic. But, for no reason at all, he was being audited.

Nothing to worry about, Harv had said. He had taken precautions. But they both knew it could be bad, really bad, for both of them. If the IRS ever found out about the surrogate-baby business, he was in real trouble. That's what he wanted to know. Was it a routine audit? How far did it go?

He realized his hand was shaking. Odd. His hand never shook. He took no prescription drugs unless necessary, drank only wine and slept at least six hours every night. Why would his hand shake? Was it a premonition? Ridiculous. He squeezed his eyes shut against the passing vision of metal bars and locked doors.

Once they went over his books, they might want to talk to witnesses. Then he remembered Flora Butler. No, she wasn't dead. They hadn't heard anything. That was another thing he had told Harv to do . . . find a better killer. Flora Butler could harm him. Harv had told him to be patient. But then why had there been a tremor in his voice if he wasn't really worried?

He looked up and saw Rochelle standing in the doorway.

"Can I talk to you, sweetheart?"

He nodded, not really seeing or hearing her.

"I've been waiting for you to come home, and then you go and lock yourself up in your study. We can go out to eat tonight if you like. I was so busy thinking all day, I didn't really cook."

He continued staring at her, but he was looking through her.

She stood, hands on hips. "I never give an ultimatum, but I have to now," she said, speaking as if her speech were carefully rehearsed. "We've talked about marriage and you've said no. Now, Borgy, if you won't marry me, I will eventually have to leave. We've lived together long enough." She bit her lip and prayed she wouldn't have to go out on her own.

Suddenly he saw her standing there.

"What?"

"I said if you don't want to marry me, I'll have to leave. Not today, but eventually." Ultimatums. She hated it, but there was no other way. She knew she had to take a stand.

"Do you have to bother me with that crap now?" he said, disgusted. "Can't you see I'm busy. Go make one of your dinners or something."

Rochelle looked at him, dumbfounded. Her lower lip trembled. "Busy? You're not busy. You're sitting there staring into space. What's wrong with you, Borgy? You never spoke to me like that."

"I have problems."

Rochelle pulled up a chair. "Okay, tell me about them."

"I'm not going to discuss business with *you*," he said, appalled.

"But that's what a wife is for."

Borg sighed and shook his head as if no one in the world understood reality and common sense except him.

Rochelle caught it and became immediately insulted. As his eyes rolled upward to the ceiling, begging for understanding from an invisible arbitrator, she stood up quickly. "I asked you a simple question before. I would like to know if you're *ever* going to marry me."

"No, I've told you over and over. I can't marry you. How can I marry you? How can I be more clear than to say no, no, no, over and over again," he shouted nastily.

"Why can't you marry me?" She felt a sickening sensation spreading all over her body. Her face felt flushed. In a way she wanted to stop, but she knew she had to find out the truth. "Why? You earn a good living, that's for sure. You can support a wife."

He scowled, not looking at her.

"And this apartment. It's gorgeous. There's room for someone else."

He looked away. His mind longed to shut out her impossible shouting and think about the audit. About the incompetents he was paying to kill the Butler woman.

"Why did you become a gynecologist, Normy? It doesn't figure."

"What the hell are you talking about, Rochelle?"

"It doesn't figure because you really don't like women. Do you, Normy?" Her voice was becoming ugly, strident. He stood up, peering down into her face. She looked up. That face was mocking him. The smile was cruel. He didn't find it sexually exciting, as before. She was threatening him.

She said, tauntingly, "Remember the boy next door, Normy? When we had that little threesome.

We did it for about six months, before his father caught us."

He looked away from her eyes. His head throbbed.

"I remember," she sang. "That must be it. You had a better time with him than with me. Any more since that, brother dear?"

Barnard Borg blinked. All he saw were her lips and her teeth. Suddenly, she looked ugly to him. That mouth. He had to shut that mouth. He put his hands over his ears, but she was still screaming at him.

"You know what I think, Normy?" she said, her tone of voice heavy with sarcasm. "Oh, excuse me for calling you by the name mother gave you. I think you're . . ." Again that smile. That ugly smile. ". . . I think you're gay. Unmistakably homosexual. Only you won't admit it. And you probably won't do anything about it."

His hand lifted and slammed her in the face, stopping that hideous smile. He had to erase that. Then his hand dropped to his side. He watched her fall across the room from the impact and shock. She accidentally landed in a chair, which cushioned her fall.

With a great deal of dignity, not daring to look at him, she got up, straightened out her skirt and ran out of the room. In their bedroom she dabbed at her face with a Kleenex. There was a tiny drop of blood on it. She was afraid to look in the mirror. She knew then that it was over. She could never forgive him. Not a man who hit a woman. No man had ever done that to her.

Amanda usually called the house every two hours if she could. It was three o'clock and she had an important meeting with the Willoughby Furniture people. It was a presentation of the new campaign.

The phone rang five times before Mavis answered it.

"I was beginning to wonder if something was wrong," Amanda said. "How's the baby?"

"Upstairs in her crib."

"Taking a nap, still?"

"I'll have to check, Mrs. Whitney."

The black woman's voice sounded odd to Amanda. "Well, where's Mrs. Butler, Mavis? Isn't she watching the baby?"

"Well, that's the thing," Mavis said with some hesitation. "That's the thing, Mrs. Whitney."

"Is anything wrong?" Amanda sat up straighter in her chair.

"Well, see, Mrs. Butler is acting awfully strange. She's out by the ravine chanting and singing."

Amanda didn't know what to say. This was the first time Mavis had said anything so revealing about what she supposed were the woman's peculiarities.

"Mrs. Whitney," Mavis said, taking a deep breath, "her dress is torn and unbuttoned and her face is dirty. Her hair is undone from that bun it's always up tight in. It's falling in her eyes. I just don't know what to do."

Amanda stood up. "I'll be right home, Mavis. Don't do anything until you hear from me. And see that she doesn't go anywhere near the baby."

Amanda ran to the back of her door and practically yanked the coat hook off getting her trench coat. What if that woman tried to do something to the baby? And then a tremor of excitement passed through her. Maybe the Butler woman was going a little mad. She thought she was something of a fruitcake, but Branch had said that was just her way.

Running out the door, she passed Murray.

"Amanda? The client will be here any minute."

"Have to go home, Mur. Trouble."

"But, Amanda," he protested, "you don't rush out the door without telling anyone. Where are your storyboards? Who will make the presentation?"

"Brad," she mumbled, and ran out the big glass agency doors.

Murray shook his head. One more trick like that and she could stay at home. Amanda Whitney or not.

Amanda buzzed impatiently for an elevator. She knew she could lose her job for something like this. The thought flashed through her mind. But what did it matter? This time Mrs. Butler had gone too far. She was sure something terrible had happened. Finally, the woman would have to leave her with her baby.

Rochelle waited. She had lost track of the time. Would he come in and apologize, or would he hit her again? She sat down on their bed. She started to cry. When she heard the crash, she jumped up, terrified. But then she realized what it was. The sound of the front door slamming. He had left.

She gulped. The phone looked huge on the dresser. Did she have the nerve? Picking up the phone, she prayed they would be home and shut her eyes gratefully when the phone picked up and was answered. "Rob?" she asked, trying valiantly not to cry, knowing her voice was breaking.

"No, it's Rog. Hello, mother," came the cold reply.

"Is daddy there, sweetheart?"

"He's cleaning the pool," her son said. There was a pause, and her fingers worked nervously with the rim of her blouse collar. "Okay, I'll get him," he finally said.

Rochelle glanced around their bedroom. In a week it would be Thanksgiving. Odd, but the same dinner she had planned to cook for him she could make for her family. She needed only to double the recipe. If they wanted her to.

"Shel?" She jumped. The voice. It was threaded with hurt.

"Hi, Victor. How are the boys? How are you?"

Then the coolness. "We're all just fine, Shel. Whatever you have to say might best be settled between our lawyers."

She began to cry. Softly at first. "I don't think so." She paused and reached for a Kleenex on the dresser. "Victor? Could I come back? I'll try. Really I will. I made a . . . mistake. I know it now. I wouldn't blame you if you said no. . . ." Tears were splashing onto her arms, dampening her blouse, and her nose was running. "Please . . ." Even with the Kleenex she nervously swiped at her nose with the back of her hand.

All the sounds in the room and the city seemed to turn up in volume. She heard the traffic noises, dogs barking, clocks ticking, neighbors walking upstairs. All in the virtually soundproof luxury apartment.

Then she heard his answer. A sob. "I . . . we want you back, Shel. Come home. How soon can you leave, Shel?" came the shaky but soft voice.

Rochelle started to cry uncontrollably and couldn't answer. He then asked her three times to repeat what she was trying to say. "The first plane I can get," she finally managed to say.

Flora scratched her arm. She hadn't slept all night. Last night her voices had spoken to her. Amy and Benjamin and Carl and Denny were waiting for their baby sister to join them in heaven.

She paced around the ravine. She had felt like this before. But she couldn't remember when or where. There was a face in the window looking at her.

"Just wait, children," she said. "Shortly now. You'll have your sister. Now, Amy . . ."

"Yes, mama," her voice answered.

"You are the mama of the family now. You welcome your little sister and see that her soul is purified, as I'm sure yours finally is."

"We miss you, mama," a chorus of voices said. Flora wouldn't cry, though. She was made of stronger stuff. But she had a strange feeling as she squinted at the bright sunlight hitting her in the eyes. She would see them all soon. They would come here for a visit, and she could have them with her.

"Ralph," she whispered.

"Yes, Flora," he said.

"I'll never marry again, you know." She wanted to add, "Or have anything to do with another man," but she thought that would bring up Emily. Ralph had never gone for the idea. She knew all along. But it was too late to stop it after they had started it. And just when she felt right about things, the Lord had seen fit to remove him from the earth. Maybe because she sinned. Her forehead began to throb. Yes, maybe she had. But she was making up for it. She was returning Emily to heaven where she belonged. Soon.

She looked down. Goodness, her shoes were muddy. She couldn't abide dirty or scuffed shoes. She scratched her head. Come to think of it, she couldn't remember if she had showered or not today. Best to clean up and be neat and tidy always. As she went upstairs, she wondered which day of the week it was.

Further back in the woods, a man scratched his head. It was a perfect shot. He had never seen the woman close up before. And he could have gotten her. Except for the face in the window. It was too risky. He would have been seen. But maybe if he and his partner took turns and hung around close to the house, this was the way to do it.

"What about her grandparents, Charles? Won't they take the girl there?"

Dr. Resnick looked across the table at the social worker. Also in on this unusual meeting, called especially for the case of Amy Butler, were the directress of the Hillcrest Home, two nurses and the recreational therapist.

Charles Resnick looked down at the typewritten sheets in his file folder. He didn't need to do that because he had written the report. "Mr. and Mrs. Nash will not drive Amy to Atlanta. And they can't afford to pay for her trip."

The day nurse spoke first. "Well, just notify her mother. If her husband died, she might have insurance. That will cover the cost. We can put her on a plane. They take care of children flying alone."

Dr. Resnick let his horn-rimmed glasses slip down around his nose as he looked over them. "Perhaps I didn't make myself perfectly clear. Her grandfather warned me that Mrs. Butler will probably not want Amy. I think the rejection will shatter Amy's already fragile ego. Furthermore, Amy doesn't like her mother. The mother is the cause of the amnesia, as far as I'm concerned."

"What are you suggesting, doctor," the directress said efficiently. "The home has a fund for such things. But a plane ride? I don't know if that would be approved. Perhaps there's another solution."

Dr. Resnick took off his glasses and rested them on the table. "I'm suggesting Amy not be returned to her mother."

"You mean remain here at the home."

"I mean, hopefully, that she would eventually be adopted. Amy is a bright, appealing child. The mother seems extremely neurotic, from all that she's told me. It's probably worse. It usually is, in these cases."

The directress looked at the young doctor rather harshly. "I think, Dr. Resnick, this is a case of the doctor becoming overly attached to the patient. Even if you and your wife wanted to adopt Amy, we can't allow it. Her mother is alive."

"And her mother will destroy her!" Dr. Resnick said angrily.

"But her mother is alive. We can't keep her in an orphanage. Would you like to call Mrs. Butler from my office, Dr. Resnick?"

He stood up, slowly putting his notes into his briefcase. Well, it was worth a try. He knew Amy would have to be returned to her mother. There simply wasn't enough time to prepare her adequately for the confrontation. He couldn't be sure of what Amy might do in her new situation. Most likely, she'd adjust after a while and follow her mother's orders. But he couldn't bet on it.

Amanda drove the car up into the long driveway. She got out, slammed the door and ran into the house. The two women were in the kitchen. Mavis spoke with her eyes. There was an apology.

Amanda looked at Mrs. Butler. She was wearing a pink shirtwaist dress buttoned to the neck, her hair was wound into a tight, shiny bun and she wore freshly polished white sneakers with nylons. She was making the baby's supper in a blender.

"Are you okay, Mrs. Butler?" Amanda asked icily.

Flora responded just as coolly, "I'm fine, Mrs. Whitney," while in the background Mavis panto-mimed a disheveled woman, putting her hair up and putting on a dress. Her face was a curious study as she finished with an apologetic shrug.

Amanda sighed. She should go back to work. But

she felt such a dragged-out feeling of disappointment. How she had hoped the Butler woman had finally gone bonkers. She was just so cagey. One minute you thought surely she was off, and the next moment she was acting so very prim and proper. How could she even explain it to Justin? He would say it wouldn't stand up in court.

She was juggling her car keys, trying to decide if she wanted to go back to the agency, when the phone rang. "I have it," she said, picking it up in the dining room.

Amanda was shocked. "Mrs. Butler?" In all the time she had lived there, the woman had never had a phone call.

Mavis yelled she was in the baby's room. Amanda went back to the phone to say that Mrs. Butler would have to call back. Or would they like to wait?

The man said no. He was calling from New York. Would Mrs. Butler call him back? He was Dr. Resnick from the Hillcrest Home. Her daughter, Amy, was alive and well. She had survived the accident, been found, suffered amnesia; and they needed some way of bringing her to Atlanta.

Amanda hardly heard the man except for the key words. This was it. Why fate had summoned her home. So she could take this precious phone call.

"Dr. Resnick, you say? No need to bother Mrs. Butler. I'll pay for Amy's flight and make the arrangements. I'll call you right back."

She took the number and hung up, smiling. No need for Flora Butler to know. It would be a little surprise. When she brought the little girl here, it wouldn't be long before she'd be leaving again. With her mother.

It wasn't until late in the evening that Barnard Borg returned to his apartment. He had just walked around the city. He had walked all the way to the

Village. Had he really walked that far? Then he had walked back uptown again. His feet hurt. And he wanted to go to sleep. Where was she?

"Rochelle! Rochelle!" he shouted.

There was no answer.

He walked by the kitchen, past the winter garden and the dining room, through the huge living room and across to his study. She wasn't in the bedroom. He could tell by just looking in the door. And she wasn't in the kitchen. He didn't need the encounter. He was still trembling at the thought of having hit her like that. His anger—well, it was uncontrollable sometimes. On the other hand, she had asked for it. He supposed he'd have to apologize.

She wasn't in the bathroom. The door was open. He drifted back into the bedroom. It was then that he saw it. The drawers to the dresser were open. Her drawers, the ones he had sacrificed for her things— they were empty.

Running to the front closet, he saw that her suitcase was gone. Then he opened the closet. There were the dresses, the skirts, the blouses, the shoes . . . everything he had bought her. She hadn't taken any of it. He looked around. There must be a note. If there was it would be on the dining-room table. That was where they left messages for each other. Running to the table, he threw aside bills, magazines, and promotional advertisements; and there it was. A note from Rochelle! Damn! It was an old note to the cleaning woman. He looked out at the midnight sky through his windows and saw a plane's lights flash on and off in the distance.

Then he stared in horror out the window. She had left him. She hadn't even said good-bye.

His face felt wet. He brought his hand up to it. He was crying. Dr. Barnard Borg was crying. She had left. And he loved her. He had never told her. She called him gay. He wasn't gay, was he? That's what he had been trying to figure out as he walked in the Village. Staring at the boys. Rochelle knew him better than anyone did.

He had also thought of his audit. Harvey was wrong. They did have a lot to worry about. Then he saw it. A cell. Jail. They would dress him in clothes like everyone else, and he would be treated like a common animal. Of all the nightmares in the world, going to prison was something he couldn't face. And those horrible men. He would be raped. He smiled. And then he laughed. Dr. Barnard Borg. It would be a living death.

That plane up in the sky . . . was Rochelle on that plane? He walked toward the windows of the winter garden. His body was filled with pain. Who cared about prison? What was life like without Shel? There was a latch on the big windows. He never opened them, but suddenly he needed air. He couldn't breathe.

"Rochelle, Rochelle!" he heard himself screaming.

The plane wasn't out of sight yet. If he hurried he could make it. Then he'd have Rochelle back. And they'd never find him. He wouldn't have to go to jail. A faint buzzing started hammering in his ears. He was all alone. The one thing in the world he enjoyed was slipping through his fingers—respect.

He put one leg over the window ledge and raised the heavy glass higher. He screamed at the plane and waved his arms. He had to get to her.

"Rochelle! Rochelle!" he screamed as he jumped out of the window to Fifty-seventh Street, realizing too late he would miss the plane because he was going in the wrong direction.

Rochelle sat, tensely biting her fingernails. She had been lucky to get on a plane this fast. Looking out the window, she watched the black diamond-studded blanket that was Manhattan. If she never came back, it wouldn't bother her. Not right now.

She had been a fool. Luckily for her, Victor was an understanding man. But that was ridiculous. He loved her. And she loved him. The seven-year itch—that's what happened to her. Well, twenty-year itch was more like it. Someone to spend the rest of her life with—that was what love was all about.

Normy . . . Borgy . . . Normy didn't know what love was. He was an adolescent man. She had only thought she loved him. Probably she should have left a note, but she didn't think it mattered to him. She had left the clothes he had bought her. Later, when she was up to it, she'd write a letter. As far as she was concerned, she didn't care if they ever spoke again. It would take time for her to recover from his treatment of her. Hitting her. Victor would never raise his hand to a woman. She wondered if he even cared that she had left without any explanation. Did he jump for joy when he found she had gone? In spite of herself, she wondered what he was doing now.

Chapter Twenty-four

Amy Butler sat on the red plastic couch and let her legs swing. She had been brought to the waiting room by a lady in a uniform. She didn't even know whom she was waiting for. Why couldn't she have stayed with Dr. Resnick?

Why wasn't her mama coming for her? And how come Grandma and Grandpa Nash wouldn't take her? Mama was here with that Emily baby. She could have told them that's what her mama would do. Come and find her other baby.

Just then she looked up into the face of a pretty lady. The lady from the airlines was standing next to her.

"Hello, Amy. I'm Mrs. Whitney." She extended her hand.

Amy looked up, absentmindedly shaking the woman's hand. She had never seen such a pretty lady. She had dark brown hair, shoulder length, and she wore makeup. Amy looked at the smooth hand in hers. The nails were polished an ambery orange, to match her shiny lipstick. She wore a navy suit and a powder-blue turtleneck sweater. Amy wondered if she was an actress or a movie star.

"Mrs. Whitney," the woman said again, "your mother is staying with us." She smiled. "I have a little girl, too."

Amy couldn't speak. She felt as if her tongue were glued to the top of her mouth with peanut butter.

"How did you like your plane trip?" the woman asked.

"Okay," she managed.

They stood up. "My, my, your mother is going to be so happy to see you."

Amy smiled as she walked alongside the elegant lady through the airport. Her mama wasn't going to be happy to see her, and she knew it.

"Have you ever been to Atlanta, Amy?" Mrs. Whitney said as they walked through the mammoth Atlanta airport.

"No, ma'am. I ain't been outside of New Jersey, except to go to New York." And then, as if her mother were sitting on her shoulder, she said, "Haven't been, I mean."

After what seemed like endless walking to Amy, they found Mrs. Whitney's car. It was sleek and polished, not like the old van they had had and not like the station wagon Dr. Resnick had taken her to Wananwa in. Wananwa. She wondered if she'd ever see it again.

Amanda started the car, one eye on the curious little girl with the unusual case history. She couldn't believe her good luck. For, once Mrs. Flora Butler realized that her daughter was alive and well, she would have to leave. Then she would have a daughter, and so would Amanda. That was only fair. The girl was pretty, to be sure. Looked just like Flora, except for those awful buck teeth. But those could be fixed. Her heart ached for the way the child was dressed. Oxfords and dark brown socks slipping down her ankles. That skimpy brown dress and the coat that was sizes too large for her. Hand-me-downs, no doubt, from that orphanage. Maybe she could take her out for a little shopping spree. But no, she doubted if her mother would allow it.

Amy looked at the scenery, too shy to say anything. When they pulled up the long, long driveway, she gasped at the size of the Whitney mansion and then closed her mouth, as if she had said something out of line.

"Stay here," Amanda said once they were inside. "I'll go up to the baby's room and get your mother."

Amy didn't say anything when Amanda left her in the front room. It was the biggest house Amy had ever seen, and it was all carpeted. She wondered if the kitchen was carpeted. Amy looked up the long winding staircase and shuddered. Mama was upstairs. Soon she would walk down the staircase and see her.

Amy looked around. The big, shiny piano. She was tempted to plunk it, but it might have waked the baby. Mama probably had her taking a nap. She wondered if Mrs. Whitney minded that mama was around to take care of their baby. Nervously, she twirled the end of one of her braids and then sucked the tip in her mouth.

There were noises on the stairs. She heard Mrs. Whitney saying, almost singing, "I have a surprise, Mrs. Butler."

Then she saw mama's shoes. No mistaking mama's shoes. She always saved them in the cellar in case Amy's feet grew big fast. She looked up into the smiling face of Mrs. Whitney. Then she looked across at her mother.

"Hi, mama," she said, aware that her voice was trembling. Maybe she would get a spanking. That's what her stomach felt like.

"Take your hair out of your mouth, Amy," Flora said sternly, and Amy spit out her braid. "I knew you'd pay me a visit. Where are your brothers?"

"They're all dead, mama. Drowned." She wouldn't say any more. How she jumped over them and swam right to the top. Mama would surely spank her then.

"I know that," Flora said harshly.

The last thing Amy saw before Flora marched her upstairs to wash her face was the astonished face of Mrs. Whitney. Her mouth had dropped open. She wondered why she looked so puzzled. She could have told her what would happen. Her mama wouldn't be happy to see her. But so far so good. Mama was just as she remembered her. So it wasn't all that bad yet.

Mavis served the soup at dinner that night. Amy was still wide-eyed and in awe of her lavish surroundings. Flora covered Amy's soup bowl.

"She'll have none and, of course, neither will I."

Mavis couldn't help but reveal the sarcasm in her voice. She had been told there was company for dinner, and here was this little girl practically risen from the dead. And not getting any soup, either.

"It's fresh, Mrs. Butler. I made it myself," Mavis said.

"Yes, I know." Mavis noticed Mrs. Butler never called her by her name. She just never called her anything. She sensed Mrs. Butler had an aversion to blacks. She could always tell.

"But with a meat bone," Flora said crisply. "Amy doesn't eat meat. And neither do her brothers." Amy looked up sideways at her mother. Why did she keep asking about her brothers? It was as if they were still here. And what if her mama knew she had not only tasted meat, but ate a lot of it? She liked it.

"Perhaps some tomato juice," Amanda said carefully.

Mavis made a face, disappeared and returned with two glasses of tomato juice. Branch and Amanda had veal. Amy had a vegetable plate but wanted the veal desperately.

Flora had vegetables, as usual, but couldn't eat

them. When, she wondered, would Benjamin, Carl and Denny join their sister for a little visit?

Branch and Amanda took their coffee cups into the library.

"I think we should ask Mrs. Butler to leave. Amy isn't entitled to stay here."

"We can't do it that way. There's room enough for her. Don't let's be nasty to the woman, Amanda."

Amanda slammed her demitasse cup down, almost shattering the little saucer. "*She's* nasty. Look how she treats her own daughter. . . . " Amanda sighed heavily. "You're attracted to her in a strange way, aren't you?"

Branch said nothing.

"No, no, I sensed it long ago. She's beautiful. But, Branch, come down to earth." She gulped. "Yes, you . . . made a baby together. But not really, and there's something wrong with that woman. She gets stronger as the days go on. Oh, Branch, we have to do something to get her to go. And I think Amy's the ticket—why, that's it!"

"What's what?" Branch asked sheepishly, knowing that Amanda was right. He did have a crush on that woman. Or maybe it was *had*. She was annoying, and it was wearing thin.

"Dr. Borg. He said he'd do something. He found out about Amy and sent her."

Branch stood up. "Okay, call him first thing in the morning and see if he knows anything else. Meanwhile, I'll talk to Justin."

Amanda looked at him, half smiling, half mocking.

"I will really, I will. First thing tomorrow. But it will be about an out-of-court settlement. Since her own child's alive, maybe we can set something up."

"You mean . . ."

"Trick her?" He threw up his hands. "Oh, well, what the hell, why not?"

Amanda smiled. "Well, that's a switch," she said. And to herself she wondered if anything would help. Would that woman take Amy and go? It just seemed endless.

Amy sat on the rollaway her mama had moved into her room. She studied her shoes. Flora was reading from the Bible, silently, and she waited patiently for her to finish.

"Mama, can we go back to New Jersey like before? Where am I going to go to school? Are you . . ." But she couldn't finish. She was going to ask if her mother was glad to see her. But she already knew the answer. She found out mama spent her time in the baby's room. All the time.

The baby. The baby. It was stupid. She wished she were a tiny little baby again. Then her mama would love her.

Flora looked at her sharply. "How come you were the only one sent?"

Amy felt a chill run through her. "Hunh?"

"Mind your manners and speak up. How come you're alone?"

Amy gulped. "The rest drowned, mama. I swam away. I'm a good swimmer." She bit her lip. She was going to get punished. Somehow mama knew the truth. That she stepped over her brothers to get out of the car and untrap herself. That Dr. Resnick was going to get it. He was the only one who knew. So he told on her.

Flora looked at the little girl and became furious. Even as a ghost she was hard to handle. Why did Amy visit her? It was Denny, her baby, she wanted to see.

Amy was so frightened she was backed up into the corner of the room. When she saw her mother's face twisted with rage, she whimpered. Instinctively, she ducked under Flora's arm when she raised it to smack her, and ran out of the room. At the end of the hall she looked around. So many bedrooms. Tears blinded her eyes. Mama didn't love her. Then she saw the room with the door slightly ajar. The baby's room.

Mavis had just finished the dishes. She had a little room she used upstairs. Since her youngest, Rita-Mae, had gotten married, she could do whatever she pleased. Her husband had left about the time old Mrs. Whitney died. She had been staying at the Whitney mansion more and more. Not because she was afraid to get home, but because she didn't trust that woman, Mrs. Butler. No, she personally thought the woman was crazed. And it wasn't too farfetched that she might take their precious little baby from them. Or worse. Mavis kept an eye out always on the baby's room. Only tonight she came up the stairs just as Amy had closed the door behind her. She saw Flora go into the bathroom down the hall and went on to her own room.

Flora returned to her room and was reading her Bible again. Her window was open to reveal a full moon. Tonight she would baptize her baby in the ravine. Tonight was the night. She could feel it.

Just another psalm and then into the baby's room. Poor little Danielle. Well, her soul would pass up tonight. And really become Emily.

As Flora left the room, she turned off the light. Downstairs, hiding under a tree, was the hired killer. Tonight the man would shoot her. If she didn't walk by the ravine as she sometimes did, he'd have to sneak into the house. He hadn't heard from Dr.

Borg or the lawyer in a long time. If he didn't get her soon, he wouldn't get paid.

Amy closed the door to the baby's room softly. Then she tippy-toed up to the crib to look at her half-sister. She had silky blond hair in little ringlets. Above her little head was a mobile of pink and yellow bunnies and chicks. Her blanket was a blushing shade of rose. Her eyes were closed in sleep, and there was a cherubic smile on her face. Amy took her forefinger and pressed it deep into the baby's pink forehead. Then she turned it around like a screwdriver. The baby whimpered and she stopped.

She went over to the white rocker and picked up a plush teddy bear. She rocked back and forth, back and forth, holding the stuffed animal like a little baby. Then she stopped the rocker and sat still. She plucked a button eye from its round face and ripped off an ear.

The baby had everything. And she had nothing. The baby was pretty, too. Looked like mama. Mama was always telling her she was ugly. Did babies have brains, she wondered? She doubted it, because Denny was always dumb and Benjamin never had a brain. If a baby had no brain, you could do what you wanted with it. If there was no baby, mama would love her because there was no one else left. She would be the only child. It was so simple. Amy jumped up from the rocker and danced around. All she had to do was kill the baby.

Mavis turned down her TV set. She opened the window and looked out. She thought she had heard someone in the bushes. But it must have been her imagination. There was no one there. And it was a full, bright moon; so if anyone was there, she would be able to see. She turned to look back at the television screen. With the sound turned off, it looked like a silent movie. She looked out again. Maybe it was nothing.

She went back to her favorite chair and turned up the set. Then she turned it off. No good. Any sound could mean something. She didn't trust it. Besides, she had had a funny feeling lately about the Butler woman. She was acting mighty strange. No, she couldn't leave anything to doubt. Maybe she had heard someone out near the ravine. That woman might be doing God-knows-what out there. Mavis grabbed a heavy sweater and flicked off her TV set. Maybe she could prove to Mrs. Whitney what she, Mavis, knew to be true: that that woman was crazy and dangerous.

Flora closed her Bible. Where was Amy? She had disappeared. She must have gone back up to heaven. There were a lot of stars out. Sometimes she thought her family were stars in the sky. Then they would be watching and waiting.

Tonight was the night. She felt a sign from the Lord. Emily's brothers and sisters were going to be pleased.

"You need wait no more. Your little sister will join you. I must see that she's purified first."

Flora walked down the hall. It felt as if she were gliding on angel's feet. Amy would tell them. Tell them all that Emily, after she had shed the Danielle part of her, would be joining them. That's why Amy was sent. As a messenger. She had wondered about that.

She walked slowly toward the baby's room. She wanted to chant a psalm, but she couldn't remember any. In fact, since she had come to this evil house, she couldn't remember any of her Bible. Sometimes she read the same page over and over.

Softly she opened the baby's room. The sweet smell of powder made her nose tingle. She smiled.

Gently she reached in the crib to pull her out from the lump of blankets. Furiously she pounded the blanket flat. There was nothing there. Someone had taken the baby.

Gasping for breath, she backed against the wall. That colored woman? Mr. and Mrs. Whitney? And then she saw it, on the pink linoleum floor. A plaid bow. Amy had worn those plaid bows when she came down from heaven. Right on the tip of her braids. Amy took the baby. But she hadn't been purified yet. Praying to the good Lord it wasn't too late, Flora clattered down the stairway in search of Amy. She had to be stopped if it wasn't already too late.

Amy stood at the top of the cellar stairs. She was going to pitch the baby down and watch her cute little head clunk down the steps one by one until she lay in a bloody pulp at the bottom. But at the last minute she changed her mind. Someone would find her. And that might be messy. No, the thing to do was hide her where no one would find her. Ever. They might think she was kidnapped, though. That would go on forever. They would be trying to find her. No, the baby had to be found. Eventually. So she and mama could leave. And mama could love her as she deserved to be loved. The woods. That was the place. Amy ran out the door. She stumbled once and almost dropped the baby, whose little face was red from crying. The baby was practically hanging around Amy's waist. All Amy needed was the right rock. Then she would bash the baby's head in and leave her to be found in her pink and white checked nightdress, under a log. With her big, adorable blue eyes wide open.

Mavis ran into the high bushes near the house. In each space of grass she looked around and into a clump of foliage. Up above the moon was full and clear. Mavis looked around. And then she screamed.

She stood face to face with the other end of a rifle. "Oh, Lordy! Lordy!" she cried. It disappeared. There was a rustle in the bushes and she could hear someone running. Thinking only of the danger to her family, without thinking of the danger to herself, she ran after the figure holding the gun, who was cursing himself for failing again.

Amy clamped a dirty hand over the baby's rosebud mouth. She hated the sound of babies' crying almost as much as dogs' barking. She didn't like the woods much, either. In fact, the more she ran the more frightened she became. She needed a rock for little, little . . . what was the baby's name? A sliver of panic rose up from her feet, racing to her heart. She didn't know which way to turn. There might be ghosts in the woods. She might see her brothers. Looking frantically, she lifted the baby higher and ran back as fast as she could.

The ravine. There was that dirty old spooky ravine. She was dragging the baby's head, and she began to cry louder.

"Bye-bye, baby. Pretty soon you'll bob to the surface. No more baby."

She held the baby in her arms and rocked her to and fro, her swings getting wilder and more dangerous. Danielle was screaming so much her cries were muffled because of her hoarseness. Her pink blanket had fallen on the grass, and she was straining to be free of the girl's tight grip.

"One for the money, one for the show, two to get ready and . . ."

Just then she saw Flora running up to her. "You give her back to me. She can't go yet. She's not purified!"

Amy looked at her mother, wide-eyed. If she

didn't get rid of the baby, she couldn't have her mama. Her mother started to grab the baby, and she pulled back. Danielle was now hanging on to Amy and clutching her with her little fists. She had no voice left, but opened her mouth and screamed silently, her tongue wagging in her mouth like a little bird.

"She's mine," Amy said.

"Not until I send her up. Now give me that baby."

"You like her better than me!" Amy wailed. With an almost superhuman force, she pulled Danielle out of her mother's arms and tried to pitch her in the ravine. Danielle's beautiful eyes rolled up as she was turned upside down. Flora grabbed her again and began chanting.

Then they heard a scream. And both stood still.

The upstairs window opened and then shut.

"I thought I heard a scream," Amanda told Branch.

"Where from?"

"The ravine. I can't see from here. Maybe I should go down."

Branch sat up in bed. He turned his remote dial and switched off the sound on the TV. "Honey, Mavis's TV set is right near the ravine. Remember the last time this happened? She fell asleep in front of the TV."

"Maybe I should check on the baby?"

"Honey, just relax. Come and get in bed with me, and we'll snuggle up and watch TV together."

"Well, that's an offer I can't refuse," Amanda said. Though in the back of her mind she thought a television scream usually has other voices in it. Then Branch pulled her close to him, and she forgot.

Mavis ran up and pulled the baby from the mother and daughter. Danielle was shaking and gasping by this time. Mavis tucked her inside her coat so she looked like a bunny. "Okay, lady. Now I've got you. What are you doing out here with this precious child, throwing her around like that? They'll put you away for sure!"

Flora had backed away about three feet and stood next to a gnarled tree trunk. She started to make a run for the baby, but her sneaker settled in some mud and she began to slip. She held out her hand for Amy to help as, horrified, she began to lose her balance and tumble backward.

"Amy, help me," she pleaded. Straining, she reached out her hand to her daughter to stop her slippery fall.

Epilogue

It was unseasonably warm for Christmas in Atlanta. The sun shone on the backyard like the promise of spring. Amy was swinging on one of Danielle's swings. She turned her face up to the warm sun and smiled. She was wearing a light blue coat, black patent Mary Janes and a shoulder bag to match, just as the big girls wore. She patted her tummy. They had just had turkey and ham and all the trimmings. She picked out a piece of sweet-potato pie that was hanging from her teeth. Just got her braces. Doctor said she was a little young, but she got them anyway.

Inside was the biggest Christmas tree she ever saw. And it was decorated so nicely, too. Not with lots of tinsel and different-colored dime-store balls. Just nice, almost bare except for little blue lights and a white angel. There were lots of presents for her. None from that old Grandma Nash. Oh, well, she didn't expect any. Grandpa had died when he found out about mama. About her tragic accident.

Amy stole a look at the ravine. "I double-dare myself," she said, then snapped her head around. She had seen the hand come out of the ravine. Mama's hand. But she couldn't punish herself anymore.

Only Mavis knew. And she and Mavis had made a deal. She wouldn't tell if Amy promised to be nice to the baby. Then she could stay.

No, she couldn't be punished. She couldn't help it

if she had little, tiny arms and couldn't reach her mama as she slipped and fell and tumbled all the way down into the ravine. And did she put in the rock that broke her head when she fell? No. She never was quick. Mama always told her she was slow. Mama was right. She didn't reach out to save mama.

Amy swung higher and higher. Oh, well, she dared herself on a triple-dare to look in the ravine. Then her legs froze to a halt. The bony hand came out of the ravine. She shook her head like a dog shaking out fleas, and it went away.

The swing came down and she jumped off. She felt a chill, suddenly. Maybe it was finally turning cold for Christmas. But not snow as in New Jersey. Well, she didn't miss it. Throwing her head back, she ran into the house, pretending she was a pony. She lived with the Whitneys now, and they were talking about adopting her.

Just as she got to the door, she swiveled her head around quickly. The hand was climbing higher out of the muddy ravine waters. She shut her eyes and willed it away. When she opened them, she saw only the sunshine slanting through the trees.

The whole thing was silly, anyway. Mama was gone. Mama couldn't punish her. Anyway, Mrs. Whitney told her that she should call *her* mama if she wanted.

TWICE BEFORE
CHANDAL HAS FACED THE UNKNOWN
TERRORS OF THE SUPERNATURAL.

AND TWICE BEFORE, MASTER
STORYTELLER KEN EULO
HAS CONJURED UP THE DEMONIC
PRESENCE OF PERFECT EVIL IN...

THE BLOODSTONE

and

THE BROWNSTONE

DON'T MISS THEM!

Wherever paperbacks are sold!

#282